ANYA
AND THE
NIGHTINGALE

ANYA
AND THE
NIGHTINGALE

By Sofiya Pasternack

Versify
Houghton Mifflin Harcourt
Boston   New York

hmhbooks.com

The text was set in Berling LT Std.
Map by Celeste Knudsen
Cover design by Jessica Handelman
Interior design by Celeste Knudsen

Library of Congress Cataloging-in-Publication Data
Names: Pasternack, Sofiya, author.
Title: Anya and the nightingale / by Sofiya Pasternack.
Description: Boston ; New York : Houghton Mifflin Harcourt, [2021]
Audience: Ages 10 to 12. | Audience: Grades 7–9. |
Summary: Thirteen-year-old Anya sets out to find her missing father but instead
travels to Kiev, where she meets the tsar, dines with a rabbi, and rescues two
brothers from a dangerous monster lurking beneath the city.
Identifiers: LCCN 2019041632 (print) | LCCN 2019041633 (ebook) |
ISBN 9780358006022 (hardcover) | ISBN 9780358157311 (ebook)
Subjects: CYAC: Magic—Fiction. | Elves—Fiction. | Monsters—Fiction. |
Rescues—Fiction. | Jews—Fiction. | Fantasy.
Classification: LCC PZ7.1.P37545 Ap 2021 (print) | LCC PZ7.1.P37545 (ebook)
DDC [Fic]—dc23
LC record available at https://lccn.loc.gov/2019041632
LC ebook record available at https://lccn.loc.gov/2019041633

Manufactured in the United States of America
DOC 10 9 8 7 6 5 4 3 2 1
4500805491

To C & C—
Find your magic.

To my husband—
For your patience
and your support,
I love you.

CHAPTER ONE

A NYA'S SUKKAH was suspiciously lopsided.

She had gone into the barn to get more rope for securing the posts of the booth's framework. The sukkah itself was in the field between their barn and the river since there were no trees out there to hang over it. That was one of the rules of building the booth: there could be nothing over it that would obscure a view of the sky. Since the fire the year before, there were also no trees at all where the new house and barn now stood, either. But it was tradition for the family to build the sukkah out in the field, and Anya was going to follow tradition.

The rope dangled from her fingers, and she narrowed her eyes as the sukkah gave a little shudder. She put her fists on her hips and said, "Zvezda, get out from there right now!"

Her goat's white horned head peeked out from around the side of the booth. He had a mouth full of the thatching she had carefully woven out of branches for one wall.

"Zvezda, no! Bad goat!" Anya dropped the rope and ran toward her half-erected booth. The goat didn't even have the decency to run away. He just stood there, chewing on thatching, as Anya stomped up and yanked it out of his mouth. "I worked hard on this, you stupid goat!"

"*Myah*," he said, indifferent to her anguish.

Anya threw the chewed thatching to the ground. Zvezda rolled his eyes up to her and, very slowly, very carefully, lowered his head to the ground. He slurped the thatching back into his mouth without looking away from her.

She sighed and pushed his rump toward the barn. "Go away. I need to build a great sukkah this year." Last year had been a disaster. It had been the first Sukkot without Papa, who usually built the sukkah they would spend a week pretending to live in. Pretending, because Babulya was too old to spend too much time in it, especially at night. They definitely took meals in it, which meant it had to be wide enough to hold all of them — plus a couple of goats, who always squeezed in whether the family wanted them to or not. Anya had built a haphazard sukkah, and then her friends Ivan and Håkon had come over to see it. Then Håkon had burned it down.

It had been an accident. Ivan never went anywhere without the staff Kin had made for him last year, so he was pretending to fight the dragon. Håkon swore he only meant to breathe a little bit of fire at Ivan. He didn't use fire much, being a river dragon, so he was out of practice. It was a *lot* of fire. It hit the sukkah and caught immediately. Ivan used his water magic to put the fire out, but by then it was too late.

That sukkah was gone, and Anya didn't have time to put up another one. She told her family that she'd set the sukkah on fire—accidentally, of course—because any excuse she had was better than the truth: that a dragon had done it. No one could know about Håkon, not even Mama and Babulya and Dyedka. The family ate outside anyway—until the sky opened up and poured rain on them. Babulya declared the rain lucky, an answer to the prayer they hadn't even said yet, but to Anya it felt like a punctuation mark to her utter failure.

Not this year.

She inspected the damage done by her stinker of a

goat. He had chewed a hole large enough for Anya to stick her arm through, but it was fixable. The other sides were untouched.

The field between the barn and the river was full of rushes and tall grass. Anya gathered some up and wove a patch for the sukkah wall, then wove its ends into the wall's ragged hole. The patch was a different color and plant species, but it worked.

Anya retrieved her rope and fortified the booth's top four corners. She made sure the poles were deep enough in the ground that a stiff wind wouldn't blow it over. Inside, she paced from one side to the other. It would be long enough to fit not only Anya's family but some guests as well.

Just a couple of guests. Anya didn't have time to build a thatch palace.

She walked a few paces away and faced the booth, one hand on her hip and one stroking her chin. She needed a roof now. But the roof couldn't just be any old roof. It had to offer shade but be see-through enough to see the stars. Papa always used pruned lengths of the roses that climbed the little house, weaving them into a very loose topping, but those roses had burned when the old house had last year. Babulya had cultivated them back, but they reached only to the top of Anya's head. She didn't want to cut some off when they were so sparse to begin with.

She thought she could go into the woods and cut a branch off a tree, probably, but hadn't yet. The roof had to go on last, and she had to make sure everything else was perfect.

Well, it was as perfect as it was going to get. As long as Zvezda didn't come back.

With a quick peek around the side of the barn, Anya determined that Zvezda was gone. Probably back inside the barn to spend time with the other goats. None of *them* ever tried to eat Anya's things.

Anya had a knife in her pocket already—she had been using it to craft the sukkah's walls—and she figured that was all she needed for gathering branches. She went back to the sukkah for one last check on it.

A little white goat butt stuck out of the door. The wall to the left of the door rippled, and then a goaty snout pushed through. Zvezda tore another piece of the wall out, then saw Anya. He stopped chewing. He just stared at her as she clenched her fists and thought of a thousand different ways to tie his mouth shut.

"*Myah*," he said.

CHAPTER TWO

Z VEZDA HAD A ROPE around his neck, and the other end of the rope was tied around Anya's waist. She wasn't going to leave him to eat her sukkah while she got branches for a *sechach*, the roof, so she brought him with her. In the forest, he grabbed mouthfuls of plants they walked by, chewing away with contented grunts.

She had just the type of tree in mind: a pretty birch tree with its wild orange leaves in contrast over white bark. There were a bunch of them up the river, north a little ways, so she followed the sound of the water away from her farm.

Away from the farm. Into the forest. She took a deep breath. It wasn't far. She'd be fine.

Every few steps, Anya had to tug gently on the rope to get Zvezda away from whatever plant he was nibbling on. He came easily, though he sometimes dug his little hooves in long enough to get a big mouthful of something delicious before allowing Anya to pull him along.

The goat's dawdling was stretching Anya's time in the woods, and she really wanted to get out fast. The forest made her uneasy. There might be traps along the path. The birds might be spying on her. An unseen enemy might come out of the trees at any moment. All those things had happened last year, when Sigurd the Varangian had descended upon the village of Zmeyreka like a dark cloud. He was dead, though. Anya had killed him.

Even so, the memory of him remained.

Her foot sank into the loam a little too much, and she jerked back, heart pounding. Sigurd had set a trap for her and her best friend, Ivan, last year. He had put them in a bag and thrown them in the river. She could smell the earthy bag again, could feel the cold water rushing in.

Anya stopped and shut her eyes to force away the memories.

Maybe it was his ghost. Maybe he was haunting her.

She felt a soft nose bump her hand. When she looked down, she met Zvezda's eyes.

"*Myah*," he said, but to Anya, the tone sounded like *What's wrong?*

She patted him with a shaking hand that steadied with every stroke across his head. With Zvezda, the forest was less frightening somehow.

Even though he was just a goat.

Anya swallowed hard and looked around. The birds in the trees watched her. With ill intent? Maybe. But who were they going to tattle to? Håkon? She wouldn't mind if the dragon showed up. He was, in theory, a ferocious monster. In practice, much less so. But he could still use magic and so would be a better protector than Zvezda.

She couldn't make her feet move forward. Every glance up the path made her skin prickle. That dark cloud gathered over her. Sigurd's ghost. Anya took a step back, then another. She turned around and tugged Zvezda with her, and the goat followed without a fight.

◆ ✳ ◆

Anya used oak branches for the *sechach*. Zvezda ate a mouthful of one, but she managed to get the branches on top of the booth before he could get much more than that.

Once the *sechach* was on, Anya stood back to look at it. It looked much better than her attempt last year, but not as good as Papa's. When he got back, they'd be able to build amazing *sukkot* together.

Last year, just before Purim, Anya's life had turned sideways when Papa had been conscripted and sent to Rûm. Then, just before Shavuot, the celebration of receiving the Torah, her sideways life flipped completely when Håkon, the last dragon in Kievan Rus', appeared in her village and saved her life. One of the tsar's knights, a *bogatyr* named Dobrynya, who had come to get rid of Håkon, promised Anya's mother that he'd send for Papa and have him brought back.

Shavuot had come and gone, and Anya turned twelve and became a bat mitzvah, which meant she was responsible for her own actions and had to answer for consequences as a result of them. Her hair was short, cut above her shoulders, as one of those consequences. She and Ivan had gotten too rambunctious practicing with the weapons Kin had given them inside her barn just after this year's Shavuot, and they'd knocked all the tools off the walls. Their house spirit, the *domovoi*, was furious, and in retaliation, he did one of his favorite punishments: knotting Anya's hair as she slept. He must have been feeling particularly nasty that night, because he'd combined pine sap with the knots. Anya, Mama, and Babulya had tried for hours to figure out how to un-knot them. When everything they tried failed, Mama sheared Anya's hair off. That had been a few months ago, and her hair only just reached her shoulders. She and Ivan hadn't brought their weapons back to the barn since.

Anya turned thirteen, short hair and all. The months swept by. Papa still hadn't returned.

Dobrynya was a hero. He wasn't a liar. He would have done what he said and sent for Papa. So why wasn't Papa back yet? He answered the letters they sent to him with his messenger hawk, Germogen. Even with magic, sometimes it took the hawk a few weeks to get to Papa and back again. The last letter they'd gotten from him had been several weeks ago, now that Anya thought about it. The hawk had been in their barn since then. Dyedka said it was nice to let Germogen have a rest, and also didn't want to alert Papa's camp superiors that he was using a magical hawk to deliver messages. Her *dyedushka* was the only one of them who could summon or send the hawk because, like Papa, Dyedka had animal magic. Anya would suggest they send more letters tonight so she could ask how far away Papa was.

She put Zvezda in the barn and shut the door. The door worked to keep him contained only half the time, but hopefully he would forget about the sukkah and eat something else. Anya went inside the house, where Mama was standing at the stove. Since Dobrynya's promise to bring Papa home, Mama had been in better spirits on most days. Today was one of those days.

She turned to Anya with a smile on her face and said, "Oh, there you are! Is the sukkah ready?"

Anya nodded. "So far. Zvezda keeps eating it, though."

Babulya and Dyedka sat at the table. Babulya was knitting a lumpy scarf near the oven, and Dyedka was grumping his way through Papa's old history book at the table, thumping his wooden legs impatiently on the floor. Dyedka looked up and squinted at Anya.

"Well, you built it too early," he said. "It doesn't start for three days. Why'd you make it already?"

Because last year Håkon burned it down, Anya thought. "Just in case," she said.

He looked back down at the history book. "That goat'll eat that whole thing before morning, mark my words."

Babulya cackled over her knitting.

"I wish he'd stop!" Anya snapped.

"Ah," Babulya said with a laugh. "Wishes. Don't wish. Pray. Pray with your feet."

Anya blinked long, exasperated. *Pray with your feet* was Babulya's way of saying *Do something about your problem* with the implied *Quit complaining* attached. "Praying with my feet is going to waste all my time with that stupid goat!"

"Well, I'm glad you put it up," Mama said. "It reminds me of your aunt Tzivyah. We used to have so much fun with your papa building ours." She cleared her throat in that way she did when she had stumbled onto something sad. "Anyway, I have some potions to make. Would you like to help?"

Anya smiled. Babulya had been delivering salves and potions all around the village for years in secret. After the magistrate had left, the villagers found out Babulya was the mysterious potions maker. Not only were they all grateful for her help in banishing illnesses, but they insisted on paying her. So Babulya and Mama both started making the potions, and since Babulya was blind and couldn't get around the village very easily, Anya delivered them. It seemed like, with the magistrate's disappearance from the village, the people were less afraid to use magic.

She joined Mama in the kitchen. Mama tapped the counter with a finger. "Let's see. Little Zinoviya is teething, so her mama asked for a potion for that. Sasha Melnik's poor face looks like he's got pox, but it's pimples, so we'll make him an astringent. Bogdana Lagounova asked for a digestive. And Father Drozdov would like something for nerves."

Anya inventoried the list of potions as Mama recited them. "Father Drozdov is nervous?"

Mama nodded. "I was talking to him a few days ago. He's from very far to the south, and the winters here make him anxious all the time. It will be winter soon, and he's already got himself worried over it."

Winter, to Anya, meant staying inside more and being careful of how she layered when she did go out. They had to watch the goats and chickens more closely, but other than the gloomy, dark days, winter wasn't terrible. "Why is he worried?"

"Oh," Mama said, "he was saying the snow makes it too hard to travel, and the days are too short and the nights are too cold. He asked if we had a potion that could cure frostbite. I told him no, nothing for frostbite, but your *babushka* has made a potion for nerves before and offered to bring him some to see if it helped."

Anya nodded. "Is he from the same south where Babulya is from?"

"I think farther," Mama said. "He might be from Byzantium. He's such a nice man. He's not that much older than your papa. When Papa gets back, maybe he and Father Drozdov can become friends."

"Maybe," Anya said. When Papa got back. Any day now.

Mama went about gathering herbs from Babulya's collection along the walls. When their old house had burned down, Dyedka and the *domovoi* managed to save Babulya's plant collection. Which was lucky. Some of the plants she had were rare and impossible to find anywhere in Kievan Rus'.

But the plant Mama brought back was a common local herb. The tiny white flowers were fun to braid into crowns to put on the goats' heads. Mama held a stoppered vial with dried flowers in it that Anya had made into tea many times.

"Chamomile?" Anya asked.

Mama nodded. "Sweet little chamomile."

"For nerves?"

"Oh yes." Mama ground up the flowers with a mortar and pestle. "We're making something a little stronger than tea today, though. Out in the garden, there's some roseroot in the north corner. I need . . ." She tapped her finger against her chin, thinking. "An inch of root. Can you get some for me?"

Anya took a knife out into the garden. The roseroot grew low to the ground along the northern fence, its fleshy leaves lining a stem topped with brushlike yellow flowers. She poked the soil with her knife until she found the dirty, thick root of the plant. She cut off an inch and hurried back inside, brushing the soil off of it and the knife blade.

Mama took the root from Anya and washed it, then ground it up with the chamomile. She added them to a small bowl, dripped some water in, and then put her finger in the mixture. As she stirred with one hand, she wove threads with the other. The potion in the bowl changed as she worked her plant magic. It turned a dark beige with swirls of white throughout, and the scent wafted up to Anya. Chamomile, yes, but barely; an afterthought of the magic. Mama pulled her finger out of the thick mixture and tilted the bowl this way and that.

"That looks . . ." Mama pulled one more string, and the white in the mixture faded into a dull silver. "That's perfect." Anya helped her pour the potion into a separate flask with a stopper, and Mama tied a tiny wooden spoon to the flask's neck.

Anya poked the spoon. "That's the dosage?" When Mama nodded, Anya said, "It's so small."

"It's powerful," Mama said. "If he takes one spoonful a day, he'll feel better. If he takes two, he'll probably miss a sermon at the church. If he takes three, he might . . ." She sighed. "Just, when you deliver it, make sure you emphasize only one per day, in the morning."

Anya nodded. "I will."

Mama kissed her on the forehead. "Good girl, Annushka."

CHAPTER THREE

ANYA HELPED MAMA make Zinoviya's teething potion and Bogdana's digestive. Sasha Melnik's astringent would take longer, Mama said, so Anya took the three ready potions out for delivery while Mama got started on his.

Even though she knew which potions were which, Anya still labeled each of them with a different colored bit of yarn tied around the mouth. Baby Zinoviya's was blue. Bogdana's was green. Father Drozdov's was purple.

She checked her sukkah before she went. No goat-bites had been taken out of it. Good.

Up the drive she went, and south on the road that ran past the property. Zinoviya and Father Drozdov lived inside the village, while Bogdana lived south of it. She and her family had extensive land down there, with a lot of bees. They were candlemakers, so Anya supposed they needed lots of bees.

A raven landed on the stone pylon of the bridge as Anya approached. It cawed at her, then cocked its head downward, toward the water. Anya had seen that head nod so many times over the last year that there was no mistaking what it meant.

Furtively, Anya checked the road behind her and across the bridge on the other side. No one was coming, so she hurried around the bridge and slid down the embankment, tucking herself under the bridge where there was a little strip of dry land on the side. A moment later, a ruby-red head stuck up out of the water, and what would probably have been fearsome teeth to someone else grinned widely at her.

"Anya!" Håkon heaved himself half onto the bank next to her. He left most of his body in the water for a quick escape if needed. The fishermen usually didn't come down by the bridge because their boats had a hard time fitting under it, but sometimes they caught bait over here, and Håkon had come very close to being found out a couple of times.

"Hey!" She arranged her dress so he wouldn't splash the potion vials in her pocket. "What are you doing all the way up here?"

Håkon doodled with one claw in the wet dirt. "I dunno. I was bored. I went by your barn, but I didn't see you. Just that little house-thing you built."

"It's called a sukkah," Anya said. "Did Zvezda eat it?"

He wrinkled his nose. "What?"

"Nothing." Anya watched his doodle turn into a crude drawing of Zvezda. The goat breathed what she assumed was fire.

"So where are you going?" Håkon asked.

"Delivering potions," Anya said. She patted her pocket; the vials clinked inside it.

"Oh," Håkon said. He continued to doodle. Now Zvezda had spines on his back, like Håkon did. His were reddish-gold, dull in the shade under the bridge but brilliant in sunlight. "That sounds fun."

"Lots." She poked his shoulder with one finger. "The deliveries won't take me long. Why don't I go pick up Ivan, and we can come to your house and play something?"

Håkon perked. "Rescue the Princess?"

Anya cringed. She'd be the princess, and that amounted to sitting in a cage he built out of stone or ice or something, and watching him and Ivan battle with magic. It wasn't her favorite, especially since she could use a weapon and didn't need to be relegated to being stuck in a cage. But Håkon seemed very down today, so she'd suffer the indignity of being caged if that made him happy.

She managed to smile. "Absolutely."

"Yes!" Håkon splashed his tail in the water, and a wave rolled up onto the shore and wet the hem of Anya's dress.

She jumped back and lifted her dress up, foot slipping on the mud near the water. Her shoe got all wet, and she groaned. "Now it's going to be all squishy."

"Sorry, Anya!" Håkon said, moving closer to her. "Here, let me—"

"Anya?"

A voice from over them, on top of the bridge, called down. Anya and Håkon both froze. Anya recognized the voice. It belonged to Verusha Dragutinovna, one of the girls Anya had become friends with over the last year.

Terrified, Anya looked up. Verusha's shadow was on the water, but Anya couldn't see Verusha's face. That meant Verusha couldn't see Anya or, by extension, Håkon. Håkon's secret was safe.

For now.

Multiple sets of footsteps moved toward the side of the bridge. Verusha wasn't alone.

"*Go,*" Anya hissed at Håkon, shoving him.

Håkon looked as scared as Anya felt. He hesitated for a breath, then slid backwards into the water with the tiniest of splashes. Just like that, he was gone, the doodle of a fire-breathing goat with spines the only evidence of his visit.

As Håkon's last ripple hit the shore by Anya's foot, Verusha rounded the corner. Behind her were two others: her sister, Olya, and their friend Mila Nikolaevna. They all had approximately the same color of light brown hair, but Verusha wore hers in two braids, while Olya wore hers in one. Mila always had hers braided perfectly around the crown of her head, and today she was carefully sliding tiny flowers into the plait as she followed Verusha.

Anya stood as Verusha peeked under the bridge. "I thought I heard you talking to someone," Verusha said. She looked disappointed.

Anya shook her head. "Just me."

"What are you doing down here all by yourself?" Verusha asked.

Anya tensed up, then pointed at the river. "Um, I was

just . . . You know, trying to do some water magic? I got my shoe wet." She lifted her soaked foot.

Verusha clapped her hands. "Oh, magic? Really? Watch this!" She reached her fingers toward the water, setting them against invisible threads in the air. She plucked, and a tiny jet of water arced out of the river and hit the bridge's pylon.

A surge of jealousy roiled Anya's belly—she still didn't have any magic, water or otherwise—but she managed to smile. "That's great!"

Verusha ran a hand down one of her braids and said, "I've been trying to get better."

Olya giggled and elbowed Mila, who said, "Because she loves Ivan."

Verusha turned a shade of red to rival Håkon's brilliance. "Shut up, Mila! I do *not* love Ivan!"

In unison, Olya and Mila sang, *"Uh-huhhhhh."*

Loudly, Verusha said, *"Actually,* we were on our way to your house, Anya. To invite you flower-picking with us."

Anya's heart did a little jump for joy. She wondered when she'd get used to this, being asked to do fun things with the other village children. It was still a thrill. "Are you going right now?"

Verusha nodded and pointed to Mila. "If she doesn't have flowers in her hair, she can't function."

"Can so," Mila said absently, weaving another tiny flower along her crown.

Anya said, "I've got to deliver some potions, but I don't think that will take long."

Olya clapped. "Oh good! You know where all the best flowers are!"

Anya puffed up. She did. It was because of Mama and Babulya. Anya had gone on flower-picking missions many times to keep up with the higher demand for potions. She knew all the richest spots.

Then she remembered what she'd told Håkon. She'd deliver her potions, then play a game with him. She couldn't abandon him for flower-picking.

"I just remembered," Anya said, "I told my mama I'd come back and help her with a really tough potion. I can't go with you."

Olya and Mila pouted, and Verusha sighed. "Oh, Anya! Really? Can't you come anyway? She'd understand."

Anya shook her head. "I can't. But there's a lot of daisies in the field north of the eastern road," Anya said, gesturing in that direction. "That would be a good place to go."

"Too bad you can't come," Verusha said. "Maybe tomorrow?"

"Maybe," Anya said, hoping it would be possible. She wished and wished for some way to bring Håkon into the group of friends she'd made since last year. When her house had burned down, the whole village had surprised her family by running to their aid. Anya had made friends with the trio standing before her now, and was becoming friends with Sasha Melnik, the miller's grandson. Mama had started to spend time with some of the other women her age in the village, swapping recipes for fish and bread and soups. Even Babulya created tenuous friendships with the collection of grandmothers whose sole purpose seemed to be creating warm garments for any child who got too close to them.

Everyone was making new friends, except Håkon. He was still alone, and Anya felt obligated to play with him as much as possible. He had no one else.

The four girls climbed to the top of the embankment back onto the road, and Anya pointed the way to the daisy field. Olya and Mila paid attention and nodded, but Verusha stared toward the village instead. Her face got red at the bottom, and the color rolled upward all the way to her ears before Anya turned and noticed who was coming over the bridge.

It was Ivan, a jaunt in his step and a cap too warm for the weather sideways on his head, swinging the metal-topped staff Kin had made for him with sloppy abandon. He'd gotten taller since he'd first moved to the village a year and a half ago with his family, who were sent by the tsar to hunt a dragon: Håkon. But Ivan wasn't like the rest of his family, and instead of hunting Håkon, he had befriended him. Today, he wore his usual attire, the uniform of a fool: very expensive clothing worn entirely incorrectly. Technically all the pieces were there: loose trousers over tall boots, a linen *rubakha*, and a stocking cap. The *rubakha* that day was particularly nice, even though it was much shorter than most men wore theirs, made of undyed linen with red embroidery around the sleeve cuffs and neck. But he had ruined it with a ratty belt tied into a bow rather than a proper knot.

Ivan waved at Anya, then seemed to see the other girls for the first time. Olya and Mila giggled behind Anya as Ivan stared at Verusha, letting his arm drop. He stopped walking.

From the other end of the bridge, Ivan yelled, "Hello, Verusha!"

Verusha squeaked, then managed to say aloud, "Hello, Ivan!"

Olya and Mila both sighed. "Awwww."

Anya groaned and kept herself from pinching the bridge of her nose. Now she was going to hear about nothing but Verusha all day from Ivan.

"I'm surprised to see you!" Ivan yelled, leaning against the bridge's side.

Before Verusha could answer, Anya called, "Ivan, why don't you come closer so you don't have to yell?"

"Don't be ridiculous, Anya!" Ivan yelled even louder.

Verusha was wringing the hem of her apron and staring at Ivan with a goony smile, so Anya took her gently by the shoulders and turned her around. "You should go pick flowers."

Verusha allowed herself to be turned around. "Oh. Yes. Of course." She tucked one braid behind her ear. "Will you tell him I said it was wonderful to see him?"

"I sure will," Anya said. "Have fun picking flowers."

Verusha nodded, grinning, and she went with Olya and Mila. They had barely stepped off the bridge when they started whispering to one another.

Ivan remained on the other side of the bridge, still

leaning against the side. Anya trotted to him and said, "Why are you standing all the way over here?"

He watched the girls walk north and didn't answer.

Anya snapped her fingers in front of his face. "Ivan!"

"Huh?" He looked down, startled, like he hadn't noticed her there before. "Oh. Hi, Anya!"

"Why didn't you come closer?"

He balked. "Come closer? To Verusha?" He whispered. "Because I *like* her."

"Exactly," Anya whispered back.

"I don't think she likes me, though," Ivan said.

Just then, the trio of girls squealed among themselves up the road. She could hear Verusha's high-pitched triumphant declaration, *"He's so handsome!"*

Anya stared at Ivan as he listened to Verusha's squeal too.

"That doesn't mean anything," Ivan said.

Anya pushed past him toward the village. "You're such an idiot."

Ivan followed her, his too-short pants riding up past his calves with every step. "Thanks!"

CHAPTER FOUR

BABY ZINOVIYA was screaming so loudly, Anya heard her while she was still out on the road. A harried Sveta answered the door when Anya knocked. Zinoviya held on to Sveta's leg, howling, face covered with tears.

"You're a blessing," Sveta breathed out. Her hair was partly braided but mostly loose, and her eyes were so dark, it looked like she hadn't slept in days. She scooped Zinoviya up and cooed with a shaky voice, "Here, Zinya; here, *myshka*," as she rubbed some of the potion inside the baby's mouth.

Almost immediately, Zinoviya stopped crying. She smacked her lips, made a sound like she was about to start crying, but then changed her mind and quieted. Sveta laughed, sounding a bit on the verge of tears herself.

"Tell your mama she's a miracle worker," Sveta said.

Anya nodded. "I will."

Sveta closed the door. Anya and Ivan continued into the village. It hummed as much as it normally did on a Thursday. It was nearly the equinox, so the villagers who were Slavists were preparing to celebrate. Dyedka would pray to some idols and get Babulya clucking at him about idolatry, like she did at every Slavist festival.

Anya was trying to figure out Ivan's reasoning for standing so far away if Verusha liked him. "What difference does it make how close you stand?" Anya asked. "I could understand if you weren't going to talk to her, but . . ."

"I don't know," Ivan said. "I get nervous. What if she smells me and I smell bad? What if I have a booger?" He rubbed his nose. "What if—"

"Verusha wouldn't care about any of that." Anya rolled her eyes.

"How do you know?"

"Because she likes you!" Anya said. "She got all giggly. Did you not notice that?"

Ivan clutched his staff as he stared into the distance and whispered, "Anya, do I smell bad?"

She sighed. As they approached the mill, the door opened, and Sasha Melnik poked his head out. Even from her distance, she could make out the pimples all over his forehead. When he saw Anya, he lifted his hand and waved at her. She smiled and waved back.

He disappeared into the mill for a second, then came out with a sack of flour over one shoulder. "Anya! Hi!"

"Hi, Sasha," Anya said. "I don't have your potion yet. Astringents take more time. Mama says it will be done later."

"Oh." Sasha looked dejected for a second, then brightened again. "That's okay. I'm just glad she's helping me at all. Here." He handed the flour to her. "Payment."

She grunted as he dropped the flour in her arms. "Thanks."

"Absolutely." He beamed, then looked a little puzzled. "I swear I saw Ivan with you when you walked up."

"He's right—" Anya turned to where Ivan had been walking beside her, but he was gone. She turned, looking around, and caught him peering out from behind the butcher shop, way on the other end of the square.

When Ivan saw them looking at him, he ducked

behind the shop wall for a moment, then peeked out again. "Hi, Sasha!"

Sasha waved a little, confused. "Hi, Ivan?"

"You look—" Ivan's voice cracked, and he cleared his throat. "You look well. Today. Sasha." He slowly scooted behind the butcher shop again. "I dropped something over here, no need to help me look for it, bye!"

And then he was gone.

Anya rolled her eyes so hard, the backs of them hurt.

Sasha scratched his arm. "I guess he must have dropped something really important."

"He must have," Anya said.

Sasha nodded, then said, "Is he . . . hiding from me?"

Anya hesitated, then said loudly, "What? No!"

"Are you sure?" Sasha touched the field of pimples on his face, an unspoken anxiety screaming directly at her.

"I bet he didn't even notice," she said, possibly telling the truth. Ivan noticed the weirdest things, and other things flew right by him. "He's definitely not hiding from you."

"Okay." Sasha didn't sound convinced.

"I'll bring that astringent as soon as it's ready," Anya said, patting Sasha on the shoulder.

"Thanks, Anya," Sasha said. He cocked a thumb at the mill. "I better get back to work."

They said their goodbyes, and Sasha returned to the mill. Anya lugged her sack of flour to the end of the butcher shop. When she rounded the corner, she saw Ivan sitting against the outer wall with his knees drawn up to his chest, the staff on the ground next to him.

"Do you like Sasha, too?" Anya asked him.

Ivan didn't look up. "So what if I do?"

"I thought you liked Verusha."

"I can like two people, Anya!"

She scowled. "Well, like them on your own time. I have to deliver potions, and then . . ." She realized she hadn't told Ivan about playing with Håkon. She said in a low voice, "Then Håkon wants us to play with him. I said we would."

Ivan looked up at her now and raised an eyebrow. "Play what?"

With a long, weary sigh, Anya said, "Princess."

Ivan grinned, grabbed his staff, and leaped up. "Let's go, then!" He took the sack from her and tossed it over a shoulder, then set off toward the middle of the square. He took half a dozen steps, then spun around and marched back to her.

"Who do you have to deliver potions to?" he asked.

Anya crossed her arms. "Bogdana and Father Drozdov."

Ivan snapped the fingers of his free hand. "No problem. Bogdana lives down by us, and Father Drozdov—you can call him Father Fyodor, Anya—he's at our house."

Calling adults by their first names seemed strange to Anya. Maybe Ivan could get away with that. He was a fool, and he also saw Father Drozdov every week at church. Anya didn't. She wouldn't be calling him by his first name, no matter what Ivan said. They set off for the south. Anya asked, "Why is he at your house?"

"Dvoyka and Troyka have finally decided that they aren't satisfied with terrorizing just this village," Ivan said. "They want to terrorize the world. They're leaving, and Father Fyodor is blessing them before they go."

Anya didn't know what to say. Ivan's eldest brothers were over twenty years old. It was about time they leave, but somehow their departure made Anya sad. They had only just moved into the village last year, but they were dynamic presences already. She couldn't remember a time before them. And after they left, there would be only five Ivans. That wasn't nearly enough.

CHAPTER FIVE

DROPPING OFF Bogdana Lagounova's digestive was complicated by the many beehives around the house. Anya and Ivan shuffled stiffly by, trying not to make too much noise and potentially anger the bees. The bees themselves buzzed everywhere and didn't seem to pay Anya or Ivan any mind.

Bogdana took the digestive from Anya as she rubbed her chest. "I've got some beeswax candles for your mama to trade." She went into an adjoining room for a minute; the sounds of rummaging reached where Anya and Ivan stood on the front step. Finally Bogdana came back with a sack heavy with candles. "Twelve."

"Thank you," Anya said, taking the candles. "Are the digestives working for you?"

Bogdana let out an enormous, weary sigh. "Yes, and it's about time something did. I'll expect you in three days with another one." She narrowed her eyes at Ivan. "Don't you touch my bees, fool."

Ivan saluted her as she shut the door on them. They shuffled silently and slowly back to the road, past the indifferent bees. Only when they were on the road did Ivan say, "I wasn't the one who knocked over the hive, anyway. It was Pyatsha."

"I don't think Gospozha Lagounova can tell the difference," Anya said.

"Besides!" Ivan said. "She had a *leshy* wandering among them! That's why we were even here in the first place. What if the *leshy* knocked over the hive?"

"I thought you just said it was Pyatsha."

Ivan drummed his fingers on the staff. "Maybe the *leshy* framed Pyatsha."

The local *leshy* didn't come out of the woods, so Anya doubted very much that the forest spirit had been doing anything with Bogdana's bees. But Anya didn't doubt that either Ivan or Pyatsha or both believed they had seen the *leshy*. They thought they saw a lot of things.

"Sure," Anya said. "Did you catch the *leshy*?"

"Not yet," Ivan said.

"Have you caught anything yet?"

He nodded; then the nod turned into a slow shake. "No. But we will. Papa says we aren't leaving until we've cleaned this village up."

Anya thought the village was plenty clean to begin with. None of the magical creatures had ever caused too much of a problem. Except maybe the *vodyaniye*, the nasty froglike river-grass spirits that liked to drown people, but even they weren't too bad as long as you were smart around the water. As far as she was concerned, the Ivanovs were trying to solve a problem that didn't exist.

But she liked Ivan's company. She was getting used to his brothers' boisterous affections. His mama was uncommonly kind. And Ivan's papa, Yedsha, was surprisingly inefficient as a monster hunter, so nothing really changed.

They crossed the road toward the Ivanov home, which had previously been Widow Medvedeva's home and boarding house. Yedsha had offered her a lot of money for the house, so she'd gone to live with one of her sons in Mologa, the next largest city. Immediately the Ivanovs had built onto it, adding rooms so each Ivan could have his own bed to sleep in—though, as far as Anya could tell, they all just slept in whatever room they felt like sleeping in. Now the original home stood in the middle with various additions, rooms, and wings stacked and piled around it, like a merchant trying to carry too many bags at once.

Ivan sauntered up to his home without a care. Anya approached cautiously. It wasn't that she didn't like the brothers Ivanov. She just usually ended up covered in dirt, or upside down, or trapped under or inside something. She wasn't in the mood for that today. She had the priest's potion in her pocket, and she didn't want it to break when Ivan's brothers inevitably tackled her to the ground.

Ivan flung the door open and went inside. Anya followed, pausing at the threshold. The house was a mess, as usual, but it was orderly in its foolish way. Two huge backpacks leaned against each other in the front room, half-stuffed with clothes and food and waterskins. The family, with all the brothers, plus Father Drozdov, were gathered in the kitchen. It made for a very crowded space. There were seven brothers in all, three sets of twins and then Ivan by himself as the youngest, all named Ivan. The oldest set of twins were Dvoyka and Troyka, Number Two and Number Three. Their father, Yedsha, was Number One. Their odd way of naming had spun Anya's head around for the first few days she'd known them, but now she couldn't imagine calling them all Ivan and being able to keep them straight.

Dvoyka—or maybe Troyka—stood beside the priest, but she couldn't see the other one anywhere. Anya had a hard time telling the eldest twins apart now that they had grown identical beards.

The crowd in the kitchen were all sitting on various surfaces, and no one was speaking. Whenever Papa had gone to the big market in Mologa, Anya's whole family had always sat around their table for a minute, silent. Even their *domovoi* would join them—not that he ever said anything anyway. It was good luck to start a journey with some silence.

Anya felt a presence behind her, and a shadow fell over the doorway. Before she could turn, arms wrapped around her, pinning her own to her sides, and she was squeezed and lifted into the air.

Troyka—or maybe Dvoyka—yelled from behind her: "Aha! Annushka! So you came after all!"

He walked into the house with her, swinging her this way and that. Everyone in the kitchen turned to look at Anya being carried inside.

Marina, Ivan's mother, yelled, "You're supposed to be silent! It's bad luck!"

Anya wheezed, "Troyka, put me down."

The twin standing next to Father Drozdov said, "I'm not holding you."

"Dvoyka, then!" Anya said, using up what breath she had left.

Marina waved a hand at Dvoyka. "Put her down! Be nice. She's practically your sister."

"That's why we can pick her up like this!" With a laugh, Dvoyka did put her down, patting her on the head after he did. "I'm glad to see you, Anya! What do you want us to bring back for you from the other kingdoms?"

Anya gasped for air. "I don't know."

"A magical doll," Ivan's father, Yedsha, said. "They have those in places, you know."

"I don't really like dolls," Anya said. The only thing she could think of to ask for was her father, and she doubted Dvoyka and Troyka were going to Rûm. "But thank you."

Father Drozdov smiled; it looked strained. "Maybe, ah, a book. Eh, Anya? You'd like a book, wouldn't you?"

"I like books." She'd take a book before a doll, for

sure. The priest's creaking smile made her remember the potion, and she pulled it from her pocket.

Before she could give it to him, though, he turned away from her and said, "Now that Dvoyka is here, let us pray."

Anya tensed up and slid the potion back into her pocket. She glanced around the room, face hot. Should she stay there and listen to the prayer? Should she step outside until they were done? She wasn't sure which option was less awkward, but before she could decide, Father Drozdov took a deep breath and began speaking a language Anya couldn't understand.

She fidgeted for a moment, then stood quietly with her hands clasped at her waist, eyes drilled to the floor. She didn't want to walk out as Father Drozdov prayed.

His singsong voice was the only sound in the room. Anya remembered how hoarse he'd been last year, days after Sigurd had almost choked him to death. He had helped Mama arrange Shavuot for the entire village, rasping out orders. She remembered him eating the cheesy bliny with a smile, and then—*flash*—she could see him dangling from Sigurd's fist, eyes bulging, choking, feet swinging beneath him, and then—*flash*—Sigurd by the river, the hand he had choked Father Drozdov with bleeding, his eyes bleeding, his teeth stained—

"Anya?" Ivan's voice snapped her out of her flashback, and she startled as he set his hand on her shoulder.

"What?" she snapped, then said, "I'm sorry."

"Are you okay?" he asked.

"I'm fine." She looked around and realized the house was emptying. "Where are they all going?"

"We're going to walk Dvoyka and Troyka to the village boundary," Ivan said. "Do you want to come?"

Anya nodded, and they followed the small procession south down the road. Dvoyka and Troyka walked ahead, big packs on their backs and a spring in their step. Ivan's four other brothers followed in a gaggle, and their parents trailed after them. Father Drozdov walked alone behind Yedsha and Marina, and Anya hurried to catch up with him.

"Father," she said as she came abreast of him.

He looked up at her with an uncomfortable expression. "Oh, hello, Anya."

She dug the vial out of her pocket and extended it to him. "My mama wanted me to deliver this to you. She said to take one spoonful in the morning, but no more."

He nodded and took the vial in trembling fingers. "This will be such a help. Bless—er, thank you. Thank you so much. You and your mama. Thank you both."

The priest's face flushed, and Anya mumbled a "You're welcome" before falling behind him. Mama said he was nervous because of the winter coming, but was that really it? Or did he still think of Sigurd the way Anya did?

She walked beside Ivan, silent, until they reached the bridge that was the unofficial village boundary. Dvoyka and Troyka hugged all their brothers and both parents, shook hands with the priest, and took turns squeezing Anya in crushing bear hugs. She caught the glimmer of a tear in Troyka's eye before the pair marched up to the bridge, then turned and took slow steps backwards over it.

"Goodbye!" Dvoyka called, lifting an arm.

"Farewell!" Troyka said, waving at them.

"We shall miss you all!"

"Some more than others!"

"Others not as much as some!"

"You shall have a place in our hearts!"

"Mostly in our hearts."

"Some in our pockets, if our hearts grow too full."

"Actually, I think we'll leave you all here."

"Anyway, we love you all!"

Pyatsha sighed loudly and yelled, "Just go already!"

"Except Pyatsha," Dvoyka continued.

"He's the worst," Troyka said, still waving.

Pyatsha took one of his boots off and threw it at his retreating oldest brothers. They both ducked, but they didn't need to. The boot went wide and hit the bridge's edge, then dropped into the river.

"Ack!" Pyatsha yelled, hobbling half-bootless over the road. The rest of his brothers followed him.

Ivan reached forward, pulling a magic thread, and the water shifted up. The boot was spat up out of the river, flew into the air, and landed on the shore in front of Pyatsha. He grabbed the boot off the ground and stood, bringing it up over his head, ready to lob it at his brothers again.

But he couldn't. The bridge was empty. Dvoyka and Troyka were gone, disappearing up the road. Pyatsha let his arm drop, and the boot slipped from his fingers. His shoulders slumped. He and the four other Ivanov brothers watched as Number Two and Number Three turned a corner and vanished.

CHAPTER SIX

IVAN'S FAMILY STOOD by the bridge for a while, watching the empty place where Dvoyka and Troyka had been. Yedsha held Marina close to him, and she rested her head against his chest. The remaining brothers drew together at the end of the bridge. None of them stepped onto it, as if doing so would have some sort of dire consequence. Anya noticed Father Drozdov turn his back to the rest of them and, when he thought no one was watching, take a spoonful of Mama's potion.

Anya patted Ivan on the shoulder. "They'll do great."

Ivan nodded. "They're both really good at fool magic."

"How does someone get *good* at fool magic?" Anya asked. "It happens when you're not trying."

"I know." Ivan's voice cracked, and he wiped a tear off his cheek. "They're so good at not trying."

Anya shook her head but kept patting Ivan's shoulder. The village would be quiet without the eldest twins, but she was confident that Ivan and his brothers would fill that void in no time.

Marina took a deep breath and said, "Well, we can't stand here all day, can we? Let's go, boys. Father, thank you so much for coming."

"Of course," the priest said. He already seemed calmer. "I'll pray for them every day."

Marina nodded, then motioned for Anya to come over. She did, and Marina hugged her tight and kissed the top of her head. "And you, Anya. You being here means so much to me. And to them. To all of us."

Anya slung her arms around Marina's waist. They embraced for a few breaths and then released each other. The group moved north on the road, returning to the Ivanov house. Ivan and Anya trailed the main group once again.

The Ivanov house came into sight just as the dull thud of horse hooves and the sharp crunch of wooden wheels over the dirt of the road rose behind them. Anya and Ivan turned at the same time. A wagon was rare in the summer, when the roads were easily passable, but it was autumn now, and snow would be coming anytime; travel so close to snowfall was nonexistent.

Usually nonexistent.

The big horse pulling the wagon was half-shaggy with a winter coat that hadn't entirely grown in yet. He tossed his head as he passed Anya and Ivan and then the rest of the family. The man driving spared them only enough of a glance so he didn't run them over. The bed of the wagon was piled with chests and bundles of what looked like furs.

"I wonder where he's going," Anya said softly to Ivan. "Usually they trap fur north and take it south, not the other way around."

Ivan shrugged. "Maybe he's delivering it to someone in Ingria, or Karelia."

"There have got to be better routes than through Zmeyreka," Anya said.

"Oh, definitely," Ivan said.

"Maybe he's lost," Anya said.

The wagon slowed, then came to a stop in front of Ivan's house.

Ivan said, "Or maybe he's delivering something *here*."

As they watched, the wagon driver turned and said something that was too quiet for them to hear. Out from between furs and chests, tucked where they hadn't seen him before, a man unfolded and stood, moving stiffly.

He had on a long, dirty coat, its fur-lined sleeves ratty and stained, that looked as though he hadn't taken it off for months. His *votola* cloak was in a similar state, with dark rusty splotches on it. The fur *shapka* on his head was grimy and clumped, pulled down around his ears. A scraggly, unkempt beard obscured the bottom half of his face.

A soldier's sword hung at his waist.

Anya was moving faster then, unaware until she was running over the road. A soldier in the village. All the men had gone, and there could be no one else coming back already. Dobrynya had promised.

Papa.

He climbed out of the wagon, collecting a backpack on the way, then shook the driver's hand. The driver slapped his reins against the horse's flanks, and the wagon moved away again.

Tears stung Anya's eyes as she ran. He was back. He was right there. He was safe. He was *alive.*

She drew nearer, bursting with happiness to see her father, and then the man turned toward her.

Not Papa.

She slowed, the speed draining out of her legs. The man before her was familiar, but not the man she'd been desperate to see. It was Demyan Rybakov, Papa's best friend and the old village magistrate, who had gone to the front with Papa.

Demyan was back. Why wasn't Papa?

Anya stopped a few paces from Demyan. Her heart fell onto the road. When she looked at him, his mouth was pinched into a line behind his dirty beard. His eyes were red.

"Where's my papa?" she asked, trembling.

Demyan clutched his bag and then dropped it. He stepped to her and hugged her, saying nothing.

He hugged Anya for what seemed to her like the rest of her life. Her arms hung at her sides. She couldn't put any thoughts into a coherent collection in her head.

"I'm sorry," Demyan said, voice hoarse.

She wanted to know what he was sorry for, but she couldn't ask. The possibilities of the answers were too grim.

Ivan's voice breached Anya's silence: "Is everything okay, Anya?"

Demyan let her go, and she turned. Ivan and all his remaining brothers were gathered behind her on the road, watching with matching expressions of concern. Ivan's parents were past them, with Father Drozdov watching carefully from their side.

Demyan cleared his throat. "My name is Demyan Rybakov. I'm your new magistrate." He hesitated. "New-old magistrate. They said my replacement disappeared."

The Ivans blinked, silent. Semya said, "What did do you?"

Shestka said, "Why would you make Anya cry?"

Demyan said, "I didn't mean to."

Anya still couldn't say anything. Papa should have been with Demyan. Papa should have come back.

"Demyan." She grabbed onto his sleeve with a listless hand. "Where is he?"

He opened his mouth to say something, then looked at the gathered Ivans and said, "Why don't we go find your mama? So I can tell you both at once."

Anya's stomach threatened to empty itself, and she was afraid to open her mouth. So she nodded and let Demyan take her hand and lead her home.

At Anya's house, Demyan pulled off his *shapka* and clutched it in his hand. His curly brown hair was matted around the sides and back from weeks of being crammed under that hat, or perhaps a helmet. He took a deep breath before knocking on the door.

Footsteps from inside. The door swung open and Mama stood there, hair messy under her kerchief. Her eyes widened and she smiled. "Demyan!"

Mama jumped forward, hugging Demyan tightly. He let go of Anya so he could hug Mama back, tucking his face against her shoulder.

It took Anya a moment to realize Demyan was crying.

Mama realized it too. "Demyan?" She clung to him. "Why are—what happened?" And then, after several seconds of heavy silence: "Where is Miro?"

Anya stared at the ground, concentrating on not crying, and thinking the same thought over and over: *Not dead. Not dead. Not dead.* She should have felt something if he died. She would know. It would be impossible for Papa to vanish from the earth without an explosion of grief from the air itself.

Demyan stepped away from Mama and wiped his wet face. "He was already gone, Masha. I'm so sorry."

Mama's face wasn't as white as chamomile petals, but it was fast approaching that shade. "What do you mean, *gone?*"

"To Rûm," Demyan said, voice cracking. "The cavalry went first. He takes care of the horses, so he went, and I stayed behind. I was supposed to leave the day after, but some messengers arrived and said I was needed as magistrate again, and Miro had permission to come back."

Mama was shaking. "What does that mean?"

"The messengers tried to catch them before they crossed into the Pecheneg territories, but the cavalry was too fast," Demyan said. "Miro is . . . not coming home. There's no way to get to him."

Mama's face crumpled. The bravery she had managed to recover in the last year disintegrated, and she would have collapsed to the ground if Demyan hadn't caught her. He helped her inside and sat her at the table. Anya shuffled after them, shutting the door softly.

Papa wasn't coming home.

She swallowed the tears away.

There was no way to get to him.

A crawling numbness spread through her as she watched Mama sob at the table. Demyan slid into the chair next to her and clasped her hand in his. They sat in tearful silence.

Mama hadn't cried in almost eight months.

Anya's sadness gave way to anger. At Dobrynya for not acting fast enough. At Demyan for leaving Papa behind. At the magistrate who had sent Papa. At the tsar for starting this war in the first place.

The house was suddenly stifling. She backed to the door, slipped out while Mama cried, and let her feet take her up the road, away from her house, toward the ravine where Håkon lived.

CHAPTER SEVEN

A T HÅKON'S HOUSE, the dragon was nowhere to be found. She searched the empty house and riverbank, hoping he'd pop out of the water so she could tell him about Papa. But he wasn't there, and neither was Kin, Håkon's human father. The house and riverside property were empty.

Well, not entirely empty. Alsvindr nickered at her from his lean-to barn as she passed it. He had been Sigurd's warhorse, but Kin had adopted him after Sigurd was gone. She paused by him long enough to rub his nose.

"Where's Håkon?" she asked him.

He rubbed the side of his face against the barn wall and stamped a hoof.

"Do you want to go ride?"

He didn't answer, but Alsvindr was always ready for a run somewhere. She'd take him, but first she needed something out of the house.

Inside, Anya went straight to where her bow and quiver of arrows hung on the wall. She didn't want Mama knowing about the weapons, or about the way she still thought about Sigurd all the time, so she kept them at Kin's. Mama knew a little about what had happened because Dobrynya had told her all those months ago. But even Dobrynya didn't really know the truth. Kin didn't either, and he was puzzled when Anya had been reluctant to use the sword he'd made for her. She didn't like the feel of it in her hands. It reminded her of Sigurd, and Håkon, and the way it had felt to stab each of them. So Kin had turned her sword into a bushel of magic arrows and a magic bow, and had taught her everything he'd learned from the Varangians about archery.

Outside, Alsvindr stamped his hooves as he waited for her. Anya didn't know if horses could have a favorite person, but she felt that Alsvindr liked her better than he did other people. He bumped her shoulder with his velvety nose as she threw his saddle pad over his back.

The old saddle Sigurd had used was still there. She

had been uncomfortable using it for a long time, because every time she saw it, she remembered him in it, riding into her barn, right before he took Håkon and set the barn on fire. But then Kin reworked it and added an embedded iron design: a little goat on the right side. It was too nice a saddle not to use, made especially for the warhorse. The front and back rose up high, holding Anya in place. It had been strange at first, but when she started firing arrows from Alsvindr's back, she understood.

She fastened the saddle to the horse, looping the chest piece around his front. Alsvindr was huge for a horse—much taller than either of the Ivanov family's horses—and since he had belonged to such a rotten man, everyone expected him to be rotten too. In Anya's experience, he wasn't rotten at all. He would steal apples from people, but other than that, he was as good a horse as she could hope for.

Anya jumped into the saddle, hiking up her dress and tucking the front beneath her. Alsvindr started walking before she got settled. She was expecting it, though. He always did. She clicked her tongue and he sped into a trot, crossing over the little bridge near the house, heading south to the archery grounds.

✦ ✖ ✦

Since the fire last year, Babulya had spoken more openly about her past: Anya's family. Babulya told her often about Ötemish, Anya's other grandfather. *Saba* was the word he would have used, Babulya said. Saba, then, was what Anya thought of him as. Khazaria, Babulya said, had been a great kingdom at its end, but its people had begun as steppe warriors. They were nomads, living on horseback, traveling to graze their herds, defeating anyone who tried to move into their cold, high territories. Saba had been a trader, but first he had been a great horseman.

Maybe that's why Alsvindr liked Anya so much. Because he knew.

The archery grounds were actually a wide field where Dyedka took the goats to graze during the warmer months, after they exhausted all the grazing nearer to their house. Anya had fashioned targets out of straw and old blankets. The targets had once looked like straw men but now looked more like straw lumps.

They would still work, though.

She brought Alsvindr to a stop at the edge of the field and pulled out her bow. She maneuvered the quiver to a good position, where she could reach her meager handful of arrows easily. Her goal was to get six in the first target and six in the second, in one pass. She had done it once, though usually she'd miss the second target by a lot.

Not today.

Alsvindr gnawed on his bit impatiently, and Anya said, "Hang on," as she pulled her bracer from where it was fastened to her quiver strap. It was leather and kind of crude, but it did the job. She put the bracer on her left forearm, positioning it to keep her sleeve from interfering with her quick draw, but also to cover the tender inside. Her bowstring had snapped against her arm once, and the long bruise that formed didn't go away for more than a week. She had blamed it on Zvezda when Mama asked what happened.

"Okay," she whispered to Alsvindr, who was dancing beneath her. She let go of his reins, draping them over the high front of the saddle, and clicked her tongue.

When the horse felt the pressure let up on his snout and heard Anya's encouragement to go, he sprang forward, hooves ripping up the grass and throwing clods of dirt behind him. He tossed his head. He ran.

Anya couldn't wait. She used the high saddle and robust stirrups to hold herself steady. Alsvindr himself, a horse bred for war, ran smooth and fast, all four hooves off the ground at the same time. Without taking her eyes off the first target, Anya pulled an arrow out of her quiver, nocked it against the bowstring, and breathed deeply through her nose.

She held her breath, imagining Saba doing this same thing in Khazaria, and Papa doing it in Rûm, and Kin doing it in the North.

She let her breath trickle out of her and felt for the *thump-thump-thump-thump* of Alsvindr's hooves on the ground. In the next breath, they would all be off, and he would fly impossibly smooth for just a second. She felt it then: him gliding through the air like a bird, and she let the arrow go. It flew true—there were only twelve arrows, but they were *good* arrows—and hit the target where its lumpy arm should have been.

She could do better than that.

Anya drew another arrow as soon as she let the first one go. Six seconds between shots was another goal. She counted eight.

The arrow whistled, its fletching catching a breeze, and it hit the target in its straw belly.

Another arrow drawn. Ten seconds. *Ugh.* She could do better.

She let go and drew another. And another. Five arrows

hit the first target. One clipped the side and tumbled into the grass.

Now it was time for the second target. She did the same thing, but she was too close, and the last two arrows missed.

Alsvindr would have run forever if not for the trees. He turned a sharp left and cantered around the perimeter of the field, snorting with annoyance at the trees blocking his path. Anya pulled his reins to slow him and muttered, "We should just cut all the trees down, right? Make a path for ourselves."

The horse snorted and tossed his head, and Anya reined him to a stop. She slid off him, and he lipped at her kerchief, impatient.

Anya grabbed her kerchief and pushed his nose away. "I need to get my arrows."

The arrows stuck in the straw men came out easily enough, but it took her a minute to find the ones in the grass. She examined each of them for damage, like Kin had taught her to. They were magic arrows, but the shafts were still regular wood, and breakable. All of them looked and felt fine.

She stood in the grass for a few minutes, staring at the arrow in her hand but not really seeing it. Papa was in

Rûm, beyond where any messengers would go to retrieve him. Last year, she had convinced a *bogatyr* to help her get him. But Dobrynya was gone now, and Anya didn't know any other knights. Who else could she ask?

Bitterly, she thought of Dvoyka and Troyka. Maybe they *could have* gone to get him. That was their job as fools, right? But they would probably just end up getting lost and stumbling upon a hoard of treasure or something. Very lucky for them. Not so lucky for Papa.

Anya got on Alsvindr again and took him back to the edge of the field. She did three more passes at the targets. Her fingers were numb and red, but even so, she made contact with all her arrows on the second and third passes.

She climbed off Alsvindr and smacked him lightly on the flank. He trotted away, then galloped around the field on his own while Anya sat down next to one of her lumpy straw men. She put her arrows carefully into the quiver, running her fingers along the shafts and fletching.

Anya pulled an arrow out and stared at its sharp point, thinking of Papa again. In his letters, he talked about learning more than just the care of the horses: the other soldiers taught him how to use a sword and a bow, how to ride, how to drill. All of that should have made Anya feel better, but it didn't. Saba knew all that too, and he still died. If a powerful-enough force went up against Papa, he would lose. And Anya would never see him again.

Sigurd's cruel, cold eyes forced themselves into her mind. The Varangian had come to Zmeyreka in pursuit of Håkon. He had wanted to drain the little dragon's blood to make himself stronger. The memory of him made her shudder, and no matter what she did to try to banish him, he wouldn't go.

In her mind, she saw his death again: blood leaking from his eyes, his nose, his ears. Then he fell, dead before he hit the ground. She squeezed her eyes shut to force away the memory. It just spun around and around in her head, along with Håkon's own stabbing at Sigurd's hands, and Ivan's near-drowning in the river.

Then Babulya's voice interrupted the terrible images in her head, speaking from the table where she knitted a lumpy scarf: *Pray, Annushka. Pray with your feet.*

Anya looked back at the arrow's tip. Pray with her feet. Ask God for help while she took action to solve her own problems.

Shaking, Anya stood and clicked her tongue for Alsvindr. He trotted over to her, breath whooshing from his big nostrils, and bumped his nose into her hard enough to nearly send her to the ground.

"Hey!" She grabbed his reins to keep from falling back. Then, after checking that his saddle was still secured snugly, she climbed back up onto him.

Papa was coming home. Anya was going to make sure of it.

CHAPTER EIGHT

ANYA RETURNED ALSVINDR to his little barn and brushed him down quietly as she let the idea of bringing Papa back swirl through her mind. She went into the house to return her bow and arrows to their spots on the wall, glad Håkon and Kin were still gone, because she didn't want to get distracted. She let her feet take her home while her mind was busy mulling over the logistics of going to Rûm. She needed to leave as soon as possible. Before anything delayed her.

In a special spot in the barn, their hawk, Germogen, slumbered on his perch. They had been using him for over a year to send messages to Papa. When he wasn't ferrying those messages back and forth, he stayed with Anya's family. According to Dyedka, Germogen liked them.

The hawk opened one eye as Anya neared him, then the other. He made his hawk-squeak sound and ruffled his feathers.

"Be quiet," Anya whispered. She grabbed one of the little scrolls of paper they kept near the hawk's perch, along with the charcoal pencil. She wrote carefully on the paper: *I'm going to find you.* Then, after a pause, *Love, Anya.*

She rolled up the scroll and slid it into the tube that the hawk wore like a pack, settled on his back between his wings. He was always amicable when Dyedka slipped it on him, but she hadn't ever tried to do it herself.

"Okay, Germogen." Anya eyeballed him. "I need you to take this to Papa. He's not going to be where he usually is. Papa says you use magic to find him. So use it. Okay?"

Germogen blinked and ruffled his feathers again.

Anya pressed her lips together and reached out to put the backpack over Germogen's wings and clip it around his chest. When her hand got near to him, he cocked his head and watched her fingers.

"Don't you dare bite me," she mumbled. If he did, he'd probably take her entire finger off. She reached for him again and touched her fingers against his soft feathers. He made his squeak and lifted his wings out.

Anya leaped back, ready for the hawk to jump and claw at her. But he didn't. He just stood there, wings out, and she realized he was making it easier for her to put the backpack on. She carefully slid the straps over his wings, smoothing his feathers down when she snapped the chest strap. Germogen shook his wings and nestled them back against his body carefully.

She put on the thick glove that protected her arm from his talons, then held her arm out. He stepped onto her carefully, his weight taking her by surprise. She struggled to keep her arm up as she walked him around to the back of the barn. She didn't want anyone to see her.

Next to the sukkah, Anya risked a stroke along the hawk's neck. He shut his eyes and leaned against her fingers.

"Find my papa," Anya whispered to him. "Please."

She didn't know what to expect. She didn't have animal magic. Would Germogen listen to her? Would he fly to Papa? Would he fly at all?

Germogen opened his big eyes and looked up at the

sky. He crouched down for just a second, then exploded off her arm. One wing smacked her in the face. The force of his flight buffeted her back, and she watched him climb into the sky, over the trees, and then he was gone into the cooling day.

He'd find Papa. He always did.

She hoped.

Anya returned the glove to Germogen's perch and then snuck to the house. She opened the side door, peeking in to see who was up and about. Mama and Demyan were gone. Babulya and Dyedka sat at the table, silent, knitting and whittling, respectively. The *domovoi* sat in front of the oven, his shoulders slumped, picking at the toe of his shoe.

Anya knew she couldn't do what she needed to do without supplies—extra clothes, at the very least—but she didn't want anyone to see her. She didn't want to talk to them and risk losing her nerve.

A hand touched her shoulder, and she spun, jumping. Ivan stood behind her, twisting his staff between his hands, eyes huge and filled with pity.

"Anya . . ." he started. She guessed he had heard about Papa.

She turned back around. She didn't want him to stop her either. "Not now, Ivan. I'm busy."

"You look like you're just standing here," he said. "Anya, I'm sorry about—"

"Don't," she snapped, then realized he wasn't responsible for any of this. He didn't deserve her anger. "I'm sorry. I just don't want to talk about it."

"Fair." He shuffled his feet. "What are you doing?"

She sighed. "I'm trying to sneak in without being seen."

He peered through the crack in the door. "Well, your *babushka* won't see you. But I think your *dyedushka* will."

"I know." She stood in the fading daylight a little longer and then admitted, "I'm going to Rûm."

He was quiet, and then slowly said, "Oh. I see." Another pause. "To get your papa?"

"Yes."

"Rûm is a long way away."

"Don't try to talk me out of it," she said. "I can't sit here any longer and let Mama suffer like she is."

"I won't try to talk you out of it," Ivan said. "I'll come with you."

She turned to look at him. "You will?"

"Obviously," he said. "You can't go on an adventure

without a fool. Plus, I've traveled more than you have. I have expertise."

Anya snorted, but smiled. "That would be nice."

"Do you want me to help you?" Ivan said, nodding toward the cracked-open door.

Anya peered back through the crack, watching her grandparents. "What could you do to help?"

"A distraction, probably," Ivan said.

Anya lifted an eyebrow. "What kind of distraction?"

He shrugged, then looked pointedly at the barn. "Are the goats in there?"

"Yes."

Ivan nodded and handed her his staff. She watched as he trotted across the yard and stopped in front of the barn. He put his hands on his hips, looked up at the top of the door, and then pulled the door handles. The doors swung open, and he threw his hands into the air.

"Distraction!" he yelled.

Anya watched. Ivan stood there with his hands over his head. None of the goats came out.

Ivan let his arms drop. "I said, 'Distraction'!"

One of the goats said, *"Myah!"*

Ivan marched into the barn. A minute later, some goats shuffled out reluctantly. Ivan appeared, pushing two of them. The one in the front turned around and went back into the barn.

"Come on!" Ivan groaned. The second goat nibbled on his pant leg.

Ivan let is head fall back. His shoulders heaved as he sighed. He patted the goat nibbling on his pants, then perked his head up. When he turned back to Anya, his eyes were bright with an idea.

That was generally a foolish look.

Ivan hurried over to the little yard around the house. Babulya's garden grew close to the house and had a good, solid fence around it to keep the goats out. He leaned over it and grabbed a handful of potato plants. He yanked on them, pulling them up by the roots, which hung heavy with potatoes.

"Ivan!" Anya hissed.

He waved a hand at her and ran back to the barn. He stood in front of the open doors and shook the potato plants in his hand. Dirt fell in clumps. A couple of potatoes dropped off and bounced across the ground.

A goat poked its head out of the barn door; then another joined it, and another. Soon the entire herd was crowding closer to Ivan.

Ivan took a step back. The goats took two forward.

He ran backwards, waving the potato plants. The goats followed, a white rush of little hooves and horns. Anya thought he was going to run past the house, but instead he turned into the yard, throwing the gate open. As he ran past Anya, he said, "Meet me at Håkon's house!"

And then he was inside, with all the goats stampeding behind him. Some of them tried to stop in the front garden, but Anya pushed them into the house and shut the door behind them.

From inside, Dyedka yelled, "What in the—"

"They've gone crazy!" Ivan screamed.

Babulya said, "Is that the goats?"

"Get out of the house!" Dyedka hollered.

"They're trying to eat me!" Ivan yelled.

The side door of the house flung open, and Ivan ran out. The goats followed. Anya cracked the front door open and peered in. Dyedka was up, his wooden legs thumping on the floor as he shooed the goats out of the house. Babulya followed him carefully.

"What's that boy up to now?" Babulya griped. "Where's Anya?"

"I don't know," Dyedka said as he followed the goats. "Of course that foolish boy let the goats out!"

"Go find Anya," Babulya said. They were both out

the side door. Ivan ran in circles around the barn, yelling, while the goats chased him.

"*You* find her!" Dyedka snapped.

As soon as they were near the barn, Anya slipped inside the house and leaned Ivan's staff against the wall by the door. She grabbed a sack from the kitchen and hurried to where some of her clothes hung by the oven to dry, fingering each piece to see which ones were the driest and which ones would just be wet lumps in her bag.

The *domovoi* appeared on the mantel near the clothing, arms crossed. He tapped one foot impatiently.

"Oh hush," Anya said to him.

The door to the sleeping room opened, and Mama peered out. Her eyes were puffy and red. She looked like she had just woken up.

"Anya?" Mama asked. "What was that noise?"

Anya froze. Mama had heard Ivan running around. In a moment of panic, she pointed at the *domovoi*. "I was talking to him."

"I thought I heard yelling . . ." Mama put her hand against her cheek. "I guess my ears are playing tricks. How are you?"

"I'm fine, Mama."

She expected Mama to go back into the sleeping

room, but she came out. Anya dropped the mostly empty bag behind her feet as Mama shuffled to her, hoping she wouldn't notice it. When Mama reached Anya, she pulled her into a surprisingly solid hug.

"I love you, Annushka," Mama whispered. "I'm so sorry your papa isn't coming back soon."

Anya's nose stung. She swallowed a few times and then managed to squeak out, "I love you, too."

Mama smelled like the hay the mattresses were stuffed with. Her hair fell loose around her shoulders and was impossibly soft. Anya could have hugged her mother all night. But Ivan could distract Dyedka and Babulya for only so long.

"I'm going to go to Ivan's," Anya said.

Mama nodded. "You do that. He's a good friend."

"He's the best friend," Anya said. She watched Mama shuffle back into the sleeping room, and then she turned back to the oven.

All her clothes were gone.

The domovoi! Anya spun, searching for the little meddler. It wasn't any of his business if she left to find Papa. He had no right stealing her clothes!

He was on the table with her clothes piled around

him. She took a step forward, then stopped as he drew a damp dress through his fist. The dress was almost too big for his little fist, but he managed to widen it out and fit the whole thing through. The dress came out dry, and he flicked his hand to the side. Water droplets spattered over the floor.

With a flourish, he folded the dress into a compact square, then dried a second dress and folded it. In less than a minute, all her clothes were dry and folded.

Anya picked up her bag and placed it on the table. Then she sat, so she could be eye to eye with the little house spirit.

He regarded her with a forlorn look.

"You miss him too, huh?" she asked.

The *domovoi* nodded. He wiped the back of his hand under his nose, then sniffed.

"I'll get him back," Anya said. "I promise."

He nodded again, then plopped down on his behind on the tabletop. He put one finger over Anya's mouth so she wouldn't say anything. They sat there, silent, until he stood back up, shoved all the folded dresses into Anya's bag, and then pointed at the door.

Go.

Anya grabbed Ivan's staff and ran out of the house, the sound of Dyedka yelling at Ivan fading away as she reached the road.

+ ✴ +

It was dark by the time she reached Håkon's house. She didn't want Kin to see her and wonder what she was doing, so she stayed on the other side of the bridge, under the trees. The night brought a deep cold—an unmistakable sign of the lateness of the season—and she shivered as she waited.

A crunching sound from the woods made her turn. She expected to see Ivan, but he wasn't on the path.

She shivered harder and took a stab at whispering, "Håkon?"

A long shadow moved, and a pile of leaves shifted as the dirt beneath it flowed up. It formed a crude dirt cage around Anya, trapping her where she stood. A dragony face peeked out from behind a tree, grinning.

"Gotcha!" he said.

Anya's heart pounded. "You can't sneak up on people in the dark. We've talked about this."

"Why are you standing in the dark, anyway?" Håkon asked. "Where's Ivan? It took you two a long time to come."

Anya realized with a jolt that she'd forgotten all about playing Princess with Håkon earlier. "Um, I was here. You were gone."

"Oh," Håkon said. "I got bored and went to your house to see if you were there, but you weren't."

"That must have been when I came," Anya said. She had really wanted to tell him about Papa earlier, but now it felt strange. He was so happy, and telling him about Papa would just make him sad.

"Is Ivan coming?" Håkon asked before Anya could decide what to say.

She nodded. "He said he'd meet me here."

"By this tree?"

"At your house."

Håkon jerked his head toward his home. It looked so nice and warm. "Why don't you wait inside?"

"I don't want your da to see me," Anya said.

Håkon shook his head. "He's not here. He's staying late at the forge. He had some big order to get done."

Anya paused for a moment, then whacked the dirt bars of the cage away. She sprinted stiffly to the house and dove inside, going straight to the fire. Håkon followed and shut the door. He joined her and made designs in the fire while she warmed herself.

Finally, he asked, "Why do you have a bag?"

If she couldn't be honest with Håkon, she couldn't be honest with anyone. "You have to promise not to tell your da."

"Promise," Håkon said.

She took a deep breath, ready to tell him about Demyan, and Papa being lost to the Pechenegs, and her plan to get him herself. *Papa.* It felt like ages since she'd seen him. She knew what Papa looked like—of course she did—but at that moment, she couldn't remember whether he had trimmed his beard short or left it long when he had gone. She couldn't remember if his eyes were green, or if she was remembering them as green because Dyedka's eyes were green. She knew that his voice got very soft when he spoke to the goats, but she couldn't remember what he sounded like when he read the Torah to her.

Instead of words, what tumbled out of her was a sob, then another, and tears down her face. Her heart felt like a stone in her chest. She couldn't make herself stop crying, and Håkon stared at her with enormous, surprised eyes as she tried to get words out.

"Muh-muh-my papa," Anya blubbered. "He wuh-was already gone wuh-when the messenger got there, and h-h-he didn't know he could come back, so . . ." She stopped, held her breath, and tried to stop crying.

Håkon hugged her. Well, he did the best he could. His dragon body wasn't built for hugs, but he made it work. His short legs wrapped around her, and he patted her on the back with his tail. Anya clung to him and pressed her face against his warm scales.

When she felt composed enough to speak again, she said thickly, "I'm going to get him." She wiped her nose with the back of her hand. "I'm going to bring him back once and for all."

Håkon continued to pat her. He said slowly, "That's—"

Someone knocked on the door. Anya and Håkon jumped apart. The dragon scrambled to answer it. He peeked through a hole in the door and looked back at Anya. "It's Ivan!"

The door swung open, and Ivan stepped in, teeth chattering. He tottered to the fire with Anya and stripped off his coat to be closer to the flames.

"Did my *dyedushka* catch you?" Anya said.

"Yes." Ivan rubbed his hands together. "He wasn't happy about the goats being out."

"And I bet Babulya was mad about the potatoes."

Ivan's eyes widened and he nodded. "She said now

the goats have a taste for them. She'll never be able to keep them out of the garden. I've single-handedly ruined everything."

Anya nodded. "I told Håkon about our plan," she said.

Ivan glanced at the dragon. "What do you think?"

"It's crazy," Håkon said.

"Yep." Ivan nodded.

"You know what?" Anya stood up. "I thought you two would understand. And you can both talk when your papas are stuck in a war zone. Until then—"

"Anya," Ivan said from his spot by the fire, "we're still going to come with you."

She blinked. "What?"

"Absolutely," Håkon said. "What kind of friends would we be if we let you go do a crazy thing all by yourself?"

"Bad ones," Ivan answered.

"Very bad ones," Håkon agreed.

Anya sat back down. "Really?"

Håkon nudged her shoulder with his. "Of course."

Ivan pulled her into a tight side hug, ending up with his arm looped around her neck. "We do crazy stuff *together*. Never forget that."

"We'd better do our crazy stuff soon, though," Håkon

said. "Because if my da comes back, he probably won't let us."

They scrambled to pack Håkon a bag then. He didn't need much — a blanket to curl up with and some dried meat — and Kin had a nice backpack that fit Håkon's blanket plus Anya's bag of clothes. Anya draped her bow across her back and hung the quiver from a shoulder. Who knew what kind of dangers awaited them in Rûm? They left after Ivan put his coat back on and retrieved his staff from where Anya had left it against the wall.

Outside, Alsvindr whinnied from his stable. Anya trotted to him and patted his nose. He smooshed it against her forehead.

From behind her, Håkon said, "Do you want to bring him? It might be nice to ride him instead of walk."

The thought of riding Alsvindr versus walking all the way to Rûm was tempting, but Anya was hesitant. Alsvindr wasn't her horse. He was Kin's. She didn't know how to take care of him if he got hurt or sick. And since Kin had gotten him, he'd been able to ride the horse to Mologa to the market there. He couldn't walk. His knee was too weak. He needed Alsvindr more than Anya did.

"You can't come," she said to the horse. "Kin might need you."

The horse snorted.

"I'll be back," Anya said, stroking Alsvindr's long nose one last time. Then she and Ivan headed south on the road. Håkon swam. He would meet them at the bridge a mile south of the village.

They got near to Ivan's home, and he said, "I guess I should get some supplies, huh?"

"At least clean underwear," Anya said, fiddling with the backpack's straps to make it fit better.

He sighed, resigned. "Fine."

Anya waited outside, not wanting to get accosted by his brothers or held up for some reason. She had some time to think while Ivan was inside the house. She was nervous about Håkon coming with them. Not that he wasn't welcome. But she worried about his safety. Last year, Yedsha had seen Anya stab Håkon in the heart. He hadn't known the dagger killed only if she wanted it to. He thought Håkon was dead. So in Zmeyreka, Håkon was reasonably safe. But beyond the river valley? If he really was the last dragon in the world—or Kievan Rus', or the Thrice Nine Kingdoms, or wherever—it would make him a target for not just the tsar, but everyone. And if anything happened to him, Anya didn't know what she'd do.

She couldn't tell him not to come, though. For starters, he wouldn't listen. But even if he did, she needed him there. She had known Ivan and Håkon for less than a year, but they were like a challah plait. The strands started separately, and wove together, but as they spent time twined together, the dough merged. Trying to unplait the bread would just result in a huge mess.

She liked her Anya-Ivan-Håkon plait just the way it was.

A shape moved around the side of the house through the darkness. Ivan held a bag slung over one shoulder as he ran toward her. He waved his arm. "Go!" he hissed.

Anya obeyed, and the two of them ran down the road for a few minutes. Then Ivan looked back, saw they weren't being chased, and slowed.

"That was close," he panted.

Anya slowed too. "Your brothers?"

"Semya and Shestka." He massaged his side. "I don't think they followed us. We'll be fine."

They walked in silence through the darkness of the evening, boots crunching on the road. At the bridge, they crossed and then waited for Håkon to appear.

"Okay," Ivan said while they waited. "This road goes south to Kiev. We have to cross the Dnieper once we get there, but they have plenty of ferries. We might even catch a boat in Kiev and go south that way. We'll go faster."

"Into Rûm?" Anya asked.

"It's called Patzinakia where the Pechenegs are," Ivan said. "I tried to grab a map, but that's when Shestka asked what I was doing, and I ran."

Anya snorted. She hadn't even thought to bring a map.

A splash, and then Håkon slid out of the river, shaking the glittering water off himself. He half slithered, half crawled to them.

"Hey!" he whispered. "Did you get what you needed?"

"No." Ivan sighed. "We didn't get a map."

"That's . . ." Håkon bobbed his head. "A problem."

Anya started down the road. "We can find one somewhere."

"And buy it?" Håkon asked. "Did you bring money?"

Anya hadn't—she didn't have any money to bring—but Ivan said, "I brought about twenty rubles. It was all I had."

"That works," Anya said, and the three of them set off down the road toward Rûm.

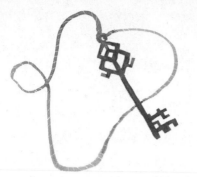

CHAPTER NINE

THEY WALKED on the road under the rising moon. Every few steps, Ivan would thump at the ground with his staff. Håkon, unencumbered with a bag at all, took time to investigate every tree they passed, every little puddle, every mound of dirt. The last time Håkon had been out of the village had been as a baby, before Kin brought him to Zmeyreka. And outside of his home's ravine, he stayed in the river as much as possible. The freedom to inspect the road and trees kept him occupied for a while, but then he tired of this constant inspection and slithered between Anya and Ivan. "How long are we going to walk? I'm getting tired."

Anya was tired too, but she didn't think it was smart to stop so close to the village. Once they exited the southern end of the valley, she'd be more open to stopping. Plus, there were caves down there, and they could use one to stay warm in.

She relayed her plan to Ivan and Håkon, and they agreed. They trudged on the packed-dirt road, breath pluming in front of them as they went. The sky was clear and crisp; distant stars blazed in the cold night. Marching down the road was keeping Anya warm, with the exception of the tip of her nose. By the time they got to the southern end of the valley and found a cave that would fit all three of them, the tips of her ears throbbed and her nose was numb.

Inside, the cave was mostly level. Anya and Ivan kicked rocks away to make a relatively smooth area to lie down on.

Ivan stuck his hands on his hips and said, "Okay, Håkon. Make a fire and we'll try to get some rest."

"Make a fire on what?" the dragon asked. "Some rocks?"

Ivan waved his hand at the floor, then out of the cave toward the trees. "A pile of wood, of course!"

Håkon squinted at Ivan. Anya said, "I'm too tired

to get any wood. We can all just lie next to each other. Håkon can keep us warm."

They tossed their bags to the ground, and Anya set her bow and quiver carefully atop them. They both hunched next to Håkon, who was comfortably warm even after the long trek. She pulled Håkon's blanket out of his backpack and draped it around the three of them as much as possible.

As soon as Anya sat, she shut her eyes. She was exhausted. But her shivering kept her awake. She burrowed up next to Håkon's warm side, willing his warmth to soak through her coat and down to her skin. It would eventually.

"We'll rest for the night," Anya said, trying to keep her teeth from chattering. "In the morning, we'll go as far as we can, until we get to Kiev."

"Sounds good," Håkon said.

Ivan just nodded.

Anya tried to go to sleep. She stared at the cave mouth for who-knew-how-long instead, thinking. She couldn't let Håkon go all the way to Rûm with her. South of Kievan Rus' was a dangerous place. And Håkon wasn't exactly subtle, with his ruby-red scales and twisting horns. Someone would stab him before she could explain that he was nice.

She swallowed hard. Last summer, she had decided that a dragon's life was worth the same as a human's. She had killed a human in order to save a dragon. Sure, Sigurd had stabbed himself with the magical dagger, but she had wanted him to die. That had been enough.

There was no way she was going to let that sacrifice go to waste.

Maybe in the next couple of nights, she could wait for Håkon to go to sleep and then she and Ivan could leave him behind. For his own safety.

Håkon shifted as he lifted his head up. He was staring, eyes hard and wide, toward the rear of the cave.

"Anya," he whispered.

"What?" she whispered back, turning to look where he was looking. In the depth of the cave, something had changed. It was too dark to tell exactly what, but it was different. Smoother. *Closer.*

What kind of cave shrank like that?

Anya shook Ivan, and his eyes popped open. "Whung?"

"*Shhh.*" She put her hand over his mouth. "Look."

He followed her pointing finger toward the back of

the cave as Håkon shifted to his feet. He slithered a tiny bit in the direction of her finger. And then . . .

Light. Orange, heavy, spilling out of a crack that widened as they watched.

Håkon scrambled backwards, dodging the light on the floor like it would burn him. Anya grabbed her bow and nocked an arrow. Ivan grabbed their backpacks and made for the exit.

A silhouette appeared in the light. Small. Human. Female. It jutted one hip to the side, jammed a fist against the hip, and said, "What are you idiots doing? You're going to freeze to death."

Anya lowered the bow and let the string go lax. She squinted at the silhouette. "The *ibbur*?"

With one hand splayed upward, the silhouette said, "Obviously. Now, get in here." And she walked away, leaving the doorway orange and empty.

From behind Anya, Håkon squeaked, "What is *that?*"

"Remember how I told you I got that magic dagger that would kill only if I wanted it to?" Anya said.

He nodded. "And you stabbed me with it?"

"Right. Well," she said, "that's the woman I got it from. The *ibbur*."

"The nice ghost," Ivan mumbled as he shuffled to Anya's side. "Are we sure she's nice? She called us idiots."

"You *are* an idiot," Anya reminded him. He nodded.

Håkon was quiet, tail flipping back and forth against the cave floor. "I think we should go in," he said.

"Me too," Ivan said.

"Yep," Anya agreed, and the three of them gathered up their bags and weapons and walked through the door in the back of the cave together.

✦ ❋ ✦

Inside, it looked the same as it had months ago when the *ibbur* had given Anya the dagger. Every inch of wall was covered with bookshelves, and every inch on the shelves was packed with books. Some of the piles on the floor had shifted around, but they were all still as haphazard and numerous as they had been last time. It was blissfully warm inside the hut, and Anya sighed as her cold face thawed.

Something flew through the air at them: a snowball. Ivan reached up and grabbed its threads, bringing it to a halt in the air before it hit any of them.

The *ibbur* cackled from the other side of the room. She was in the same white dress as last time, with the same beautiful hair and eyes like spring pools. She wiped a wet hand off on her white apron, which had blue waves embroidered across the top.

"Good, Ivan," she said. "You're getting better."

"I am?" He blushed. "I guess so."

"Definitely." She pointed a finger at Anya. "Any magic for you yet?"

That familiar sick feeling of being left out rose up in Anya, and she managed to push it down before she said, "No."

"It'll come," the *ibbur* said, almost dismissively. She had moved on to Håkon, who shrank back at her attention. "I didn't get to meet you last time."

"No," he said. "I was—"

"Being killed, I know." She smiled. "You're so big."

"Uh . . ." Håkon's blue eyes shifted back and forth, looking from one end of the floor to the other. Anya wasn't sure if dragons were capable of blushing, but to her, he looked a shade of deeper red. "Thank you, Gospozha."

"Gospozha, pah!" the *ibbur* said. "Call me Lena. Will you do that?"

Håkon brightened a little and said, "Of course."

"Hey!" Ivan said. "You never told *us* your name!"

"That's because you two aren't dragons," Lena said, sticking her tongue out at him.

Håkon perked. "Do you know other dragons?"

Lena clasped her hands at her waist. "No," she said. "There aren't others. You're the last, Håkon."

Håkon's cautious smile dropped. "The last . . . Are you sure?"

Lena nodded sadly. "Very."

Håkon curled up on himself, tucking his nose inside his coils. Anya put her hand between his shoulders and said nothing. What could she say about that?

Ivan knew what to say. "Sorry, Håkon."

The dragon tucked his nose farther down.

Lena stood quietly, teeth on her lower lip, watching Håkon. She sighed. "I didn't mean to bring you such upsetting news tonight. Your story ends happily, Håkon." She smiled. "Probably."

He withdrew his snout enough from his coils to glare at her. "Probably?"

"Yes, I think so." She motioned for them to follow her to the fire, where she sat in her chair and the children gathered on the floor. Anya opened up her coat to keep from sweating, and Ivan stripped off his and collapsed to his knees in front of the fire. Håkon slithered up and coiled again, tucking his legs inside the coil so he just looked like an enormous red *zmeyok*.

"Going to find your Papa, Anya?" Lena asked.

Anya gaped. "How did you—"

"I know because I know," Lena said. "Where is he?"

"Patzinakia," Anya said, remembering what Ivan had called it.

Lena blinked. "That's very far away."

"I know," Anya said, then pointed to Ivan and Håkon. "*We* know."

From his spot on the floor, Ivan said, "We didn't think it out very well."

Anya frowned at him. "I had to do something. My family has already waited a whole year, and more. And he's got to come back. Mama can't . . ." Her nose stung, so she rubbed at it. "Mama misses him."

Lena nodded, her face troubled. Anya was certain the *ibbur* was going to make her go home, and Anya was trying to figure out what she'd say to Lena to convince her not to do that. The four of them sat in silence but for the crackling of the fire. Then Lena said, "I'll help you."

Anya, Ivan, and Håkon looked at her. Anya said, "Really?"

"Of course," Lena said, then stood. "And I won't send you empty-handed." She went to one of the bookshelves. She dug around for a moment, looking behind and under books, and finally she pulled a necklace with a pendant from behind a stack of texts with flowers drawn onto their spines. She turned to Anya with a smile.

"A gift for you, Anya," Lena said.

Anya didn't really want a necklace, but she figured Lena had her reasons, so she stood and reached for it. Then she realized the pendant was actually a large metal key.

"What's it open?" Anya asked.

"A door," Lena said.

Anya looked at Lena, exasperated. "What's special about the door, then?"

Lena laughed. "Nothing. The door is ordinary. It's what's behind the door that's special."

Anya swallowed. Was this a key to the cell where Papa was being held? How would Lena have a key to it?

"How will I know which door?" Anya asked, nearly whispering.

Lena shrugged. "You may not. You'll just have to try the key everywhere."

Lena handed the necklace to Anya, and she pulled it over her head, careful to tuck the key under her dress. It sat on her chest against her skin, comfortably cool and heavy.

Lena motioned to Ivan, who shuffled to her. She plucked a book off the shelf and handed it to him with a smile.

Ivan opened the book and flipped from front to back. "It's empty," he said.

"Is it?" Lena asked, stroking her chin. "I suppose you'll have to fill it, then." She pulled a charcoal pencil out of the air and handed it to him.

He took the pencil with a suspicious squint. "Are these magical?"

"Absolutely," Lena said.

"Really?" Ivan grinned. "With what magic?"

Lena whispered her answer: "Voice. You may have heard it called charm magic."

Ivan studied the empty book and the pencil. "*Written* voice magic?"

Lena lifted a finger in the air. "Not all speech is spoken, Ivan. I know that doesn't make sense, but it will."

Ivan shut his mouth. "I see."

"Whatever you write in that book will influence those who read it," Lena said. "But not forever. So be careful."

Ivan nodded, clutching the book and pencil to his chest.

Then Lena turned to Håkon. He was still coiled with

his nose tucked down. She knelt in front of him and put a hand on his scales where his nose was hidden.

"I have something for you, too," Lena whispered.

He pulled his nose out, eyes hopeful. "Something magic?"

"Better." Lena wagged a finger at him. "But you're not going to like it."

Håkon frowned. "It's better than something magic, but I'm not going to like it?"

She nodded. "But it's important. They need your help."

"Who?" Håkon asked.

"You'll figure it out." Lena slipped her pale hands on either side of Håkon's red face and touched her forehead to his. "Be so, so careful," she whispered. "He'll do anything to have you. Anything to turn you back."

Anya watched, and her skin prickled at Lena's words. Turn Håkon back? Turn him back from what?

Before Anya could ask, Lena kissed Håkon on the forehead. Where her lips touched, a bright light burst out, growing brighter and more dazzling until Anya couldn't bear to look at it anymore, and a warm flash enveloped her as she hid her face in the crook of her elbow.

CHAPTER TEN

T HE WARMTH FADED, and Anya looked up. Lena's hut was gone, replaced by an unfamiliar road with trees on all sides; half the trees had decided to put on their fall colors, but the other half stubbornly clung to summer green. The sun shone into Anya's face out of a clear blue sky. Ivan stood next to her, likewise blinking away the brightness, and he mumbled, "What happened?"

Anya looked around. "I think she brought us to Patzinakia."

"How does she do that?" Ivan yelled.

"Be quiet!" Anya hissed. "Håkon, hide."

She realized then that Håkon wasn't there. She spun,

her heart seizing in her chest, and she almost tripped over a pile of coats and bags on the road next to her. The pile was a hodgepodge of the things they had worn into Lena's hut, but also new coats and hats that didn't belong to them.

She pointed. "There's your coat . . ." She bent closer, staring.

A foot poked out from under the pile. A human foot.

"Ivan!" She gasped and knelt. She threw his coat at him and pushed the bags away. Underneath it all, a boy lay face-down on the road.

Oh no. When Lena had let them out, they must have landed on top of someone. She rolled the boy over, grimacing, hoping he was alive.

Ivan pulled on his coat as he bent to peer at the boy. "Does he look familiar to you?"

Anya shook her head. She had never seen him before in her life. He had deep golden hair curling around his ears and at his neck. His clothing was too big for him, threadbare, and he wore oversize, scuffed boots. A smattering of freckles colored the rosy skin at the tops of his cheeks. She reached out to touch his face when his eyes snapped open. They were a familiar shade of brilliant blue.

Anya jerked her hand back. "Håkon?"

He looked up at her. "An—Any . . ." He ground his teeth together, and a look of panic crept across his face. His lips moved like he had a mouthful of honey. "An. Ya."

She couldn't speak. She just stared at him with her mouth hanging open. Ivan stood by, equally agape.

Håkon—Was it really him, though?—looked back and forth between them. His panic was plain on his face, and mounting. "I f-feel . . . strange."

"You look strange," Ivan mumbled, and Anya swung her fist at his leg. "Ow!"

Håkon's breath hitched, and it took him a few tries to get out, "Wh-what did she do?" He tried to roll off his back but only moved from the waist up. He swung his arms up, then froze. He brought his hands back, trembling, in front of his face.

Then he screamed.

"Håkon!" Anya slapped her hand over his mouth. His breath blasted against her palm as he continued screaming. She shook his head back and forth. "Stop! Stop it. Someone's going to hear you."

Finally, he quieted, and Anya took her hand away from his face. His mouth was still twisted in a silent scream. He didn't blink.

"What—?" he squeaked finally, looking down at himself. At his human body. His breathing got faster and faster the longer he looked. He kicked one foot and started keening, like he was going to scream again.

Anya put her hands on his arm. "It's okay."

"Okay?" He crossed his eyes, looking down his face, at where his dragony snout no longer stuck out. "Whuh-whuh-where is my face?"

Ivan pointed to his own. "You've got one like this now."

"I hate it!"

"You haven't even seen it," Ivan scoffed. "It's not a bad face."

Håkon still lay on his back, hands up in front of his face with the fingers curled in. Anya hooked her hands under his shoulder and tugged him, trying to prompt him to sit up. "Come on, Håkon."

He was dead weight as she tugged him forward. Sitting up, legs straight out in front of him, wasn't a good position. He started to lean to one side and did nothing to stop himself from falling over.

He let his arms flop against the road and wailed, "I don't have a tail!"

"Humans don't," Anya said.

"How am I supposed to walk?" Håkon said. "Why would she do this to me?"

Anya almost said she didn't know why, but then she realized she did. "I bet the Pechenegs are just as hostile toward dragons as the tsar is. We couldn't bring you here as a dragon. They'd kill you. So she changed you."

Ivan crouched in front of Håkon and studied him. "How did she do it? Where'd the dragon parts go?"

Håkon glared at him, looking miserable lying on his side with his face in the cold dirt. He was much more expressive as a human.

"Magic, obviously," Anya said. "Håkon, come on, stand up." She reached down to help him stand, but he remained in the dirt of the road.

"May I have a moment, please?" he asked. He curled his arms in close to his body.

"Are you cold?" Anya asked.

Håkon grumped, "My skin is tingly."

"That's goose bumps," Ivan said. He grabbed the remaining coat off the pile Lena had left with them. "It means you're cold." He wrapped the coat around Håkon as tightly as he could while the dragon-turned-boy lay on his side.

Anya felt bad for rushing him, but they couldn't afford to just sit there. They needed to figure out where they were and find the door that fit the key Lena had given her. But Håkon looked so wretched and lost, and Anya decided that letting him find himself for a minute wouldn't hurt. "Um . . . take your time, Håkon." She caught Ivan's eye, looked pointedly at the other side of the road, and walked a few paces away to stand there.

Ivan patted Håkon's shoulder, got up, and joined Anya. They stood with arms crossed, heads together, and Ivan said, "I wasn't expecting that to happen."

"What were you expecting?"

"I dunno." He shrugged. "Not that."

"This doesn't change our plan, right?" Anya said. "Rescue Papa, bring him back to Zmeyreka?"

Ivan looked unsure. She cleared her throat.

"I mean, clearly," Ivan said quickly. "But Håkon—"

"Håkon is fine," Håkon said. He pushed himself uneasily into a sitting position, pulling his legs up in unsure, jerky motions. He clutched the coat around him like a blanket. He tried to get his feet under him, but he couldn't figure out how.

Ivan darted to him and fastened the coat shut over Håkon's meager clothing as Anya gathered up their bags and weapons from the road. Then Ivan sat by Håkon's side. "Like this." He tucked one foot under his behind, then leaned forward, balancing himself as he brought his other foot up and straightened out.

Håkon tried to do what Ivan did, but he got his feet tangled together and fell forward onto his hands. He grunted with frustration.

"Or you could try . . ." Ivan mimicked Håkon's position, on his hands and knees, then walked his feet up and used his hands to push himself to standing.

Håkon did better with this method and almost stood, but then stumbled as he tried to straighten up. His knees buckled and he went down. Anya and Ivan ran to him, each grabbing an arm and helping him up.

Håkon laughed. There was something grim in it. "I need my tail back."

"At least you're getting better at talking," Ivan said. "Here." He took his staff from Anya and wrapped one of Håkon's hands around it. "You can use this to help you walk."

"I don't think that's going to help much," Håkon said with a grimace.

"I'll be on your other side," Ivan said.

Håkon shook his head. "I'll never get used to this."

"You'll figure it out," Anya said. "Let's find somewhere safe to sleep before it gets dark."

Anya and Ivan searched up and down the road. Its packed earth was much more heavily traveled than the roads in Zmeyreka. The trees crowded close to the road, their leaves rustling in a breeze that sounded like the whole forest sighing. That sigh and birdsong were the only sounds that disrupted the forest's quiet.

"Is this what Patzinakia is like?" Anya asked. "I imagined just open steppe."

"It's probably mostly steppe," Ivan said. "But she left us in a forest because it offers some shelter. We can get wood for a fire." He scratched his cheek. "It seems familiar, though. Like I've been here."

"You've been a lot of places," Anya said. "Are you sure Patzinakia wasn't one of them?"

"Yes," Ivan said. "We were always north of Kiev, not south of it." He wrinkled his nose. "But still . . ."

They helped Håkon stumble up the road, and he said, "I don't know if it was a good idea for me to even come. I mean, the tsar definitely wants to kill me. And Sigurd did. The Pechenegs probably would too."

"A Pecheneg king, maybe," Anya said. "I don't know.

We'll have to be really careful. Make sure no one is planning to hurt you."

"Lena said whoever it is will do anything to change me back," Håkon said.

Ivan nodded. "Yes! Someone who knows you're a dragon and wants to kill you, but not when you're a human. So we have to watch out for someone who wants to kill dragons and knows how to reverse Lena's magic!"

Anya blew a breath out slowly. "We need to focus on getting my papa. The faster we get him, the faster we can get out of here, and Håkon won't be in danger anymore."

They walked until they reached a fork in the road. A crude log fence was half blocking the left fork. Dirt from the road itself had been dug and shored up as a wall, blocking the way even further.

"Well, we go this way, right?" Anya said, pointing to the unblocked road.

"Maybe," Ivan said, but he sounded unsure. "There are highwaymen in places like this. They might block the road to drive us toward them." He fidgeted. "This happened to us when we were traveling from Ingria. My papa was with us and he took care of the highwaymen, but we're not . . ." He paused. "He's not here."

Håkon was panting from the exertion of walking in his new body, so they let him sit on the road to recover. Then Anya approached the haphazard fence alone. She spotted something carved into the wood of one log. She brushed rain-caked dirt off it, surprised to read Russian there.

"Ivan, do the Pechenegs speak Russian?" she asked.

He shrugged. "Maybe. Nomadic peoples rarely have one language they all speak. I'm sure a lot of the Pecheneg bands nearer to the Kievan border speak Russian. Why?"

Anya read the scrawled message out loud: "'Beware. Keep Out. Go Around.'" An arrow pointed in the direction of the right fork.

Ivan frowned. "It's in Russian?"

"Something must have happened to the road," Anya said. "We have to go around."

Ivan scrunched his face. "No. This is Patzinakia. Why would the sign be in Russian?" He chopped the edge of one hand against the palm of the other, answering his own question before Anya or Håkon could. "Because Pecheneg highwaymen are setting a trap for Kievan travelers! If we go right, we'll walk straight into an ambush. We need to go left."

"But the sign says 'Beware,'" Anya said.

"Of course it does!" Ivan said, gesturing. "To scare you!"

Anya glanced back at the carved words in the wood. "What if it really is dangerous?"

Ivan puffed out his chest. "We beat a Viking and a *bukavac*. Plus, we have a dragon."

"Ah." Håkon bobbed his head from where he sat on the ground with the staff across his lap. "Not really."

"You can still do magic, though, right?" Ivan asked.

Håkon held up his hands and squinted at them. "I do it with hands now?"

Ivan nodded. "Yes."

"With strings?"

"Yes."

"Well, I don't see any strings," Håkon said, waving his fingers. "And I can't feel any. So probably not."

Ivan's confident look melted off his face. "Oh." He straightened. "We still should take the left road. I can feel it. If we come up against a Pecheneg ambush, we won't be able to run while we're carrying you, Håkon."

Håkon looked about to argue, but then he deflated. "That's fair. I'm sorry I'm a burden."

Anya glared at Ivan, then turned to Håkon. "You're

not a burden. You have a new body. You'll get used to it."

They helped Håkon up again and supported him around the blockade.

A bird landed on one of Håkon's shoulders, and the former dragon smiled at the little feathered thing. The bird chirped at him, and Håkon opened his mouth. No sound came out, and his smile dropped into a severe frown.

Anya nudged him, and when he looked at her, she pursed her lips and whistled.

Håkon looked absolutely disgusted, but he tried to whistle anyway. He didn't do well, but it was better than the nothing that had happened before. He whistled at the bird, and the bird warbled back. Anya watched as Håkon and the bird went back and forth, having a conversation.

She looked past him to Ivan. "I don't think Lena would leave us too far away from where Papa is being held. Do you?"

"No." Ivan glanced around. "I mean, I hope not. She took us almost directly to Håkon when Sigurd was going to kill him, but a little way off. Maybe that's what she did this time. Far enough away from where she wants us to be that we don't get spotted jumping out of a magical cottage."

The key thumped against Anya's chest with every step she took. "You said the Pechenegs are nomads?"

Ivan nodded.

"But she gave me a big key to a solid door," Anya said.

"Maybe it's just to a padlock," Ivan said.

"Maybe," Anya said. "But she mentioned a door too. I think we'll know we're in the right place when we find a solid building with solid doors."

"And a guy who wants to kill dragons," Ivan said.

Anya sighed, wishing they hadn't brought Håkon into danger. "And that."

"Um, friends?" Håkon said from between them. Anya and Ivan turned to him. His bird friend flew off his shoulder, streaking into the forest. Håkon's face was pinched with worry. "The bird told me to be careful here."

"We already knew that," Ivan said.

"Yeah, but we aren't really being careful," Håkon said, lowering his voice. "The bird said . . . It doesn't make a lot of sense. She said, 'The nightingale makes them bleed, makes them pay.' And then she flew off."

"A killer nightingale?" Ivan laughed. "Those are tiny!"

He demonstrated with his free hand. "They're just little birds."

Håkon fidgeted. "Maybe we should go back."

"But the highwaymen," Ivan argued.

"You don't even know if there are highwaymen."

"If there are," Ivan said, "you won't be able to run away from them. You can't even walk on your own!"

"Well, let me try!" Håkon pushed away from both of them, standing steadily for a few moments before buckling. He tried to use the staff to keep himself up, but his hands slipped down the smooth wood. Ivan caught him and let him slide to the ground.

Anya turned around, her gaze searching the forest. She could feel someone watching them. Or was it her imagination? Down the road, just around the next bend, she could make out the trunk of what looked like an enormous tree.

Ivan stuck his hands on his hips. "This is the right way. I know it is."

"Your foolish intuition is guiding you?" Håkon puffed breath in and out, still managing to sound skeptical through his panting.

"Probably, yes," Ivan said.

"I've heard the stories about your da!" Håkon said. "He

always gets into trouble before things work out for him. There are probably highwaymen down this road!"

Anya wandered away from their bickering. She got nearer to the bend, bringing more of the huge tree into view. It was truly gargantuan—wide enough to fit Anya's barn inside it, and twice as tall as the trees surrounding it. She gaped at it, stepping carefully closer. As she did, details in the trunk became clearer, until she realized it wasn't a single huge tree, but dozens of smaller trees that grew so close together, they acted as one.

"Wow," she whispered. A breeze swept through the tree's leaves, and they all moved in unison with a single whisper. She stopped in its long shadow, marveling up at it, wondering what could have made so many trees grow so tightly lined up.

The breeze blew again, and Anya saw the dark shape of a person crouched in the branches for a breath. She blinked, and the shape was gone.

She stumbled back. Ivan and Håkon were still arguing on the road as Anya ran back to them, skin prickling.

"Stop your stupid fighting!" she yelled at them. She pointed at the tree. "There's something in the branches."

Ivan and Håkon turned to behold the enormous tree. Ivan scratched his head.

"That tree is huge," he mumbled.

"It's not one tree," Anya said. "It's a whole bunch grown close together."

"Wow," he said. "Incredible."

Håkon shrank down. "'The nightingale makes them bleed,'" he repeated to himself.

"Giant tree, giant nightingale, maybe," Anya said.

Ivan snorted. "I'm still not scared of a big bird." But his voice was a little higher than usual.

"It didn't look like a bird, though." Anya remembered the humanoid outline. "It was like a man crouched in the tree."

"A man is not a bird," Håkon said.

"Thank you." Ivan sighed. "Well, let's just run past it."

Anya shifted. "I don't know . . ."

"I do," Håkon said. "I can't run. Let's take the other road."

He turned around to look back the way they had come, then froze. He gulped and stared. Anya and Ivan turned as well.

A man stood on the road behind them. Barely a man. More a boy, really. Probably only a couple of years older than Ivan. He was angular, gaunt almost, and not at all dressed for the season in a dirty, torn *rubakha* and leg wraps. He didn't even have a hat on. His skin was a gold so pale, it resembled sun on snow. Anya squinted. Along his arms, exposed through the rips in the *rubakha*'s sleeves, were swirls of slightly darker gold. Tattoos? She had only ever seen a real tattoo on Kin, and his didn't look swirly or golden at all. The boy's hair was grayish-brown, cut short in the front around his face but left long and stringy on the sides. His eyes glared, and dark rings circled them, like he had smeared mud there. His boots were scuffed and stained, and he had no weapon on him.

Håkon shrank down further. The boy's eyes ticked back and forth among the three of them.

Anya whispered, "Is he a Pecheneg?"

Ivan breathed fast. "He must be." He cleared his throat and called, "Hello! Good day!"

The boy on the road didn't respond.

"This might be why the road is closed," Ivan said out of the side of his mouth. "Some kind of crazy guy harassing people."

"Oh," Håkon said, "like a highwayman?"

"Good observation," Anya said, rolling her eyes. "Now, what do we do about him?"

Ivan took a deep breath. "We have a dragon?"

As a response, Håkon climbed, wobbly, to his feet. He

managed to stay upright by leaning heavily on Ivan's staff, but he was pitched forward on his toes and looked like he was going to fall over at any moment. He swam the fingers of one hand around in the air, clumsy in his grasping.

"There's nothing here," Håkon muttered, canting to the side. Anya caught him before he stumbled to the ground. "No magic at all."

The boy on the road moved. He brought his hands up and leaned his head back. He pursed his lips and —whistled?

Ivan laughed a little, and then the boy grabbed something in the air. Strings. Magic. He whipped his arm through the air like he was getting ready to throw a rope. The whistle sound didn't dissipate like sounds should. It got louder and shriller until it was too loud to bear. Anya clapped her hands over her ears to block out the sound, but it was still there. How was it so loud?

The boy squared his shoulders at them and released his hand. Anya could see the autumn air parting as the weaponized whistle rocketed toward them. Ivan crashed into her, knocking her to the ground. Their bags scattered across the ground as the whistle screamed overhead. Håkon dropped the staff and hit the road; whether intentionally or not wasn't apparent. The whistle went past them, shoving air out of its way and flattening Ivan and Anya to the ground. It hit the road near the huge tree, blowing a crater in the packed earth.

Anya stared agog at the hole. She had never heard of sound magic before, and seeing what it could do made her breath stick in her throat.

"Run!" Ivan shrieked.

He didn't have to tell her twice.

They both jumped to their feet and tugged Håkon to his. Ivan stopped long enough to snatch up his staff, and the three hobbled away from the sound sorcerer, farther up the right road. Anya didn't dare look back to see if he was following, but then another booming whistle exploded behind them. A wave of air and sound hit Anya's back and threw her forward. Her forehead slammed into the dirt. She scrambled up, head pounding, breath hitching. Ivan and Håkon had been thrown too, and they pushed up with more difficulty than Anya did. Ivan's forehead bled from a gash.

They were up, supporting Håkon, running again. Around the corner, the road hit a bridge over a narrow river. Ivan stopped, his eyes drilling into the babbling water.

Anya slowed. "Ivan, come on!"

"Go," he said, waving her and Håkon on. "Keep going. Find shelter. Get Håkon safe. I'll slow him down."

"But—" Anya's protests were eaten by another screaming whistle. It exploded in the air near Ivan, throwing him to the ground. Anya scrambled toward him, but before she could reach him, Ivan got to his feet and whipped his staff through the air.

A column of water shot out of the stream, and Ivan yanked his magic threads with the magic metal on the ends of his staff. Anya took her bow from where it hung across her back and nocked an arrow into it, aiming at the boy, who walked a dozen or so paces behind them.

"Håkon," she said as she held the boy in her sights, "go."

"Go where?" he hissed.

She didn't answer. Her arms trembled. She didn't usually hold the arrow for this long, but she couldn't make herself fire at the boy. He was going to kill Ivan, kill all of them, and she still couldn't let the arrow fly at him.

Sigurd's ghost leered at her from the back of her mind. "You'll all die this time."

Ivan's water column blasted toward the sound sorcerer. He didn't even try to get out of the way. Anya knew for sure the water would hit him hard, knock him down, make it possible for them to escape. But then the boy jumped.

No, he didn't jump. It was more of a casual hop, but he didn't come back down. His foot hooked on something in the air and he hopped again, bounding up an invisible set of steps as Ivan's water column thundered through where he had just stood.

Anya lowered her bow, letting her arrow go slack against the bowstring, gaping at the boy flying above the road.

Then he dropped to the ground and whistled again.

Håkon yelled at Ivan. "Get behind a tree!"

Ivan didn't. With his staff, he grabbed another ribbon of water and hurled it at the whistling sorcerer, then grabbed another and another. He flung water balls frantically, panting. He was getting exhausted.

The boy lifted his hands—and caught the water balls. He rolled them all into a big water ball, then threw it back at Ivan.

Anya lurched forward and grabbed Ivan. She yanked him out of the way of the water. The ball blasted where Ivan had just been, smashing into a tree on the other side.

Anya dragged Ivan after her to where Håkon staggered

away on the road. They hooked Håkon under his armpits and pulled him as fast as they could over the bridge. Ivan stumbled; the gash in his forehead still bled. As they rounded another curve in the road, the ground under them rumbled.

"No, no, no," Anya muttered to herself. Did this mean another ball of explosive noise was on its way? They had to outrun it. So far, all the sound magic had hit the ground eventually. If they could just get past it . . .

Five men on horseback thundered toward them. Anya screamed and clasped Håkon to her, hugging him and Ivan in the middle of the road as the horses galloped past. They threw dirt up in sprays. Four of the five riders had bows with arrows nocked and drawn. The fifth held a torch aloft.

Anya watched the sound sorcerer storm around the bend, hands up, ready to throw more magic at them. The riders didn't hesitate. The first one swept his arrow through the torch, lighting the end on fire. He let the arrow fly, and it hit the ground in front of the boy.

The flame didn't hiss out like Anya thought it would. Something in the arrow's tip broke and spattered, and the flames caught the liquid. The fire jumped to the road. Anya stared, mouth open. What kind of arrows could do that?

The second archer fired; then the third, and the fourth. Their arrows landed in a row across the road, making a flaming barrier. Anya fully expected the sorcerer to control the fire as he had Ivan's water, or hop over it on steps of air. But he recoiled, his face twisting at the sight of the flames, and he glared at the riders who stood between him and Anya.

An archer aimed an arrow at the sorcerer, and the boy lifted his arms. But he didn't do magic this time. He darted into the air, hopping toward the trees, and then . . .

He vanished.

Anya blinked at the spot he had been in. He had just evaporated.

What kind of sorcerer could control elements and sound, then vanish into thin air?

Ivan dabbed his fingers into the blood dripping down his forehead and mumbled, "I hit my head."

"Yeah." Anya watched two of the archers trot their horses to where the sorcerer had disappeared, while the other three turned their steeds to her and Ivan.

The torchbearer was closest. He wore armor similar to Dobrynya's—made of small scales fixed together that flexed as he moved—but his was shinier than the *bogatyr*'s had been. His chain-mail shirt beneath the armor was more of a long, hooded tunic. It covered his head and face from the nose down and went all the way to his knees. The metal helmet over his chain-mail hood had a nosepiece that obscured the middle of his face, leaving only his eyes visible, a bright blue shade similar to Håkon's. The helmet shone in the sun, and Anya made out intricate designs smithed into its brim. A rich scarlet cloak covered his back and fell past the saddle behind him.

The others were dressed similarly but lacked helmets. Their cloaks were a different shade of red—duller—and while their armor was just as shined, it was more dented.

Why did these Pecheneg archers have armor that looked just like that of a *bogatyr* of Kievan Rus'?

With a voice that was equal parts youth and unquestioning command, the torchbearer barked, "What are you doing on this road?" It was the voice of a woman.

She spoke Russian, not whatever the Pechenegs spoke. It sounded fluent and native, not like Babulya when she spoke with her heavy accent. And her dialect was that of a bigger city—very much like Ivan's.

Anya, Ivan, and Håkon exchanged alarmed, disbelieving looks. The torchbearer was a girl? And Russian?

Anya licked her lips. "We, uh—"

"This road is off-limits!" the torchbearer snapped.

"I know," Anya said, struggling to find an excuse. She definitely wasn't going to bring up Ivan's highwayman theory. She motioned to Håkon, who was hunched down, hair hanging over his face. "My friend is sick, and we got lost—"

The torchbearer narrowed her eyes. "How?"

"How what?" Anya said.

"How did you get lost so close to Kiev?" the torchbearer barked.

Anya stared with disbelief. She couldn't speak. Why would Lena send them to Kiev?

"Of course, Kiev!" Ivan said, forcing a laugh out. He smacked Anya lightly on the arm. "Yes, Kiev is where we wanted to go. Absolutely."

The torchbearer glared at him. "What's your business in Kiev?"

"Our business?" Ivan asked. He looked at Anya, face paling, then back at the torchbearer. "Our business is with the tsar, of course."

Anya winced. Ivan must have hit his head especially hard. Business with the tsar? They couldn't do that! What business could they possibly have with him?

The torchbearer pulled her cowl down and let it rest under her chin. She was as young as Ivan, likely not even sixteen yet, with red cheeks topped with freckles. Her mouth was curled into a stern frown.

She looked familiar.

Anya glanced at Håkon, who still hunched with his hair hanging over his face. Was it Anya's imagination, or did Håkon look like this torchbearer who barked questions at them?

The torchbearer said, "What business?"

Ivan gasped a little, then threw his arms up in the air. "Your Highness!" He bowed low to her. "It's so good to see you!"

Anya froze, eyes wide, staring at the torchbearer before her. The princess of Kiev? Out riding around, fighting a monster in Patzinakia?

The princess wrinkled her nose. "Do I know you?"

Ivan laughed. "Princess Vasilisa! Always the comedian!"

To Anya, Vasilisa didn't look like a comedian. She looked like a person about to tell Ivan that he was stupid.

Anya let Ivan talk as she scooted closer to Håkon. She didn't want him to look up. What would the princess of Kiev say if she saw Håkon's face? The more Anya looked at the princess, the more she reminded her of what Håkon looked like now . . . They were so similar. Why would

Lena do that? And why would she send them to Kiev? Had she been confused?

Was Papa in Kiev, instead of Patzinakia, for some reason?

Ivan continued on like the princess wasn't glaring at him. "Ivan Vosmyorka Ivanovich Ivanov." He bowed low again, with a flourish this time. Blood flipped from the gash on his forehead to the road. "Son of Ivan Yedinitsa Ivanovich Ivanov, your blessed father's imperial fool."

Anya wondered if invoking his father's name was going to cause trouble for Ivan's family at all. But he didn't seem worried. Wasn't that the point of fools, anyway? To be unpredictable and do foolish things?

Princess Vasilisa's eyebrows lifted. "And *you* have business with my father?"

"We do, Your Highness."

"Of course," she said. "Your business with the tsar is to explain to him why you're trespassing on a forbidden road."

Anya and Ivan balked at the same time. "What?"

The princess looked down her nose at them, and with arctic coldness in her voice, said, "Seize them."

CHAPTER ELEVEN

THE FOUR OTHER ARCHERS leaped off their horses and came toward where Anya and Ivan supported Håkon. Håkon clung to Anya, his eyes wide and terrified.

"Anya," he whispered, the rising panic in his voice unmistakable, "don't let them take me."

"We'll be okay," Anya said, even though she had no idea if they actually would be. "This is just a misunderstanding."

The archer who reached them first was only a little taller than Håkon, and Anya suspected he was about Ivan and Håkon's age. It was hard to tell exactly. All the archers still had their chain-mail cowls up, obscuring everything but their eyes. The one in front of them had a pink scar marring the olive skin next to his left eye.

One of the archers took Ivan's staff away from him, and another took Anya's bow and quiver of arrows. Without their weapons, they had nothing: Anya had dropped their bags while they ran from the sound sorcerer.

The archer with the scar put his hand on Håkon's shoulder. In a surprisingly soft voice, he said, "Can you walk?"

Before Håkon could speak, Anya said, "He's very sick. That's why we came this way. We thought it would be shorter."

The archer met her eyes. "That's a good way to get yourself killed."

Anya didn't know if he meant killed by the sorcerer or killed by the tsar. She swallowed hard.

Håkon stumbled to his knees as the archers walked him toward where the princess waited impatiently on her horse. After exchanging looks and a few quiet words, one of the archers let Håkon ride with him on his horse. Håkon clung to the saddle and clenched his jaw as the horse walked forward. Once they saw Håkon being helped, Ivan and Anya went with the archers without a fuss.

The other archers mounted their horses, and the princess set off down the road. The archer with Håkon followed her.

The archer who had asked Håkon if he could walk extended a hand to Anya. She stared at it for a few moments before he sighed and said, "Do you want to ride with me or walk?"

"Oh." Anya reached for his hand, then withdrew. "Can Ivan ride with someone too?"

The archer laughed. "Sure. He can ride with *our* Ivan." He nodded toward another archer, who leaned down to pull Ivan onto his horse, and then took Anya's hand when she grabbed his.

Anya climbed behind the archer, holding on to the saddle at first. When he clicked his tongue, the horse trotted forward and Anya almost slid right off its back. She grabbed the archer around his chest long enough to get balanced, then released him quickly.

"Sorry," she said. "I was falling off."

He cleared his throat. "Wouldn't want that. Uh, my name is Mikhail."

"I'm Anya," she said.

"Anya," he said, "have you ever ridden a horse before?"

Anya laughed before she could stop herself. Hours

on Alsvindr, back and forth across the valley, feeling her ancestors down to her bones. She pressed her lips together, took a breath, and then said, "Yes, I have."

"And it's funny that you have?" He sounded amused.

"I guess," Anya said. "I ride Alsvindr pretty much every day."

Mikhail swiveled to look back at her. "Alsvindr?"

"I didn't name him," Anya said. "He's a Varangian horse, so he has a Varangian name."

His eyes widened. "You have a Varangian horse?"

"Yes." She fiddled with the edge of her coat's sleeve. "Are we in much trouble?"

Mikhail looked forward again. "I think your friend being sick is going to get you some leeway. But the tsar closed off this road for a reason. For safety."

Anya thought it was unfair to close a road for safety and then punish people who trespassed on it. Maybe they'd just get a talking-to and be released. Hopefully nothing more. She needed to get to Papa soon.

In front of them, the fool Ivan sat silently behind the archer Ivan, and farther ahead, Håkon hunched on his archer's horse. The princess still held up the torch, fiery and writhing in the wind.

"Why doesn't she put the torch out?" Anya asked. "That sorcerer is gone."

Mikhail laughed a cold laugh. "He's not gone. He's just watching."

"Watching?" Anya's skin prickled again.

The archer nodded. "He'll leave us alone as long as we have fire. He hates fire."

"Why?" Anya asked.

"I think it's because he's some kind of forest creature," Mikhail said. "And fire burns the forest. So he doesn't like fire."

She turned to look at the trees. No insidious movement drew her eye. She scanned the trees for a few breaths, then turned back to Mikhail.

"Who is he?" she asked. "Why is he attacking people?"

Mikhail shrugged. "He showed up two years ago and started to attack travelers on the road. He would throw his magic, whatever it is, at them. He destroyed hundreds of caravans. The tsar would send soldiers out here to find and catch him, but he can disappear when he wants to."

Anya nodded, remembering. She had seen it with her own eyes. One moment he had been skipping through the air and the next . . . gone.

"We can't ever find him," the archer continued. "One

time, the tsar tried to chop down that big tree. We're pretty sure that's where he lives. But the trees attacked the lumbermen."

"The *trees* attacked?" Anya asked.

"Yep." The archer was more animated. "Tore out of the earth and walked. Fire didn't stop the trees, even. So the lumbermen ran. The trees followed all the way to the river and died there. But no lumbermen will come into this side of the forest anymore."

Anya pressed her lips together, mind whirring. What kind of magic could animate trees? Mama and Babulya could make the trees use their branches, but could they pull a tree from the earth and make it walk around? Anya hadn't even known there was such a thing as sound magic. How many other magics were there that she had no idea about?

She glanced at the archer in front of them. He had Ivan's staff and Anya's bow strapped to his saddle. She pointed. "I want my bow back."

Mikhail snorted. "You can't have weapons in the presence of the princess."

"*You* do," Anya said.

"We're different," Mikhail said. "We're her vanguard. We have special permission."

"Ivan has special permission to use magic," Anya said, "and he uses the staff for magic. So he should get it back."

Mikhail said, "What about your bow? Do you use that for magic too?"

Anya held her breath for a moment, then let it out silently. "I don't have magic."

Past the trees, Kiev appeared. The tall stone wall rose up on the other side of a brown river about half as wide as the Sogozha River was at home. Guards patrolled on top of the wall, peering over at the archers, and more stood on the stone bridge over the river. The guards stood aside as the five horses and their riders passed. She caught some of them giving her curious glances.

To the side of the bridge, a stack of dead trees rotted, branches hanging into the murky water.

The shadow of the massive gate passed over them, and on the other side, Anya's breath caught in her chest. The city of Kiev stretched in front of her, climbing up a gradual slope to a plateau that overlooked the lower city and the river beyond. The houses around her were all taller than Widow Medvedeva's house. Taller than the village church. Anya gazed open-mouthed at them, wondering how buildings so tall managed to stay upright. Many of the buildings were made of stacked logs with cracks filled with mud—like Anya's own home back in Zmeyreka. But others were brick and stone with wooden roofs towering over her head. The top of her head throbbed, ready for these tall buildings to come down on her as she rode by.

They passed over another bridge, swift waters running beneath it. The road angled up to the plateau, cutting a line through more tall houses and shops. On Anya's left, a huge space had been cleared out, obviously in preparation for construction of some kind. Workers labored, carrying bricks and wood beams from carts and stacking them on the site.

Anya poked her archer again, and he turned with a raised eyebrow.

"What's that going to be?" Anya asked.

"A church," he said. "Tsar Kazimir has commissioned hundreds of new churches across the kingdom." After a long pause, he said, "He's truly a great man."

Anya watched the laborers haul building materials as the archer's horse carried her up the hill. She thought of Dyedka's Slavist worship, and of Mama's prayers on Shabbat, and wondered what the tsar's new churches were crowding out.

They crested the road, emerging onto the tallest part of the city. Anya could see the wild Dnieper River behind her, its waves thrashing against its shores as it hurtled past. The forest reached to the horizon on her right, and she tried to pick out the giant tree. In the distance, its crown rose over the others like a mother standing over her children.

The road curved left against a tall wall, and a fortified gate creaked as soldiers pushed it open. The archers went through with a casualness bordering on boredom, but Anya marveled at every little thing they passed: the royal guards in their brilliantly colored uniforms, the spectacular neatness of the cobbled road beneath the horses' hooves, and even servants hurrying from one task to another.

The royal palace. The realization hit Anya hard. She was about to meet the tsar. The same man who had sent a *bogatyr* to capture Håkon, and whose war had taken Papa from her. He was the son of the man who had destroyed Khazaria and killed Saba. Her mouth was dry. She didn't want to meet the tsar.

The road turned into a wide courtyard lined with magnificent buildings. To the left, the unmistakable shape of a church rose up, the teardrop tops of its towers glowing in the sun. On the right, winter-slumbering gardens were partly obscured behind a low wall; within the garden, across wide lawns of short brown grasses, was a wide tower made of white stone. And in front of them, a long building stretched. It had more windows on one wall than the entire village of Zmeyreka possessed. A magnificent door that was two stories tall stood open, guards flanking either side. The beauty was overwhelming, even muted in the late fall, and Anya had to look down. How did the people who lived here stand it? How could someone get used to living in a paradise?

A long line of peasants like Anya waited at the windowed building's huge doors, nervously tugging at shirts or hats, holding long scrolls of paper, or talking in hushed voices to a person beside them. In the company of the archers, Anya rode straight past them. Every single one of the peasants dropped to a knee as the princess passed. She didn't look at any of them. It was like they weren't even there.

Anya felt eyes on her as the peasants stood. What were they thinking?

They rode into a courtyard, where the princess dismounted. She walked inside, not in a hurry but not waiting, either. Just outside the door was a wide bucket full of sand, with several torches jutting out of it. She slammed her own torch, flame side down, into the sand, extinguishing it. Then she disappeared into the building.

Mikhail slid off his horse and then helped Anya down. A scrape and cry from nearby made her stomach clench. Anya ran toward the sound, darting around horses. Håkon was on his knees, the archers on either side helping him back up.

Håkon gritted his teeth as Anya ran up to him. "I'm just useless, aren't I?"

"No," she said. "You're weak from the transformation. It's not your fault." She found Mikhail and said, "Is there somewhere he can wait for us? He needs to get his strength back."

Mikhail looked uncomfortable. "Maybe later. You must all report to the tsar."

Håkon looked terrified. He gripped Anya's hand awkwardly in his new one. "Anya, don't leave me alone!"

Anya held his hand. "I won't." She looked up at the archers. "He'll need help walking, then."

Håkon trembled as Mikhail looped Håkon's arm around his shoulders and walked him into the building. Anya followed behind, and a moment later, Ivan fell in behind her.

Two of the archers followed them, a wordless presence

hedging them in. The princess waited with an irritated face, and as soon as they neared her, she walked down the hall again. She removed her helmet and cowl as she walked. She had brilliant gold hair braided into a circle at her crown, with wisps catching on the cowl and poking wildly out of the plait. Servants materialized to take the armor away from her. Everywhere she went, people got out of her way. Still, she acknowledged none of them, her blood-red cloak brushing the stone floor of the castle.

Anya tried not to gawk at the castle as they moved through it, but it was nearly impossible not to. The hallway they walked through was as wide and tall as Anya's entire house. The floor was stone blocks fitted together, and the walls were a different type of hewn stone, the huge blocks so solid, she couldn't imagine anything knocking them down. Every now and then a long, woven tapestry would be seen hanging from the walls or a braided carpet would stretch beneath their feet. Otherwise the halls were dim and undecorated.

The hallway ahead ended with tall double doors, flanked by three guards on each side. Another man stood in the middle of the doors, effectively blocking the way. His *rubakha* was longer than any Anya had ever seen, almost to his ankles. In contrast, the archers and Ivan

—even Håkon, now that he was wearing clothing—had a *rubakha* just down to their knees. Ivan's was even shorter, but as a fool, he could get away with that kind of thing. The embroidery on the hem of the doorman's *rubakha* flashed in the meager light of the hallway. Anya squinted. Gold thread? Her mind boggled at the wealth gold-embroidered clothing must require.

The doorman stood with his back straight, his chin up, staring down his nose at the approaching archers and prisoners. A black cloak fastened across his throat with yet more gold, covering his left arm and falling down to his knees. He stood with his free arm across his body, disappearing under the left side of the cape. There was only one reason Anya could think of for him to be standing like that: he was holding the handle of his sword. Ready.

She expected the doorman to remain upright, but he dropped his right hand and executed a deep bow to the princess. When he straightened, he said, "Good afternoon, Your Highness."

"I'm here to see my father," the princess said. She moved to step around the doorman, but he shifted to block her.

"He's not seeing an audience today," the doorman said.

The princess stepped very close to him and snapped, "I am not *an audience*, Pyotr. Now, get out of my way!"

The doorman—Pyotr, apparently—didn't even glance at the furious princess. "His Majesty instructed me that no one should enter the throne room."

"He didn't mean *me!*" the princess said.

Pyotr repeated, "He's not seeing an audience today." He turned only his eyes to where the princess seethed and, with the barest smile, added, "Not even you."

The princess spat, "If you don't move, I'll—"

"Your Highness," Pyotr interrupted, and Anya felt the archer next to her stiffen. Another sucked in a breath. Anya gulped. Who was this man who interrupted the princess so carelessly? "His Majesty is preparing for your betrothal banquet tonight. He has invited your fiancé—"

"I don't *have* a fiancé," the princess snarled.

"—for a celebration of your future marriage. I would recommend doing some preparation yourself," Pyotr finished as though the princess had said nothing. He smiled at her, cold and cruel.

The princess and the doorman held each other's eyes for a few breaths, one furious and the other smug. Finally, the princess whirled, stomping back down the hallway, and the archers all followed her at a scamper.

CHAPTER TWELVE

PRINCESS VASILISA SWEPT down hallway after hallway, saying nothing but leaving a trail of sizzling wrath in the air behind her. The archers followed at a distance, removing their cowls as they hurried after her. Anya expected them all to be about Vasilisa's age, but only Mikhail was. The other three of them were older, probably about Dvoyka and Troyka's age, twenty years old or so. One of the older archers had to support Håkon so he could keep up with the princess's breakneck pace.

Walking next to Anya, Ivan pulled the notebook that Lena had given him out of his coat and began scribbling in it. Anya peered over and said, "What are you doing?"

"Insurance," he said.

When she looked, she saw that he had written, *We are nice!* on the paper, alongside *Agree with me, Håkon is normal,* and *Miroslav Kozlov should come home.*

Their path through the castle took them from the opulence outside the throne room into gradually less grand areas. The princess threw open a heavy, scratched-up door, and the archers followed her through. Inside, Anya gasped at the weapons lined up along the walls and on top of tables. Shields stacked ten deep formed columns jutting off the floor. A whole row of unstrung bows in varying stages of repair or build rested on a worktable, and hundreds of bushels of arrows were stacked into pyramids on the floor beside them.

Next to Anya, Ivan whispered, "I think we're going to be executed."

"Don't be ridiculous," Anya said, but fear settled into her belly.

The princess grabbed a dagger off a table and hurled it at a stack of shields. The dagger hit—*bang!*—and the pile of shields tumbled to the floor—*crash!*

Anya startled at the noise. She hadn't ever seen another woman ride a horse like the princess did, or wear trousers like a man, or hurl a dagger with such rage. In stories about the Polenitsi, women warriors from the East, they were always described as being enormously tall and supernaturally strong. Anya had always assumed that, to be a warrior, a woman would have to be as tall and wild as the Polenitsi, but Vasilisa wasn't tall at all. Her wildness, though . . .

Three of the archers remained by the prisoners. Mikhail hastily smoothed his curly black hair, tangled from having been under the cowl, and approached the princess carefully. "Vasya . . ."

"I should have just stabbed him right in his face!" the princess yelled.

Mikhail shrugged. "You could. That's a possibility. But he's fairly decent at fighting. I think he could have stopped you."

She growled something under her breath, and Mikhail put a hand on her shoulder. Anya watched the tension in the princess's body drain out with a long, exasperated sigh. She glanced back and forth between the archer and the princess. He called her Vasya. He put his hand on her. Was that how people in Kiev acted? Like they were family?

The princess spun and walked to where the remaining archers held Anya and her friends. She stopped an arm's length away and said, "I never introduced myself. Vasilisa Tsarevna, the heir to the throne of Kiev, no matter what my father's henchmen think."

Ivan bowed deeply and foolishly. Håkon tried to imitate him, but his was weak and shaky. Anya did the same, bending at the waist. When she straightened, Vasilisa was staring at her, puzzled.

"What was *that?*" Vasilisa asked.

Anya's stomach churned. "I, um . . . was bowing to you?"

"Women don't bow," Vasilisa said. "Women curtsy."

Anya didn't know how to curtsy, but she didn't want to admit that. She felt adrift, like she really had gone to Patzinakia among the Pechenegs. At least there she'd have an excuse for not knowing things.

Vasilisa continued. "Anyway, don't do either." She pointed a finger at Ivan. "You said you were here to have an audience with the tsar. What was it for?"

Ivan froze. His eyes widened. Anya's hands slowly curled into nervous fists as everyone watched Ivan, waiting for an answer.

Finally, Ivan said, "We came about that guy on the road. Obviously."

The archers exchanged confused looks. One of Vasilisa's golden eyebrows lifted up.

"Obviously?" she asked.

Ivan nodded. "Oh yes." He pulled out the notebook Lena had given him and flipped it to the first page. He pointed to where he had written *Agree with me*. "See?"

The princess narrowed her eyes at the paper. Anya held her breath, hoping the notebook actually worked. If it didn't, she wasn't sure Vasilisa would appreciate the attempt to charm her.

But Anya didn't need to worry. Vasilisa hummed and said, "I do see." She drew a dagger out of her belt and began to run her finger up and down the ridge along the center. "In that case, I think you can help me. And I you. Mutual benefit."

Anya watched Vasilisa's finger go back and forth, singing along the shined metal blade. She swallowed hard.

"Absolutely, Your Highness!" Ivan said, grinning. "Whatever you need, we'll—"

"I need the Nightingale," she said. "Alive."

Ivan's grin was frozen to his face, tacked there uncomfortably as he stared at Vasilisa. "The Nightingale. Because that's what he's called. I knew that." He cleared his throat, grin falling way, and he stroked his chin. "Why alive?"

Vasilisa regarded him with calculating, brilliant eyes. "Do you not think you can do it?"

"Of course I can do it!" Ivan said.

Vasilisa continued to hold him with her eyes. "That's interesting. I think I remember something about your father. He was sent up north to a village to investigate a dragon. How did that turn out?"

Ivan swallowed hard. Anya scooted to be next to Håkon, who was so pale that his freckles looked like they'd been drawn on with ink.

"There wasn't a dragon," Ivan said.

"We got a letter that there had been," Vasilisa said slowly. "But that it was dead."

"That's what I meant," Ivan said. "It, um . . . there was a Varangian."

Vasilisa nodded. "Do you see why I ask? If you can do it? That dragon was very important to my father. To me. And your father let it die."

"I can bring the Nightingale alive, no problem," Ivan said. "I was just curious, that's all."

"From what I hear, fools aren't supposed to be curious." She focused on the dagger's tip now, balancing a finger against it with the barest pressure. "You *are* a fool, aren't you?"

Ivan shifted uncomfortably. Anya winced for him. Was he a fool? By family right, he absolutely was. By magic inheritance . . . not at all.

"I'm the best fool you'll ever see," Ivan mumbled.

"Wonderful." Vasilisa slid the dagger back into her belt. "If you can bring me the Nightingale alive, I'll grant whatever wish you ask." She waited, staring at Ivan expectantly. When he didn't say anything, she sighed. "What do you *want*, fool?"

"Oh!" Ivan hesitated, and then pointed to Anya. "Her father was wrongfully conscripted. We'd like him to be brought back."

Now Vasilisa turned her penetrating eyes to Anya. Anya tried her best not to shrink away from the princess, but it was hard. She felt as though Vasilisa could see straight through her and out the other side.

"Wrongfully how?" Vasilisa asked.

"Um." Anya wasn't sure she wanted to tell her that Papa was Jewish. Vasilisa was the granddaughter of the tsar who had wiped Khazaria off the map and killed Saba. Her father was building churches as fast as he could quarry the stones. What did Vasilisa think of Jews? What would she do to Anya?

Anya straightened her back. She had to be brave. For

Papa. Whatever Vasilisa's opinion of Jews, she had said she'd do whatever Ivan asked. And there were witnesses. She'd have to keep her word. Wouldn't she?

"My papa's name is Miroslav Kozlov," Anya said. "He's Jewish. The magistrate in my village lied. He told the conscription officers that Papa was Slavist so they'd take him. He never should have gone in the first place."

Vasilisa glanced for half a breath at Mikhail. It was so fast, Anya might have imagined it. But the archer's eyes were wide, and Anya caught him staring at her before hurriedly looking away.

"Wrongful by law," Vasilisa said. "But I think anyone should be able to serve as a soldier if they want."

Mikhail shifted but stayed silent.

Vasilisa asked, "Where is he?"

Anya trembled. "He's working with the cavalry. They went into Rûm through the Pecheneg territories some time ago. That's all I know."

Vasilisa recovered her surprise quickly. "If he's already in Rûm, extracting him will be difficult."

Anya's shoulders slumped. How was she supposed to convince the princess that bringing back her papa was worth it?

Before Anya could speak, Vasilisa continued:

"Difficult, but not impossible." To Mikhail, she said, "Take the three of them to the guest suites. They can stay next to that idiot *bogatyr* who thinks I'm going to marry him."

"Yes, Your Highness," Mikhail murmured, bowing his head.

Vasilisa strode to the door, pausing halfway across the room to turn and glare at Ivan. "Make it worth my effort, fool." And then she was gone out the door.

Mikhail turned to them, smiling unsteadily. "Well. All right, then. I'm Mikhail Yakovovich." He gave them all a slight bow.

Ivan had already introduced himself, but he did it again for good measure.

Anya said, "Anya Miroslavovna."

They all looked at Håkon, who said nothing. He fidgeted with the hem of his *rubakha*.

Ivan clapped Håkon on the back. "My shy friend here is Håkon Jernhåndssen. He's afraid you're going to think his name is strange."

Håkon looked up then, and Mikhail stared at him wordlessly. His eyes ticked to where Vasilisa had stormed out, and, too late, Anya remembered that Håkon looked like the princess. She moved to get between Mikhail and Håkon, but then Mikhail managed an unsteady smile.

"There are plenty of strange names in Kiev," he said through his unsure smile. He glanced at Anya. "You can call me Misha. I'll be showing you to your rooms."

CHAPTER THIRTEEN

MISHA ESCORTED THEM out of the armory. This trip through the halls was slower, and Misha was a very amiable chaperone. Without his cowl on, he looked much friendlier. His dark, curly hair was cut short, and his eyes twinkled. There was something about him that put Anya at ease.

"So, you're going to apprehend the Nightingale," Misha said after walking in silence down several hallways. "That's a bold statement."

"If anyone can do it, Ivan can," Anya said. Like Ivan, she was curious about why they needed to bring him back alive, but she was fine with not shedding any blood. She didn't want to press the issue in case it made the princess change her mind.

Misha peered over at Ivan. "Are you a great fool, then?"

Ivan exclaimed, "Of course I am!"

Misha looked skeptical but didn't say anything. He directed his attention to Håkon, who was trailing a step behind everyone else. "And you. Are you a fool too?"

Håkon just stared at him, so Anya said, "He's not a fool. He must still be feeling sick."

Misha nodded. "He looks unwell."

Håkon's face darkened. "*You* look unwell."

"I look . . ." Misha's brow furrowed. "What?"

"Nothing!" Anya said. "He's just tired. *Right, Håkon?*"

Håkon huffed and said nothing.

The group went back to walking in silence, with Ivan breaking it every now and then to point at something he found interesting. They returned gradually to opulence, and then Misha halted by a door and pushed it open. "This room is for the gentlemen."

Ivan dashed in, looking around the huge room. "Nice!"

Håkon shuffled in behind him. Anya wanted to see what was so nice, but Misha was already moving down the hall. Anya hurried after him. He opened the next door and said, "And this is yours."

Anya peeked in. The room was the size of the main portion of her barn, but instead of being filled with hay and goats, it was filled with a huge, tall bed and a massive carved wardrobe. The windows were shuttered against the cold, so the room was dim. There were unlit lamps mounted on the walls. A stone dais under one window was carved into a bowl on top, and a pitcher with a towel over it sat on the edge of the dais. On the wall opposite the bed was a deep fireplace as tall as Anya was; a fire rumbled within it and warmed the room nicely.

"Wow," Anya whispered. She was almost afraid to touch anything.

She stood at the threshold until Misha chuckled from behind her. "You can go in if you want," he said.

"Are you sure?" Anya said. "This is . . ." She didn't know the words to describe it.

"It's a castle," Misha said.

"Do you live here?"

"No," he said. "I live in the city with my family."

"Oh." Anya edged into the room. "Is your family nice?"

He shrugged. "Usually. I'm going to let you get settled. If you need anything, I'll see you at the banquet tonight."

She whipped her head to look at him. "The what?"

"The banquet," he said, as if it were the most obvious answer in the world.

"Are we invited?"

Misha nodded. "All guests of the royal family are invited, and now you're guests of the princess."

"Oh," Anya mumbled. "Good." She looked down. "You know, Misha, I don't think I'm dressed well enough for a banquet. None of us are. And we don't have any nice clothes, so—"

Misha waved his hand around. "I'll bring some clothes for you all!" He grinned.

"You don't have to do—"

"I want to," Misha said, scooting off down the corridor. "I'll go arrange that. The banquet is in two hours. I'll see you there!"

✦ ✹ ✦

Misha vanished, and Anya lingered in the hall, mind whirling.

How were they supposed to capture that sound sorcerer—the Nightingale, apparently—without getting themselves killed? He had been nasty enough while they had been trying to run away. What would he be like when they retaliated? She thought of him grabbing Ivan's water magic and turning it against him, and what Misha had said about him making trees walk.

Hair the color of dirty rocks and cut utterly bizarrely. Eyes painted black. Skin tattooed gold. What *was* the Nightingale, anyway?

Under Anya's dress, the key Lena had given her hung heavy against her skin. She pulled it up, holding it in the palm of her hand. Lena had brought them to Kiev, not Patzinakia. Papa must have been here for some reason. Imprisoned? Why? Where? And Anya understood why Lena had turned Håkon into a human, but why had she made him look so much like the princess?

The thought of Håkon propelled her to his and Ivan's room. She knocked on the door, and Ivan answered. The gash he'd gotten from the Nightingale was purpling around the edges, bruising deeply.

"How is he?" Anya asked, slipping in to search for Håkon. Their room looked very much like hers, except the bed was on a different wall. Håkon was on the bed, lying on his back, hands up in the air.

Ivan shut the door. "He's um . . . What did you say, Håkon?"

Håkon's hands twitched. "Everything feels."

"'Everything feels,'" Ivan said to Anya.

She climbed on the bed and sat next to Håkon. He looked haggard. Dark circles made his glittering eyes sunken. "We got invited to the banquet. You probably shouldn't go."

He looked at her. "Why?"

"Because"—Anya ticked off on her fingers—"you can hardly walk. You've never eaten anything with a human mouth." She pointed to his hands in the air. "And 'everything feels'?"

"Everything," Håkon mumbled. "I touch the door, it feels one way. I touch the bed, it feels a completely different way. They're rough and smooth and cool and warm and how do you *live* like this?"

"You get used to it," Anya said. "Maybe you should take a break right now, though. A banquet is going to be a big deal for Ivan and me, and we've been human our whole lives. I don't want you to get overwhelmed."

Håkon was quiet for a few moments, and then he said, "I think I'm hungry."

"You think?" Anya asked.

He indicated his abdomen with a feeble hand wave. "Is this where my stomach is?"

"Yes."

"It hurts. So I think I'm hungry."

Anya sighed. "Ivan and I can bring food back from the banquet for you. I don't really want to stay long. We have to talk about how we're going to handle the Nightingale so we can get my papa back."

"Bring him to the princess alive," Ivan said. "Obviously."

Håkon sighed. "Alive. Just like the dragons."

Silence hung over the room like steam, heavy and sticky. Finally, Anya said, "Yes. Like the dragons."

Håkon lay still, silent, and then murmured, "If she knew I was a dragon . . . I wonder what she would have done to me."

Anya and Ivan exchanged a look as Håkon rolled over. He winced when his hands touched the bedspread, and he slid off onto unsteady legs.

"I want to go to the banquet," Håkon said.

Anya shook her head. "I don't think—"

"I want to see him," Håkon said, his face dark. "The tsar. I want to ask him why he killed us all."

Ivan said, "Håkon, that's crazy."

"I think it's a valid question!" Håkon said.

"We know why," Anya said. "A dragon killed his son."

"Well *I* didn't kill his son," Håkon said, furious. "Why do I have to die?"

Anya tugged on her dress. "We don't agree with the tsar. You don't have to get mad at us."

Håkon glared at her, exasperated, and Anya was struck by how he and Vasilisa even had the same facial expressions.

"There's something else," Anya said.

"What?"

"It's the way you look," Anya said, peering at Ivan, trying to see if he was following her.

He didn't seem to be. He was picking at a scab on his arm.

"Ivan," Anya prompted.

He looked up. "Huh?"

"Don't you think Håkon looks like . . . someone?" Anya asked.

Ivan nodded. "Oh. Yeah. He looks exactly like Vasilisa."

Håkon's exasperation evaporated. "I do?"

Anya and Ivan both nodded.

"I mean, you're a boy and she's a girl," Ivan said, "but you're practically the same person."

"Why?" Håkon asked.

Anya shrugged. "We'll have to ask Lena when we see her next," she said. "But for now, that's something we've got to deal with."

"How much like her, though?" Håkon asked.

"If we braided your hair, put you in a red cloak, and you scowled enough, you could fool anyone here," Ivan said.

"I just don't think it's smart to parade you around looking exactly like the princess," Anya said, not adding that Misha had already noticed. "I think you should stay here and practice being a human. Then later, you won't make anyone suspicious." When Håkon looked like he was going to argue, Anya said, "I'll go really fast, grab some food, and come back here. Okay?"

Håkon slumped back onto the bed. "Okay."

He looked very sad, and Anya took a step toward him. She intended to hug him, pat his horns, run her hands over his scales —

But he didn't have those anymore.

He was a human now. A boy. She couldn't pat his horns or run her hands over his scales. So she did what she would have done with Ivan. She pulled Håkon into a hug, arms wrapped around him tight. He brought his arms up and hugged her, then laughed.

"This is a lot easier with long arms," he said.

Anya laughed with him. Her heart thumped. "I'll be back soon."

CHAPTER FOURTEEN

A KNOCK CAME at the door, and Anya remembered that Misha had said he would bring them clothes to change into. When she answered, though, Misha wasn't there. A steward with a sour face stood there, a bundle of clothes hung over one arm.

"I was told this is the gentlemen's room," the steward said.

"It is!" Ivan waved an arm. "The gentlemen are here!"

Anya blushed at the steward's disapproving glare. She slipped out of the room and escaped to her own, where a few dresses were already laid out on her bed. She picked the simplest one of the bunch: a black linen *rubakha* with a long red silk *sarafan* gown to go over it. The *rubakha* had red embroidery around the sleeve ends and the collar, matching the design of black embroidery on the *sarafan's* hem. A matching embroidered belt cinched at her waist, and the black head covering was held in place with another matching embroidered cloth.

It was easily the nicest thing Anya had ever worn, and she was afraid of ruining something somehow. She decided she would have to be extra careful.

Someone knocked at the door. She stepped carefully to avoid tripping on the gown's long hem and opened the door. Ivan stood on the other side, dressed in finery as Anya was. His *rubakha* was white, embroidered with red, and the tunic over it was deep blue silk. His trousers were black silk tucked into black boots. He would have looked absolutely regal if the rich clothes weren't fastened incorrectly. The beautiful belt was tied in a messy knot off to one side. His hat was tipped so far askew, Anya was sure it would fall off. His collar was tied crooked. He still had blood on his face.

Håkon stood behind him, dressed in simpler clothing that actually fit him: a white *rubakha* over black pants, which were tucked into brown boots. His hair was combed down over his eyebrows, and it made him look less like Vasilisa. Probably thanks to Ivan. "Can you make *him* dress like a proper human?" Håkon asked.

She sighed. "No. He's a fool." She used her fingers to comb Håkon's hair out of his face.

"I look fine!" Ivan said. "You're lucky my trousers are on the right way around!"

"He tried them backwards," Håkon said to Anya, "but they wouldn't fasten."

"Ha, ha," Ivan said.

Håkon smirked, the first non-grimace Anya had seen on him since he'd changed into a human. The half-smile looked good on him.

"Let's go," Ivan said to Anya.

"Hold on." She waved him into her room and to the stone washbasin. She dampened the cloth in the water, then scrubbed at Ivan's bloody face.

"Ah!" Ivan yelled.

"Hold still," Anya said through gritted teeth. "You've still got a big gash and a bruise, but at least I can clean the blood off."

She cleaned his face until the steward knocked. He eyeballed Ivan's attire, clucked his tongue at the gentlemen in Anya's room, but didn't say anything. Anya and

Ivan said goodbye to Håkon and followed the steward through the castle, heading back toward where the throne room was. They turned before they got there, and found themselves in another enormous, tall room. This one held a dozen long banquet tables, all packed with what Anya assumed were the tsar's noble boyars. Torches burned in sconces, their flames scorching the stone walls behind them. Diners spoke with animated arms, some pacing between tables as they ate and spoke and laughed with others. Servers hurried here and there bearing goblets, platters, and bowls, dodging the roaming boyars. More food than Anya had been prepared for covered every banquet table. There was hardly room for the diners' own bowls.

The steward walked easily into the fray of scurrying servers, and Ivan started after him. Anya managed to grab onto Ivan's sleeves, clinging to him as they crossed the room and sat in empty spots near a far window.

The tsar sat at the front table, facing the entire room. He was tall even sitting, with hair like bronze, and eyes like fire. His beard was trimmed impeccably, the golden diadem on his head flashing with every movement. Vasilisa sat to his right; the tsarina, his wife, sat to his left. Anya had never seen a woman as beautiful as the tsarina.

Even from a distance, she was glowing perfection: long golden hair in an ornate braid, a high forehead, graceful eyebrows, a delicate nose. But she looked fragile and pre-occupied. Like an injured bird that dreamed of another sky. The tsar held her hand, resting their entwined fingers on the table's edge in front of them. A golden ring inlaid with a diamond flashed on his finger.

Two others sat at the table on Vasilisa's right. The one closer to her was the younger of the two men. Vasilisa had her shoulder turned to him, pointedly ignoring him. He didn't look bothered about that, though. And he didn't look much like he belonged at the table with the royal family, either. He was dressed appropriately in a richly colored *rubakha*, and though he wore it easily, he seemed too rough for it. His shoulders were very broad, like he could lift up a horse with one hand and regularly did. His hair and face were unlike any fashion Anya had ever seen before. Both sides of his head were sheared almost down to the skin. The dark hair remaining ran in a wide strip down the top of his head, and he had braided it down to the top of his neck. One of his dark eyebrows was cut in half by a long white scar that curved like a scythe across his forehead and into his shaved hairline. And his beard . . . his beard was nonexistent. Like he shaved it off on purpose. Anya wrinkled her nose. Who would do that? Maybe he couldn't grow one. And he smirked constantly, like someone had just told him a funny joke that was too impolite to laugh openly about.

The man next to him was older and dressed well, and unlike his companion, he looked actively uncomfortable in his clothing. He sat with his hands clasped politely, his blond hair and beard in fashion with every other grown man in Kievan Rus'. He was huge as well, but he crunched in his shoulders to make himself seem less like a mountain of a person. He reminded Anya of Dobrynya: imposing but kind, powerful yet gentle.

Earlier, Vasilisa had mentioned an idiot *bogatyr*. Anya suspected she was looking at a pair of them, and that the younger one was the idiot she had spoken of. Anya assumed Vasilisa didn't use the word to describe the *bogatyr* as a fool but instead meant he was actually stupid. He didn't look stupid to Anya. He just looked inexplicably smug. But who was the older one?

She reached for a loaf of bread, but a server swept it out of the way to make room for a new dish: a huge platter with a suckling pig on it. An *entire pig*, trussed and cooked, its mouth open and stuffed with some kind of fruit. Its empty eye sockets stared at her.

She pulled her hand back from the table, trying desperately not to make a face. Neighboring diners dug into the pig, cutting pieces off it with careless abandon.

Ivan reached for the pig, noticed Anya, and let his hand drop. He pulled a dish from his other side—a deep tureen with some kind of stew in it—and he said, "I think this is just vegetables."

She swallowed hard, wishing someone would take the pig away. "Thanks." The stew seemed to be cabbage-based, and she inspected it for any meat as she spooned it into her bowl. Nothing apparent surfaced.

Ivan managed to grab some rye bread and fried fish for her, and some pirozhki for himself. He opened up the pirozhki's pastry crust and inspected the filling. "Meat," he said. "I don't know what kind."

When he looked at her, eyebrows up, questioning if she wanted it, she shook her head.

"It'll be for Håkon, then." Ivan took another bowl and piled extras of everything, plus some of the pirozhki. He snagged a small bowl of honey as it made its way around the table. A server took away the remains of the pig and replaced it with a heaping pile of crescent-shaped, fried *chebureki*.

Anya was about to spoon some of the stew into her

mouth when the tsar stood and shouted, "My friends! My subjects! My loyal boyars! I'm so blessed and happy that you have joined me here tonight!"

The gathered crowd cheered and clapped for him. Anya set her spoon in the bowl so she could clap too. Ivan left his spoon hanging out of his mouth as he clapped. Anya would rather not applaud the man who would kill Håkon, and when she glanced at Ivan, his face said the same thing.

The tsar waited for the noise to die down, and then he continued speaking: "We are doubly blessed today. Two of my mightiest *bogatyri* have joined us here! The mighty Ilya of Murom, my dear friend and loyal knight!" He swept his arm toward the big blond man, who waved uncomfortably from his seat.

Anya sat up, stock-still and wide-eyed.

Ilya of Murom. Ilya Muromets. A sickly peasant who was healed by magic and went on to perform the greatest of deeds. Anya's hero. Eating a piece of meat with one hand and waving with the other.

The tsar said, "We are also blessed to have Alyosha Popovich, he of unending strength and power, visiting us from his northern city of Rostov!"

The young *bogatyr* with the bizarre half-shaved head

jumped to his feet and waved at the assembled crowd. He was certainly tall and looked strong, but he wasn't as enormous as Dobrynya or Ilya. Vasilisa scowled and leaned even farther away from him.

The tsar swept a hand toward Alyosha. "His father is the priest of my newest cathedral in Rostov. Alyosha is not only a mighty *bogatyr* but a devout and dedicated man of God." He turned to Vasilisa and grinned, beaming like the actual sun. He put his hand out to her. Slowly, the princess set her hand in her father's and stood up. The tsar reached around her, taking Alyosha's hand. He set Vasilisa's tiny hand inside Alyosha's much bigger one. "And a magnificent future tsar!"

The boyars gasped and cheered. Vasilisa's jaw clenched, and she pursed her lips together. Alyosha lifted their combined hands upward, tugging her closer to him. She wrenched her hand away from him and shoved her chair out of the way, stomping away from the table and out the door with a slam.

Alyosha started after her, but Ilya grabbed his arm. When Alyosha turned to look at Ilya, the older knight shook his head slowly.

The boyars began to lean close to one another, mumbling questions.

The tsar looked between where his daughter had vanished and the now-empty seat she had left behind. "Ah," he said with a laugh. "She's so overwhelmed with gratitude! And so excited to start a new life as a wife and mother!"

Anya winced. She had known Vasilisa for mere hours, but even she knew that being a wife and mother was the last thing the princess wanted to do.

The tsar motioned for the *bogatyri* to sit, and someone slid into the seat across from Anya. When she turned to give a nervous smile to whoever it was, she recognized the pink scar beside his left eye.

"Misha." Anya was surprised at how glad she was to see him.

He smiled. "I'm glad you came."

Anya said, "Where did the princess go?"

Misha pressed his lips together for a second. "Probably to stab something."

Anya nodded. That was the vibe she'd gotten as well. It was probably good that Ilya had stopped Alyosha from following. She nodded toward the tsar's table, where the *bogatyri* sat. "That's the 'idiot' she was talking about earlier, right?"

"Yep," Misha sighed. "Alyosha Popovich. Vasya

—Vasilisa is . . . not fond of him. The first time they met, he broke her favorite sword. Bent it right in half. I think he was trying to impress her. She got angry instead. He refused to apologize. She's refused to speak to him since." He shook his head wearily.

Anya nodded along with him and reached for the cabbage stew. Misha stopped talking so he could put his hand out, covering the bowl. When Anya glared at him, he smiled weakly.

"They use pork fat as a base," he said.

Anya sucked in a sharp breath and whispered, "You're Jewish! I knew it!"

He blanched. "You what? How?"

"Vasilisa looked at you when I said I was Jewish," Anya said. "Just for a second. You were both too surprised."

"Oh." He breathed out in relief. "That's observant. I mean . . . it's safe here. Pretty safe. Not like other places. Still." He touched two fingers to his hair above his ear. "Better to be cautious."

"And not wear your kippah?" Anya asked.

"I wear it at home," Misha said. "Just not here."

Anya poked the fish on her plate and raised her eyebrows in a silent question to Misha.

He shook his head and said, "Fried in pork fat."

"What?" Anya groaned. "Is the bread at least safe?"

He laughed. "So far."

Anya scowled and slid the fish away. "So all I can eat is bread?"

Misha shrugged. "I'm going home for dinner. Do you want to come?"

Anya held her breath for a second. "I don't know," she said. "My friends . . . I don't want to leave them."

"It will only be for a little while," Misha said. "Please. I know my family would love to meet you."

"Why?" Anya asked. They didn't even know she existed. How could he know they'd love to meet her?

Misha laughed like she'd made a joke. When she didn't laugh back, he furrowed his brow. "Because you're one of us," he said. "Anyone who's Jewish is welcome in our home. Especially on Shabbat."

Anya had felt an ominous prickle up her spine during the tsar's speech earlier, and now she felt another prickle. But this one was different. It felt nicer. Warmer. She smiled. "Really?"

"Of course," Misha said. He stood and waited expectantly.

Anya didn't want to leave Ivan and Håkon behind, but

she really wanted to meet Misha's family. She wouldn't really be leaving them, she decided. They had each other. They could work out some kind of plan for the Nightingale while she was gone.

"Hang on," she said to Misha, and leaned toward where Ivan continued to stuff food into his mouth like his brothers were on their way to take it from him. "Ivan."

He looked up at her, cheeks stuffed. "Muh?"

"I'm going to go eat with Misha."

Ivan's brow furrowed. "Whuh?"

"He's Jewish," Anya said. "None of this food is kosher." She swept her hand out. "I'm just going for dinner and then I'll be back."

He swallowed frantically. "What about Håkon?"

"You two will be fine without me," Anya said. She reached for the bowl of food Ivan had put together. "I'll drop this off. I need to get a coat, anyway."

Ivan looked very sour as Anya and Misha stood. They exited the hall, and Anya stopped. She couldn't remember which direction the rooms were in.

Misha did, though. He moved through the halls like he had been there his entire life.

"So, how . . ." She didn't know how rude it would be

to ask him why he could serve the royal family *and* be Jewish. "I mean, I thought we. . ." She lowered her voice. "Jews. I thought we couldn't be in the military."

"You wouldn't be in the military anyway, because you're a girl," Misha said with a smile.

Anya frowned. "Vasilisa is a girl."

"Well, yeah," Misha said. "But she's not just *any* girl. She's the tsar's only child, and she'll inherit the kingdom one day. So she gets to do whatever she wants."

Except not marry a person she hates, Anya thought. "So is that why you're in her personal archery detail?" Anya asked. "Because she gets what she wants?"

He laughed. "Yes, kind of. We used to play together when our fathers would meet. We're friends now."

So he was some sort of noble. A Jewish noble? "Who is your father?"

Casually, nonchalantly, like it was a totally normal thing to say, Misha said, "The head rabbi of Kiev."

Anya's mouth dried up and her heart thumped faster. "A rabbi?"

Misha nodded.

A rabbi. She was going to meet a rabbi. The first rabbi she'd ever met.

"But why would he meet with the tsar?" Anya asked. "Isn't he worried that something will happen?"

"Something did happen," Misha said. "That's why he spoke with the tsar in the first place. The tsar was a Slavist up until a few years ago. Then he decided to convert, but not just himself. The whole country. Everyone in Kiev went to the river to be baptized. But my father protested. We had bags and wagons packed just in case. But the tsar seemed fine with our refusal. They used to meet a lot to talk about how to keep Jews and Christians happy with one another."

Anya looked at his exposed hair. "But you still don't wear a kippah?"

"It never hurts to be cautious," Misha said.

Before Anya could say anything else, Misha said, "Where did you come from? The same village as the fool? Or a shtetl close to it?"

Anya blinked. She had no idea what a shtetl was but felt stupid admitting that to him. "I'm from the same place as Ivan."

"Did you ever see the dragon?" Misha asked.

Anya shook her head, feeling cold inside. "Never."

"That's probably a good thing," Misha said. "Is that village far?"

Anya nodded. "North. Ivan says we're close to Ingria."

Misha thought for a few seconds. "That's really far, isn't it?"

"Yes."

"How long have you been traveling?" He tugged at the end of his sleeve. "Alone with them this whole time?"

Anya didn't want to tell Misha they had been transported in a magical house in a matter of minutes, so she said, "It didn't seem that long."

Misha frowned, clearly not entirely approving.

"We were safe," Anya said in an attempt to make his frown go away.

"I'm sure," he said, sounding skeptical.

"They're my friends," Anya said. She wasn't sure why she was trying to justify her friendship with Ivan and Håkon to Misha. "We've been through a lot together. A Varangian came to our village to get the dragon, and he tried to kill us. Ivan and Håkon saved my life." It was so much more complicated than that, but she couldn't very well tell Misha the truth.

Misha's eyes widened. "Tried to kill you? Why?"

"He was a bad person." And she was hiding the dragon from him.

"What happened to him?"

Anya's stomach clenched as Sigurd's bloody face flashed behind her eyes. "He died."

Misha was quiet. "I'm sorry that happened."

Anya shrugged. She didn't want to talk about it anymore. "Tell me more about serving in the military," Anya said.

Misha laughed before she could continue. "Why? Do you want to join?"

"No," Anya said. "I just find it interesting. A Jewish man being allowed to serve."

Misha nodded. "Ah yes. I'm something of a rarity."

"What makes you so special?" Anya asked. "You're friends with the princess?"

He nodded again. "Yes. Vasya asked for me." He cast a sideways glance at Anya. "I know she's mean. She doesn't have a lot of friends. The tsar and tsarina have been trying for a long time to get her to marry someone, but she's rejected all of them. She'll reject Alyosha, too. She says if anyone's going to rule Kievan Rus', it will be her. A couple years ago she asked me to teach her archery, and you don't say no to Vasya. She put me on her detail then. I mean, of course I'm going to be a rabbi. But this is nice for now, and I think she needs me."

"Of course?" Anya asked.

"Yes, of course," Misha said. "Does your rabbi not have sons?"

Anya was embarrassed to admit that the only clergyman she'd ever met was the priest, Father Drozdov. "No. I mean, that's not . . . You don't have any brothers?"

Misha shook his head. "Two sisters, both younger. No brothers."

"I don't have any brothers or sisters," Anya said, and Misha looked very surprised.

"Why not?"

Anya shrugged. "I don't know. I never asked."

"That's unfortunate." Misha stopped by a familiar door. "This is your friends' room."

Anya knocked on the door and waited for a few seconds before pushing the door open gently. She peered in. Håkon sat on the floor, back against the bed, legs stretched out in front of him. He looked up forlornly as Anya peered in.

"I forgot how to stand up," he said.

She looked at Misha, forced a grin, and said, "Just one minute." And then she slipped into the room with the bowl and shut the door in his puzzled face.

With some hoisting and grunting, Anya got Håkon on

his feet. He leaned against the bed, face-down on the top, and mumbled, "This body is the worst."

"It's temporary," Anya said. "We just need to bring the Nightingale here alive, and we can go back to Zmeyreka, and you can go back to . . . being you."

His eyes shifted to the door. "Is someone out there?"

"Yes." Anya held up the bowl. "Here's your dinner."

"Where are you going?"

"With Misha," Anya said.

Håkon stood up straight. "What? Why?"

"He's Jewish."

"So?"

"So?" She snorted. "I've never met someone Jewish who isn't my family."

Again, louder, Håkon said, "So?"

"*So*," Anya said forcefully, "I want to know what it's like for him. For them. He invited me to dinner."

"You're leaving me twice, then?" Håkon said.

"I didn't leave you," Anya said. "Why are you angry?"

"Because I look like a human being and I *still* have to hide from everyone," Håkon said. "That's my whole life. *Håkon, don't let them see you. Håkon, don't talk to the villagers. Håkon, the tsar will kill you even though you never did anything wrong."*

Anya said, "I don't—"

"I want to meet him." Håkon walked unsteadily toward the door. "Is he out here?"

"Yes," Anya hurried after him.

Håkon yanked the door open and almost fell over. Misha startled, eyes wide, but he recovered and said, "Hello."

"You're the archer." Håkon glowered.

Misha nodded and held out his hand. "Mikhail. Misha."

Håkon examined Misha's extended hand, then put his out in the same way. "Håkon." Misha took it and shook, and Håkon ground his teeth together so hard, Anya heard them squeak. She wasn't sure if that was because *everything feels*, or if it was because of Misha specifically.

Misha didn't seem to notice Håkon pulling his hand away as fast as he could. "Håkon, I've got to tell you. You look . . . a lot like the tsarevna." He laughed.

Anya's breath stopped in her throat. Håkon seemed to hold his, too.

"That's just remarkable," Misha said, reaching a hand up. "You've even got the same freckles just there."

Håkon swatted Misha's hand away and said, "I'm

going to be sick everywhere," and slammed the door in Misha's face. He spun to face Anya, which was a bad idea. It caused him to teeter and almost fall. "You're trying to be friends with him? Why?"

"Not friends," Anya said. "I just want to see what it's like to talk to an actual rabbi."

"He's going to figure it out," Håkon said. "He's going to turn me back into a dragon. Maybe *he's* the one Lena talked about. The one who would do anything to change me back."

"There's no way," Anya said.

"Think about it," Håkon said. "The princess, in the armory. She said the dragon was very important to her father and to her. That's *me*." His voice shook. "I'm that dragon. I'm very important. If Misha took me to the tsar, he'd probably be rich for the rest of his life." Håkon jabbed his finger at the door. "He'd kill me, Anya."

"He wouldn't—"

"He would so."

"Only if you looked like a dragon."

"I *am* a dragon!" Håkon snapped, and then looked at the door. Quieter, he said, "If I didn't look like this"—he motioned at himself—"he'd be trying to drag me to the tsar, and I'd die. Like all the others. Like *all the others*.

He's not different from the rest of them. He's not like you and Ivan."

"I felt bad taking you to the tsar *because* I'm Jewish! Because of the Talmud!" Anya said. "And he probably knows it better than I do. I bet he wouldn't hurt you."

Håkon blanched. "Don't you dare tell him."

"Tell him what?"

"What I am."

Anya frowned. "Do you really think I'd tell a stranger about you?"

"You're going to go eat dinner with a stranger," Håkon pointed out.

"That's completely different," Anya said. "Eating dinner is not the same as telling someone a huge secret."

"A secret that's not even yours to tell," Håkon said.

Anya put her hands up. "You know what? If you're going to stand here and be unreasonable, I don't want to deal with it. I'm going."

"Fine," Håkon grumbled.

"Fine," Anya said.

"Go."

"I am." And she opened the door, stepped out, and slammed it behind her.

CHAPTER FIFTEEN

MISHA ASKED ANYA if she was okay, and she yelled that she was, and he didn't say anything else as she collected a coat from her room. He also didn't say anything as they walked out of the castle and away from the city's upper town and into the southern area. Anya could see out of the city, out to the Dnieper and the forest, both tinted orange in the setting sun's light. The day was starting to pick up a nighttime bite already. They would be cutting it close with Shabbat.

Misha ran his fingers along the closure seam of his coat, then cleared his throat and said, "I hope your friend is—"

"I don't want to talk about him," Anya snapped in the dimming afternoon light.

"Okay." He fidgeted with his coat seam and then said, "Did I make him angry?"

"He's feeling sick," Anya said. "He's just grumpy in general. It's not you." Even though it definitely *was* Misha. Thinking about it rekindled Anya's annoyance. Håkon wasn't her papa. He couldn't tell her what to do, or who to be friends with. Misha wouldn't hurt Håkon. If he met him and knew how nice Håkon was, there was no way Misha would hurt him.

Right?

Misha smiled. "Oh. Well, good." He looked skyward. "We'll get there with plenty of time to spare. My mother is going to kiss your entire face, just so you know. And my sisters—"

"Wait," Anya said. "Kiss my *entire* face?"

"Yes." Misha nodded. "And my sisters will not stop talking unless you specifically ask them to. They're going to want to know everything about you. But you don't have to tell them. They're just nosy."

"What about your father?" Anya asked.

Misha shrugged. "He'll be fine."

To Anya, that sounded very ominous.

They followed a road down the hill Kiev was built on, but they didn't descend that much. Misha followed the river's curve north and zigzagged back and forth between tall buildings. Eventually they passed through a gate, and something on the other side changed. It might have been the smells, or the colors of the wood on the doorposts, or the arrangement of the stones on the road. Whatever it was, it felt familiar.

Misha stopped at a clean wooden door with flowers carved into the doorpost. He reached into his coat pocket and withdrew a folded half-circle of cloth; he unfolded it, kissed it, and smoothed it over his hair. A black kippah, smaller on Misha's head than Papa's was on his. When Misha opened the door, it swung out rather than in, and just inside the right-hand jamb was a small rectangular box, nailed on a slant above Anya's head. It was plain, mostly, wood or metal painted blue, but a single Hebrew letter—shin—had been inscribed in gold on the front. Misha touched it as he passed through the door, and Anya's hand twitched to follow. But she didn't know what it was, didn't know if it was special only to his family, so she just balled her fists and marched inside.

The door swung shut behind her, and a puff of warm, delicious air wafted against Anya's face. Someone had baked bread—Anya could smell the unmistakable aroma that filled her own home once a week. Besides the bread smell was something fruity and flowery, plus something else. The air smelled *alive*. It smelled like Babulya's most delectable tinctures, when she took the most aromatic of her plants and stewed them into good magic.

The room they stood in was small but cozy, with a fire burning in a fireplace to their right. Wooden chairs with pillows on the seats faced the fire, and bookshelves covered the opposite wall. The shelves were jammed full of books and stacks of scrolls, but tidily—a neat kind of clutter. One shelf held nothing but writing tools: quills, parchment, bottles of ink, and several boxes with probably more of the same inside. A long sideboard sat in front of the shuttered window, and five graceful candlesticks with white candles were lined up in the center. Anya thought of Mama lining up her own candles, without Anya by her side. A silver chalice of dark red liquid sat between the line of candles and two large, deep bowls with squares of cloth folded in front of them, and smaller cups sitting on top of the cloth squares. Anya stared at them, mind whirring. What were those for?

To their left, a long table was set for at least a dozen people, and a couple of smaller children sat on the long bench down one side. The little boys wore black kippot like Misha's.

Past the table, a door led into a brightly lit room, and lively conversation drifted out to Anya as she lingered by the doorway.

Anya fidgeted nervously with her coat sleeve and looked around the room another time. On the wall between the bookshelf and the fireplace, a taller bookshelf stood apart. It was emptier than the other, holding a collection of almost two dozen tomes that matched in size and color. A set of . . . Anya held her breath. She had two pieces of that set at home. The Talmud. Misha had the entire thing in his sitting room.

One of the little boys at the table spun, and when he saw Misha, he stood up on the bench with his arms up and yelled, "Mikhail!"

But he said it differently than a Russian would have, with a hard *ch* sound that made Anya's heart ache for Babulya and Mama and their hard *ch* at the back of their mouths.

Misha rushed the table and scooped the boy into his arms, spinning him in a circle as the boy squealed with delight.

She didn't watch Misha and the little boys for long.

The Talmud crooked a finger at her, drawing her toward it. She stepped slowly to the tall bookshelf. These books were bound differently from the ones Babulya had pulled out of her burning synagogue. Rich, brown leather covers were glossy in the candlelight. The scent of old paper and leather wrapped itself around her, kissing her skin. She reached out a hand and touched one finger to the spine of the closest book; a warm shiver passed through her finger and up her arm, and it settled in her heart. One day, she'd have a shelf in her own home with a complete Talmud, and she'd read them with Papa, and they'd discuss the wisdom within like they were rabbis.

A scream from behind made Anya jump and whip her hand away from the books. She turned to see Misha dangling one of the little boys upside down, swinging him in circles. The boy held on to his kippah with one hand and was screaming with delight. The other little boy jumped up and yelled, "Me next! Me next!" And Misha obliged, grabbing one in each arm and turning wide circles with them. They shrieked and giggled, and Anya couldn't help but smile.

A woman poked her head through the doorway from the kitchen. She was probably as old as Mama, wearing a festive green kerchief over light brown hair. "Mikhail!

You're going to get your cousins all riled up before dinner! Put them—" She stopped midsentence when she saw Anya.

Misha set the boys down and said, "Mama."

She stepped into the room, eyes wide. "And who is this?"

Misha approached her cautiously. "This is Anya. I invited her to—"

Misha's mother smacked his arm with the back of her hand. When she yelled, it was no longer in Russian. It was something else, but with Hebrew words sprinkled throughout, and Anya caught the tiniest pieces of the conversation.

Misha put his hands up while his mother continued to berate him and whack him with the back of her hand. "But Mama, I didn't have a way to tell you! I know I—yes, I should have—but she's not—Mama, she *is!*"

Misha's mother pushed him out of her way and charged at Anya, hands up to cradle her face and hold her there while she—just like Misha said she would—peppered Anya's entire face with kisses.

When she spoke, her words came out all at once, like if she stopped talking, she'd never be able to start again: "I'm so sorry! I wasn't expecting you. My idiot son didn't tell me someone so beautiful was coming to eat with us tonight. Of course you can have dinner with us. You're so skinny, it looks like you haven't eaten dinner in weeks! And look at your pretty face. Your mama and papa must have the hardest time keeping the boys away from you. *Mikhail!* Did you walk her here all by yourself? What am I going to do with you? What am I going to do with him? Absolutely the death of me. My only son, a deviant, walking good girls through the dark streets without a chaperone at all."

Anya looked toward Misha in time to see him scooting out of the room through the door his mother had come through. He was barely through it when his mother turned her head and barked, "Mikhail, you'd better be sneaking away so you can set another place for her!"

"Yep," Misha squeaked as he escaped through the door.

His mother yelled, "And come back here to take her coat!" She started fussing with the seam on the front of Anya's coat as another handful of faces peered out from the kitchen. Three women, all approximately Misha's mother's age, gasped with delight when they saw Anya standing by the door. Two younger girls that seemed closer to Anya's age followed, one looking just as enthused as the adults, and one looking sour.

They hurried over to Anya as Misha's mother gathered Anya's coat into her arms. One of the older women elbowed Misha's mother out of the way and grabbed Anya's face, kissing her cheeks between words: "Shabbat. Shalom. What. A. Lovely. Little. Girl."

The next one replaced the first. "Look at her, though! So skinny!"

The third one lingered back with the two younger girls, arms crossed, and said, "Dvorah, you let Mikhail bring home the goyim like stray cats now?"

"Don't be ridiculous!" Dvorah said. "She's not a goy. You can see it in her face." To demonstrate, Dvorah pinched Anya's chin in her fingers and turned her head side to side.

Anya nodded, even with her cheeks being squished by overly friendly hands, and her chin being swung left and right. "I'm Jewish, just like—"

But they were talking over her, exclaiming excitedly a hundred different things, some in the language Dvorah had yelled at Misha in. The third woman grabbed Anya in a hug and kissed her a few times before releasing her, and the two younger girls slid up beside Anya while the older women talked around them.

"Your name is Anya?" one of them asked.

"Yes."

The girl smiled. She looked a lot like Misha, and Anya guessed she was one of the sisters that he'd spoken of. "I'm Ilana." She grabbed Anya's hand and tugged her out of the room, toward where all the delicious smells were coming from. "We're decorating the sukkah! Come help!"

Anya let Ilana pull her through the kitchen, bustling with even more people, out a back door and into a walled courtyard. A fiery orange tree stood in one corner. Most of the courtyard was cobblestones, but a small, neat garden took up a significant part near the door. In the corner opposite the tree was the sukkah, or what Anya assumed was the sukkah.

It was tall and long, at least twice as long as the one Anya's family built every year. Its walls weren't made out of tree branches and grasses gathered from the forest, but from reed mats woven with colorful ribbons tied down at the bottom. The poles were all even—unlike Anya's crooked and twisting poles at home—and lashed at the corners with more colorful ribbon. The covering was the same brilliant orange as the tree in the corner, like what Anya had wanted to do with her sukkah.

The inside of the sukkah was occupied mostly by a wooden table and chairs. Garlands of dried flowers hung on the backs of the chairs, and a couple of them sported squash. The covering on the inside was hung with little trinkets and decorations. Anya spied a doll tied around its waist with a string, bundles of wheat cut short and tied with festive bows, and several apples with simple pictures carved into the skin. The decorations even extended to the walls, where grapevines had been cut and woven into wreaths, and then peppered with fall leaves and dried flowers.

Ilana stood by Anya's side, bouncing on her toes as Anya beheld the sukkah. Finally, she couldn't contain herself any longer and squealed, "Isn't it beautiful?"

Anya nodded. "It's much prettier than mine."

"Oh, don't say that!" Ilana chirped. "We're all beautiful in our own way!"

The other girl stepped beside Anya and said, "That's Ilana's way of calling someone ugly."

Ilana put her fists on her hips. "Nava, don't be such a sourpuss."

Nava ignored Ilana and turned her solemn face to Anya. "Are you going to marry my brother?"

Anya choked a little, and Ilana gasped from her other side. "Do you think?" she gushed.

"Of course," Nava said, eyeing Anya. "They came here

by themselves with no chaperone." She narrowed her eyes. "Were you two holding hands on your way here?"

"No!" Anya blurted. Her cheeks were hot. "No, we didn't. And no, we're not going to get married."

Ilana wiggled her fingers in the air. "Oh, but he'd make such a good husband!"

"I don't want to marry him," Anya said. "I'm thirteen. I'm not—"

"Perfect!" Ilana said, twirling in a circle. "Misha's sixteen! And he's so nice, and caring, and he knows the entire Torah by heart, and—"

"He does not," Nava said. "He's always too busy riding around with the princess to get any proper study in." She jabbed Anya in the side. "Do you know the princess?"

Anya whapped Nava's hand away. "Not really."

Nava's suspicious glare intensified. "What kind of name is Anya, anyway? That's short for Anna. That's a Christian name."

"It's short for Channah," Anya said, meeting Nava's glare with her own.

Nava narrowed her eyes even more and scrunched her mouth. After a few moments of silence, she said, "You're not good enough to marry my brother, anyway." And she spun around, marching away into the house.

Anya didn't know why Nava's words upset her. She didn't actually want to marry Misha, but Nava's assertion that Anya wasn't good enough to marry him sat unsteadily inside her, poking her with sharp edges. Why wasn't she good enough?

Ilana leaned her head against Anya's shoulder. "Ignore her. She's such a grump. Anyway, *I* think you're good enough to marry Misha! Oh, I want a sister-in-law!"

"I'm sure you'll get one," Anya said. "I'm not . . . uh. I couldn't marry him. I'm from very far away."

"Oh," Ilana said cheerfully. "We have extra space! You could move here and live with us! I mend all his clothes right now, but that could be your job when you marry him." She clasped her hands under her chin and sighed. "I'm going to embroider hearts into my husband's clothes when I mend them. Because I'll love him so much!"

"That sounds . . ." Anya managed to smile at Ilana. She didn't mind mending her own clothes, but it was time-consuming. And she already did Babulya and Dyedka's mending, too. Adding someone else's clothing onto that pile would take up her entire day. "I mean, you seem like you love mending. I bet you're very good at it."

Ilana beamed. "I am! Did Misha tell you?"

"No," Anya said. "I just . . . got a feeling. That's all."

Ilana sniffed. "That's the nicest thing anyone has ever said to me."

Anya had no idea what to say to that, but she was saved by Dvorah sweeping out into the courtyard and waving a hand at Anya and Ilana. "Girls!" She hurried to the sukkah. "Anya, Nava said you're a bat mitzvah. How wonderful! I simply must meet your mother, and the rabbi would love to speak to your father." She grabbed Anya's face and kissed each cheek. "It's time for dinner. You can decorate the sukkah more later!"

Ilana looped her arm through Anya's and whispered, "I can't wait for you to marry Misha!"

Anya kept her beleaguered sigh to herself, and the two girls followed Dvorah back inside.

◆ ✹ ◆

More people had gathered in the front room, and one of them was undeniably Misha's father. He and Misha stood side by side, and the only difference between them was that Misha would eventually be taller than his father. And his father had a long beard. Misha didn't have that.

The rabbi smiled at Dvorah when she entered the room, and then turned his smile to Anya. Without breaking eye contact, he walked to her with Misha in tow.

When he reached her, he put one hand on his chest and bowed a little to her.

"Shabbat shalom," he said. "Anya Miroslavovna, is it?"

Anya nodded, finding herself clinging to Ilana, wondering how he knew both names. But then she remembered: she had told Misha. He had told his father. Her chest was tight then, and she couldn't stop thinking of what Nava had asked: *Are you going to marry my brother?*

"I'm Rabbi Galanos," he said. His voice was soft but powerful. Like he could calm a rabid bear with just words. "Misha tells me you're not from Kiev."

She shook her head and opened her mouth to answer, but then Dvorah said, "We're going to miss the sunset, and I'm not going to light an extra candle for the rest of my life because of chitchat." Dvorah herded them all into the sitting area in front of the sideboard. On the fireplace mantel was a long, smallish box, and from within she removed a long, wooden wick. As she lit one end, Nava shouldered past Anya. Ilana quietly scolded her younger sister as she followed. They both stood to the side as Dvorah came back with her lit wick.

She held it out to Ilana. But before Ilana could take it, Dvorah pulled it back. She turned to the gathered group and found Anya with a smile. "Come here," she said, motioning with her free hand.

Anya shrank back, swallowing hard. Ilana waved her forward too, smiling broadly, and Nava glared. Misha and his father watched Anya with matching smiles, and she shuffled forward to join them. Her heart was pounding so hard, she could feel the pressure inside her ears.

Anya stepped beside Ilana, and Dvorah turned back to the candles. She handed the wick to Ilana, who took it and lit one of the candles, then handed it off to Nava, who lit another candle. Nava handed the wick back to her mother. Dvorah lit the remaining three candles, then dropped the still-burning wick to the sideboard's top—just like Mama always did—and lifted up her hands.

Ilana and Nava followed their mother's example, so Anya did too. Dvorah swept her hands through the air, like she was grabbing the glow and warmth of the candles and bringing it to wash over her. Just like Mama always did. Nava and Ilana moved to do the same thing, so Anya did too.

Then Dvorah sang the same melody Mama sang, the same melody Anya had been singing since she had become a bat mitzvah.

"*Baruch atah Adonai, Eloheinu, melech ha'olam,*" Dvorah sang, and Anya could hear Mama's voice in Dvorah's
as well, and Babulya's, and her own. She felt warm, like
sweeping the light toward herself had lit candles inside
her.

Dvorah continued on with the blessing, and Anya
heard Ilana beside her singing along, very softly: "*Asher
kidishanu b'mitzvotav vitzivanu l'hadlik ner shel Shabbat.*"

From behind her, the others murmured, "*Ameyn.*"

Dvorah let her hands drop and turned, beaming. She
reached her arms wide, like she was going to hug everyone at once. "Shabbat shalom!" she said.

"Shabbat shalom," everyone said back to her.

Anya expected everyone to go to the table then, like
her family always did, and say their quick prayer over
the wine and bread. But no one moved. Rabbi Galanos
walked carefully to where Dvorah stood, kissed her on
the cheek, and turned to everyone.

He began to pray.

But not in Hebrew.

Or was it? Anya could pick out words here and
there. No. It was whatever Dvorah had spoken earlier:
half Hebrew, half something else. And the melody was

different from anything she had ever heard before. Everyone around Anya sang along too, but she couldn't. She just stood there, silent.

"*Ameyn,*" everyone said, and Anya had to mumble it after them, when Rabbi Galanos had begun another prayer. Anya strained her ears, trying to figure out what he was saying, what part of the blessing he was on, but she couldn't catch up before everyone else said, "*Ameyn*" again. Anya managed to say it faster that time, but she still caught Nava glaring at her.

Anya squeezed the fingers of her right hand in her left fist. She could feel her face getting hot. When she heard everyone say "*Ameyn,*" she muttered along with them. These blessings were so much longer than what Babulya and Mama said at home. Or maybe they weren't. Maybe dying from embarrassment was just making everything slow down.

The singing stopped. The rabbi turned and picked up the chalice. He held it up in front of him. Good. Kiddush. Anya knew that blessing, at least.

But when he began, it was in words Anya didn't know. And it, too, was so much longer than the Kiddush she said at home. The warmth that the candles had kindled in her was fading.

The cup of wine made its way around the congregation. Misha's little cousins each touched their tongues to the wine and then passed it on with a grimace. Rabbi Galanos returned the chalice to its spot on the sideboard, then walked to where the two bowls sat. Misha stood at the second bowl beside him. They both picked up the little cups from on top of the folded cloth, then dipped the cups in the water. They murmured more prayers Anya didn't know while they poured water over one hand, then the other, and then, silent, they dried their hands on the cloth squares. They walked away, and two other people stepped up to wash their own hands.

With horror, Anya realized everyone was going to wash their hands. Everyone was going to say that blessing. She didn't know it.

Anya strained her ears to hear what everyone was saying, but they were all being so quiet, she could make out only a word here or there. Misha was all the way at the table on the other side of the room, standing silently. She wished he were closer so she could ask him what on earth was going on.

Someone put a hand on Anya's arm. When she turned, Dvorah smiled at her and said softly, "You look like you've just been sentenced to death."

Anya swallowed hard against a dry throat. "I . . . I've never done this before."

She expected Dvorah to look surprised or exclaim her disbelief, but she didn't. She just nodded a little bit and said, "I'll go with you. Stand by me."

Anya did, and the two of them waited until everyone else was done and gone to the dinner table. Dvorah and Anya stood side by side, and Dvorah talked Anya through the steps. Fill up the cup once and pour it over her entire right hand. Fill the cup again and pour it over her entire left hand. Set the cup down. Say the blessing.

"After you say the blessing, you don't speak until after Ha-Motzi," Dvorah whispered. In her soft singsong, Dvorah said, *"Baruch atah Adonai, Eloheinu, melech ha'olam, asher kidishanu b'mitzvotav vitzivanu al n'tilat yadayim."*

Anya repeated each word, comforted at the familiarity of most of it. She dried her hands on the cloth and followed Dvorah to the table. Rabbi Galanos pulled the cover off two perfect golden loaves of challah, picked up one, and held it in careful hands while he said Ha-Motzi in exactly the way Anya's family did. Halfway through, he set the one down and picked up the other, then tore off a piece of the challah and passed it to Misha. Misha passed it to the person next to him, and around they went until everyone had a piece. Together, they ate the bread, and Dvorah pulled Anya close in a sideways hug and whispered, "You did great." And Anya believed her.

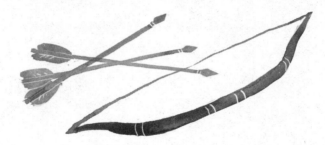

CHAPTER SIXTEEN

T HE ENTIRE CONGREGATION didn't stay for dinner. There were about a hundred handshakes and head nods and declarations of "Shabbat shalom" as the room emptied. Misha's little cousins tackled Misha's legs, and he waded to the door with them after their parents, who collected them and waved goodbye. Soon it was just Misha and his family, plus three of Dvorah's friends, and two men who were likely friends of Rabbi Galanos.

And Anya.

Dvorah sat on Anya's right, and Ilana slipped into the seat at her left. Misha sat by his father, across from Anya, and Nava sat on Misha's other side. Misha smiled at Anya, and Nava tried to stare a hole into her forehead.

To distract herself from Nava's glare, Anya studied the food. The two challah loaves were passed around and pieces torn off. A long, deep dish held fried fish that had been cooked in what appeared to be onions and . . . other things Anya had never seen before. Small, wrinkly, dark purple nuts? Nuts, perhaps, if nuts were squishy. They smelled sweet and tangy, and the dish was colored rich gold in places and olive green in others. Beside the fish was a smaller bowl with red jam inside it. The fragrance out of that bowl was heavenly — that was where the fruity and flowery scent was coming from. It smelled too good to eat. In the last bowl, dark green leaves mixed with cooked onions and the wrinkly purple things and some smallish white things. It smelled wonderful too, and as Anya struggled to keep herself from openly drooling over the food, she found herself realizing they might be celebrating something she had intruded upon. Besides Shabbat, of course.

She counted on her fingers under the table. If it was Friday, that meant Sukkot was in two days. Would she be done in Kiev and back to Zmeyreka in time for Sukkot with her own family? Was her sukkah even still intact? She assumed that without her supervision, Zvezda had eaten most of it by now.

From the table's other side, Rabbi Galanos smiled and said, "Anya. So. Where did you come here from?"

Her tongue stuck to the top of her mouth. Where had she come from? Not a shtetl, whatever that was. Not Kiev. Just Zmeyreka, a tiny village with a grand total of four Jews in it—three, with Papa gone—who all prayed differently than this community she sat with.

The raised eyebrows around her told her she'd been quiet for too long. She blurted, "Mologa."

Rabbi Galanos nodded slowly. "Where is that?"

"North." She answered faster that time. "By Ingria."

"I'm not familiar with that area," the rabbi said. "How long did it take you to travel?"

Anya didn't know. Again, she couldn't say a few minutes, so she guessed. "Ten days on the road."

Rabbi Galanos's eyes widened, and Dvorah's head snapped toward Anya.

"*Ten* days?" Dvorah gasped.

Maybe that was too long. But Anya was sold to the lie now. She nodded.

"All by yourself?" Dvorah said.

"No," Anya said. "Two of my friends came."

Dvorah leaned back in her chair, fanning herself. "Three little girls all alone? For ten days? In the winter? Where are they? Are they still in Kiev?"

While Dvorah spoke, something hit Anya's leg. She started and looked up. Misha was on the other side of the table, his eyes big like his father's. He shook his head side to side, just a tiny bit.

Had he kicked her? He must have. And what was he shaking his head *no* to? There was no way to ask him, so she answered Dvorah, "Uh, no. They got scared when the Nightingale—"

Ilana and Nava both gasped out loud, and Dvorah and the other three women all spoke at once in various volumes.

"The Nightingale?"

"You saw the Nightingale?"

"That maniac?"

"How did you get away from him?"

Anya ran through the actual events in her head, and the first one that didn't involve Ivan's magic was . . . "The tsarevna and Misha and some other archers chased him away."

Misha's face lost its color as Dvorah and the other women turned to him.

"What a brave son I have!"

"Our Mikhail is out saving pretty girls from monsters?"

"Is that what you do with the tsarevna all day?"

"Dvorah, are you comfortable with him risking his life like that?"

While Misha shrank back in his seat, Nava slid out of hers and disappeared under the table. She resurfaced a moment later between Anya and Ilana, and whispered to Anya, "What actually happened?"

Anya cleared her throat. "That's what happened."

Ilana hissed, "Nava, you're not supposed to crawl under the table like that!"

Nava ignored her sister. "What *else* happened?"

"Nothing," Anya said. "Do you not believe your brother could do that?"

"Of course he could," Ilana said.

Nava put up her hand, fingers splayed, in Ilana's face. "That's all he wants to do. He knows bowstrings and arrow shafts like he *should* know Torah." Her eyebrows lifted. "Mama and Papa let him stay with the tsarevna because the tsar specifically asked for him, and they don't want to make enemies in the castle."

Ilana knocked Nava's hand out of the way. "You're such a gossip, Nava." But she leaned closer to their conversation and whispered, "I was cleaning Misha's bed one time and I found some texts on military strategy hidden under his mattress. I didn't tell Mama or Papa about them."

Anya peeked at Misha, who was still being interrogated about his heroics against the Nightingale. His father had said nothing and just sat with his lips pursed. The other men at the table had also said nothing. She regretted saying anything about the Nightingale.

Finally, Rabbi Galanos said, "Well, Mikhail, we're very glad you were there for Anya and her friends when they needed help." Dvorah and the other women sat back, trading glances back and forth.

Softly, Misha said, "Thank you, Papa."

With a smile, Rabbi Galanos turned to Anya. "Tell us about your family, Anya. What does your father do?"

This conversation was taking a turn for the worse. Anya wanted to slide under the table like Nava had, but not resurface. "Um . . . he's a farmer."

"A farmer," Rabbi Galanos said. "Interesting. What does he farm?"

"Goats," Anya said. "I guess that's not farming, really. Mama is the farmer. She grows onions."

Rabbi Galanos nodded. "Goats and onions. Do you have any brothers or sisters?"

"No," Anya said, and everyone turned their heads at her.

Everyone except the rabbi. He said, "Do your parents know where you are?"

Anya took in a slow breath. Did she admit she had basically run away? Or did she lie to the rabbi? Either one was equally distasteful, because she didn't want to lie to the first and only rabbi she'd ever met, but she also didn't want anyone to send her home. She thought about pretending to be ill and escaping back to the castle, but Dvorah had put her coat somewhere and she didn't know where. Also, Misha knew where she was staying. He'd be able to find her.

And so Anya found herself fibbing. "Mama knows. She didn't like me coming"—that would be true—"but we didn't really have a choice."

The rabbi lifted an eyebrow. "Didn't have a choice?"

Anya shook her head. "My papa . . . got conscripted. Our village's old magistrate lied to the conscription officers. We just found out about it, and I came here to ask the tsar to send him back from Rûm."

Several people around the table gasped. Rabbi Gala-nos didn't, but he looked surprised anyway.

"I'm sorry that happened," he said. "But *you* shouldn't be asking the tsar. One of the men should be. What does your rabbi think about this?"

Oh no. Anya tensed as she said, "We don't have a rabbi."

The surprised stares weren't accompanied by gasps that time. Misha's cheeks and throat were bright red.

Rabbi Galanos recovered and said, "No rabbi for the moment?"

"No rabbi ever," Anya said.

The rabbi was contemplatively quiet, and this gave Nava the opportunity to blurt, "Why would you live somewhere with *no rabbi?*"

"Nava!" Dvorah scolded.

"Does that mean you don't have a synagogue?" Nava asked, and then she said, "Have you ever seen a Torah?"

Anya winced. "Of course I've—"

"When?" Nava demanded, and then said, "I knew you weren't good enough to marry my brother!"

Misha blanched, and his mouth dropped open.

Ilana smacked Nava on the back of the head. "You're

so rude! She is *so* good enough! It doesn't matter if she's never seen a Torah!"

"I *have* seen a Torah!" Anya was on her feet. She didn't even remember standing. "I've held it! I've read the whole thing! Babulya brought ours from Sarkel, from their synagogue, when it was burning!" She fumed, then realized everyone at the table was staring at her again with matching expressions of shock and embarrassment.

She decided she'd rather freeze walking back to the castle, and she scrambled out of her seat. "Thank you for dinner," she mumbled, even though she hadn't eaten anything, and escaped out the door into the cold night.

CHAPTER SEVENTEEN

ANYA MADE IT one street with her arms curled into her chest before she desperately regretted fleeing without her coat. The nights here were so cold. A frigid wind whipped up and down the streets like it was racing itself somewhere. But she wasn't about to go back, so she just hiked up her dress and ran up the street, trying to remember which turns Misha had taken to bring them there. It would be easy to find her way back to the castle, she reasoned, because she could see it up on the hill, and she just had to keep heading that way. But the streets twisted and seemed to always scoop her back down the hill, away from the castle, and she felt like she was about to just lie down and turn into an ice maiden when she heard someone call, "Anya!"

Misha. She turned toward his voice. He trotted up the street, holding her coat. When he got to her, he wrapped the coat around her shoulders and, after a slight hesitation, pulled her to him and rubbed his hands up and down her arms.

She stood there, hunched, shivering, expecting him to scold her for running around in the cold like an idiot. So she was surprised when he said, "I'd rather freeze to death than get judged by my family too."

Anya let out a laugh that ended with an audible chattering of teeth, and Misha said, "I'm sorry. Let's get you back to the castle."

She nodded, and they walked side by side up the hill. He pulled off his kippah before they crested the hill and stuck it in his pocket again.

"So Kiev is safe," Anya said, "but you hide your kippah anyway."

He shrugged. "My family moved here from Spain a long time ago. The king there made Jews convert to Christianity or he'd kill them. He took the children away from their parents so Christians could raise them. It was bad. So my family left and wound up here."

Anya listened with a profound ache of understanding in her heart. "My saba died in Sarkel. If Babulya hadn't run away, she would have died too."

Misha nodded. "My father says we have to be proud of what we are. Even though he mounts the *mezuzah* on the inside of the door instead of on the outside, where it should be. And I am. But I . . ." He sighed. "I don't want to be a rabbi. Vasya said she wants me to stay in her guard and one day be the captain of it. She wants me to lead the army's archers."

"That's incredible," Anya said.

Misha stared into the distance. "Yeah. It is. It's my dream."

"Not being a rabbi?" Anya asked.

He shook his head. "If my father knew, he'd never let me go back to the castle." Misha fiddled with his coat seam. "And if the other archers knew I'm Jewish, I don't know if they'd accept me. So I wear my kippah for my father, and take it off in the castle." He laughed, the sound humorless. "I think that makes me a bad person."

Anya shook her head. "I think the magistrate who lied about my father being Slavist is a bad person," Anya said. "He would rather Papa be dead than Jewish."

"That's pretty bad." Misha walked in silence for a few

feet, then said, "So . . . you and your friends didn't come here for the Nightingale?"

Anya chewed on her lip. Ivan had told Vasilisa they'd come for the Nightingale, but Anya had just told Misha's entire family something different. "We, uh . . . I mean, Ivan came for the Nightingale. And I tagged along because of Papa. And . . ."

Misha patted her arm. "I'm not going to tell her," he said. "If my father was caught up in a war, I'd do whatever I could to bring him back."

Anya's lip trembled as she said, "Thank you."

Misha smiled, cleared his throat, and said, "My father is the first rabbi you've ever met?"

Anya grimaced. "I wish I hadn't told everyone that." She thought of Nava's outburst. How could Anya have seen a Torah without a rabbi? Without a synagogue?

A question rose in her mind, digging claws into her. If she had grown up without a rabbi and synagogue, did that make her less Jewish than they were?

She didn't want to think about it, so she changed the subject before Misha could press on. "So, since I don't actually know anything about the Nightingale, could you tell me about him?"

Misha snorted, sending puffs of white air into the

cold night. "I really hope your friend can get rid of him. I could have shot the Nightingale a couple of times. I might have killed him. But Vasya stopped me. Alive, she said. Because that's what her father wants." He shook his head. "He's terrorizing us. I don't understand why we can't just kill him."

"Is he human?" Anya asked. "Or is he . . . I've just never seen a human being with so much magic before."

"He's not human," Misha said. "Do you know much about history? About the war with the Drevlians?"

Anya had no idea what the Drevlians were, so she shook her head.

Misha took a deep breath. His cheeks were bright from the cold, and his eyes sparkled. Either he really loved history, or he really loved this war in particular. "When my grandfather was a young man, the Grand Prince of Kiev was assassinated by a tribe to the west called the Drevlians. They aren't men. Not really. They look like us, like people, but then you get close and they look more like trees. They live in the trees, tend them, and change colors with them. My grandfather called them the tree people."

Anya straightened. The tree people? Hadn't Dyedka lost his legs and his eye to the tree people? Was it the same ones?

"The Grand Princess was widowed and alone with her very young son, the future tsar," Misha continued. "She knew the Drevlians would kill him, so she acted first. She sent troops to the Drevlian capital and burned it to the ground, leaving no one alive."

Anya grimaced. "That doesn't really sound like a war."

"They fought back," Misha clarified. "With all their magic. It wasn't an easy victory."

"I guess," Anya said. "So is that what the Nightingale is? One of the Drevlians?"

Misha shrugged. "I don't think so. They all died. The Grand Princess made sure of that. But he's one of the tree people. He changes colors with the seasons. They're supposed to hibernate in the winter, though, and he doesn't. Vasya and I think he's from another tribe, related to the Drevlians. There are a few. Some from the north, the Alvolk. And some even farther north, from the lands of the Varangians. Fierce, all of them. And in the forests they can vanish"—he snapped his fingers—"like that."

"Why is he here?" Anya asked.

"To avenge the Drevlians, maybe," Misha said. "To collect information for a future attack. We don't know. It doesn't matter. He's dangerous."

"Has he killed anyone?" Anya asked.

"No." Misha shrugged. "But he will."

His words made her skin prickle. Last year, before she really knew Håkon, when everyone was hunting him, that argument was thrown at her by men much older and wiser than she. *The dragon hasn't attacked anyone here, right?* she had asked Ivan's papa. *Not yet,* he had said. Every dragon in Kievan Rus' had died because one had hurt the tsarina. Every Drevlian had died because some had assassinated the Grand Prince.

The Nightingale hadn't killed anyone, even though he could have. Easily. She had seen the power he held. Why hadn't he used it for real damage? What did he really want?

+ ✦ +

The guards nodded to Misha and stood aside for him, and soon they were back in the hallway Anya recognized. They walked past Håkon and Ivan's door, and she wondered how her friends were doing.

Misha opened her door for her, stepped back, and said, "Gospozha."

Anya rolled her eyes and laughed as she passed by him. Her skin tingled, but in a good way? Was that a thing? "Thank you for inviting me to dinner."

"I'm sorry my family is so nosy," he said, a blush rising

in his cheeks. "And that, um, apparently my sisters were trying to be matchmakers."

Anya shrugged, embarrassment sizzling in her chest. "That was Ilana, mostly. Nava told me how unworthy I am."

"Nava is . . ." Misha pursed his lips. "She has opinions."

Anya nodded. "You should tell Ilana you think she does a good job mending your clothes."

Misha lifted one eyebrow. "I should?"

"It would mean a lot to her."

He laughed. "Okay, I'll do that." He smiled. "Good night."

Anya smiled back. "Good night."

Misha bowed a little and left. Anya waited until he was almost gone, and then she leaned out of her door to watch him go. His long coat danced as his calves hit it, and his dark hair shone in the torchlight. She liked him better with his kippah on. He fiddled with his gloves, tightening them on his fingers as he rounded the corner. She imagined him as she had met him, mounted and firing flaming arrows with such precision. So good that the warlike tsarevna had asked for him personally. Jewish. A future rabbi, or captain of the guard.

She realized he was the first Jewish boy she had ever met.

Anya leaned back to make sure he didn't look and see her blushing.

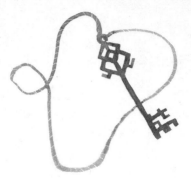

CHAPTER EIGHTEEN

ANYA CHANGED out of the nice dress she had worn to dinner and Misha's home. Her old dress was still on the bed where she had left it, so she pulled it on. It was worn and shoddy in comparison to the resplendence of the castle, but it was comfortable, and it was *her*. She pulled the necklace that Lena had given her out from under the dress fabric, appreciating the smooth weight of the key. She wondered if the key would open a door in the castle. Maybe that's why Lena had brought them here. But was it to rescue Papa? Why would he be locked up in Kiev? When he answered his letters, he never talked about being in Kiev. He talked about the horses, and how he was still not very good at sword fighting, and about how the camp food was fine but he really missed Anya's challah.

Maybe Papa wasn't in Kiev at all.

But then why had Lena sent them there? And if the key wasn't to find Papa, what was it to find? She studied the key for a few more seconds, stuck it back under her dress, and walked out of the room.

She knocked on Ivan and Håkon's door, and Håkon answered. He was much steadier than he had been when she had . . . yelled at him. A couple of hours ago.

He didn't look mad, exactly. But he didn't look happy. He looked the way Mama did just before she said, *I'm not angry, Anya. I'm just disappointed.*

"Yes?" he finally said.

"Can I come in?" Anya asked.

He narrowed his eyes. "How was dinner with *Misha?*"

Now he looked mad. Anya clenched her jaw and said, "Better than dinner with you." And she shoved past him into the room.

Ivan was in his nightclothes, lying upside down on the bed with his feet in the air. He cranked his neck to look at Anya when she stomped in.

"Anya!" He rolled over and slid off the bed. "How was—"

"I'd rather talk about how we're going to do what we need to do with the Nightingale," Anya said.

Ivan flicked his eyes to Håkon, who shut the door and crossed his arms. Then Ivan looked back to Anya, smiled cautiously, and said, "I think we figured out how he took my magic."

That was good news, anyway. "How?"

"Well." Ivan laced his knuckles together. "I—we, Håkon and I—were trying to figure out how Håkon can get his magic back. And we . . . didn't. But we still figured some things out!"

He jumped off the bed and ran to the stand with the bowl of water on it. He pulled a ball of water out, floating it in the air, and Anya scooted away. She was about to get soaking wet. She could feel it.

Ivan walked the water nearer to Håkon and said, "Håkon described to me how it's possible to take magic away from someone."

Håkon nodded. "I used to take metal threads away from my da sometimes, as a joke."

"See," Ivan said, "when I threw the water at the

Nightingale, I let go of the threads. And he picked them up to stop the water from hitting him."

"What if you didn't let them go?" Anya asked. "What if you held on to them?"

Ivan snapped his fingers. "Right! If I don't let go of the strings, then he won't be able to control the water!"

Anya put her hands on her hips. "What if he tries to take the threads that you're holding? Can he take them even if you don't let go?"

Ivan looked unsure. He said slowly, "Nooooooo?"

"Yes, he can," Håkon said. "I'm not as strong with metal magic as Da is. So he could always pull the threads back from me eventually. I had to surprise him."

The three of them exchanged worried looks. The Nightingale seemed pretty strong. Could Ivan overpower him if he had to?

Anya tapped her fingers against one another. "Håkon, you have no magic at all?"

He shook his head. "Ivan says he sees threads in the air, and I don't see anything."

Anya knew that feeling. "If only someone could practice stealing threads from you, Ivan. So if the Nightingale tried to steal yours, you'd know how to stop it."

Håkon said, "It's not about knowing anything. It's about being strong enough."

"You get stronger with practice," Anya said, annoyed. "I know you've never had to practice any magic in your whole life, but that's just how it is when you're a human."

Håkon's face got red. "I'm *not* a human."

"You're human enough for now," Anya argued, spinning toward him. "So act like it."

"Should I act more like Misha, then?" Håkon spat. "Your precious soldier boy?"

Anya stuck a rigid finger at him. "He's not my precious anything. But sure, why don't you act more like him? He's responsible, and he's noble, and he's good because he tries and he . . ." In her anger, her mind was going blank. She struggled to find another thing Misha did. "He reads!" she finally blurted.

"I can read!" Håkon yelled.

Ivan scooted between them, hands up, water still hanging in the air over him. "We can all read."

"That's not what this is about!" Anya leaned around Ivan so she could speak directly at the annoying dragon-turned-boy glaring at her from the fool's other side. "We've got to figure out how to stop the Nightingale so we can get my papa back, and you're just focused on Misha for some stupid reason. He didn't even do anything to you!"

"He would!"

"He wouldn't!"

"Hey," Ivan said, putting his hands up higher. "You're being really loud."

Anya stomped past them both. "I'm going to bed. Get over whatever problem you have with Misha and figure out how to keep the Nightingale from stealing Ivan's magic. Or else . . ." Or else they wouldn't be able to survive a fight against him. Or else they wouldn't be able to bring him to Vasilisa. Or else Papa would stay in Rûm even longer. Or else Papa might never come home.

She couldn't bring herself to say any of those, because she didn't trust herself not to burst into tears. So she turned away and wrenched the door open, leaving it ajar as she hurried down the hall to her room.

They couldn't afford to fail.

CHAPTER NINETEEN

ANYA SLEPT FITFULLY, even though the bed was the most comfortable thing she'd ever touched in her life. She dreamed that Håkon was a dragon again, and that he and Ivan were with the Nightingale in his tree. Vasilisa and Misha were at the base of the tree, and they set it on fire. As flames licked up the sides, Anya stood by, unable to help.

Then, in the dream, someone grabbed her shoulders and spun her around. Sigurd. With blood coming from his eyes and ears and nose, just like when he had died. He grinned, his teeth pink and bloody, and then laughed as Anya's friends screamed for help from the fiery tree behind her.

She woke up damp with sweat. Her heart pounded in her fingertips. She slid out of the bed and splashed water on her face from the bowl. Her hands shook as she did.

"Stupid dream," she muttered, as if that would banish the fear that still sparked up every part of her. She hated the helplessness she had felt in the dream, and the way it carried into waking life. If she were in Zmeyreka, she would have helped Mama make potions, or ridden Alsvindr back and forth on the roads. It made her feel better to *do* something.

What could she do here, though? There was no one to make potions with here, and no Alsvindr to ride. She didn't even know where the archers had put her bow and Ivan's staff. So she just stared at her rippling reflection in the bowl's surface. Babulya said dreams were usually nonsense, but some were God's way of helping someone with a problem. In Anya's dream, Ivan and Håkon had been with the Nightingale. Vasilisa and Misha had been hurting them. Since the Nightingale was with her friends, did that mean he was, or could be, her friend too? And why wasn't Anya with them in the tree?

Her reflection in the water offered no answers.

It was dark outside, but she wasn't going to be able to

go back to sleep. She got dressed and realized she hadn't eaten anything the entire time she'd been in Kiev.

Anya left her room, intending to find the kitchens and get something to eat. On her way, she passed a lot of doors leading off into rooms or other halls. The key felt heavy around her neck. She pulled the chain over her head, wrapping it around her wrist, and went to the closest door.

The key and the door's keyhole didn't match, but she tried to unlock it anyway. She slid the key in as quietly as she could and turned it.

Nothing. The key didn't go to this door.

Anya tried every door in the hall. None of them worked.

She snorted and returned the key to her neck. Of course it wouldn't open these doors. What would even be inside them? More rooms for royal guests? Some tapestries? Uncomfortable dresses?

She made her way toward the banquet hall. The kitchen would probably be somewhere near there. She passed by more doors, fingers itching. Maybe one of these was the door Lena had wanted her to open . . .

Anya tried to unlock every door on her way to the banquet hall. None of them opened.

She stopped trying to unlock doors when she smelled cooking. She followed the scent to the kitchen, which was bustling. No one glanced at her as she entered. She snuck some bread and a hunk of cheese, and she hurried off before she got caught. Her hurry turned into an amble, and she eventually found herself at an outer door. As she peered out into the dark morning and chewed on her bread, she thought about her dream.

The Nightingale had been in the tree with Ivan and Håkon. He was grouped with them: friends. Vasilisa and Misha weren't. The Nightingale had screamed for help, too.

Was Håkon right? Would Misha try to kill him if he found out Håkon was a dragon? And why had Anya been standing apart from them all? Had she been standing with Sigurd, or did he appear to her because she was all alone?

She didn't know the answer to any of those questions. But she did know fighting the Nightingale wasn't the answer. If he was a friend—or a potential friend, anyway—the answer was in helping him. But how was she supposed to make friends with an aggressive forest elf who could make trees attack people?

The dragon hasn't attacked anyone here, right?

Not yet.

The Nightingale had attacked people, but he hadn't killed anyone. Misha had said so. Even though he easily could have killed loads of people. She thought back on their flight from him on the road. How he aimed around them and over their heads. He knocked them down, sure, but he could have done so much worse. He had jumped through the air like he was taking invisible stairs upward. He could have done that straight over the city walls. He could have used his sound magic to blow up buildings or kill people. He could have made trees walk the streets like invading giants.

But he didn't.

She crammed the last piece of bread in her mouth with resolve. She'd make friends with him the same way she had with Ivan and Håkon. She'd go to his tree. She'd say hello. She'd be nice to him. She didn't have any magic or weapons. She was harmless. Hopefully he would realize that, and not squish her with a tree.

The morning was purplish, dark, and still, with the sharp, biting cold that had settled during the night. Anya pulled her coat tightly around herself and marched toward the gate into the city. She passed by the stable and paused, glancing at the grooms and servants going in and out. A trio of goats stood idly by the open doorway, chewing on hay with their eyes half-closed.

Anya changed trajectory toward the barn. A little detour wouldn't hurt. She missed Zvezda. She missed Alsvindr.

The goats barely acknowledged her when she approached them, but when she scratched one behind her ears, the other two crowded up to Anya. She smiled and scratched each of them in turn, wishing she had more hands.

Inside, the grooms were brushing down beautiful, glossy horses, or cleaning their polished hooves, or braiding their long tails. A horse near Anya nickered and stretched its nose out to her. She stretched a hand toward him and patted the end of his nose with a small smile.

Someone holding a bucket of apples rounded the corner and came toward Anya. She snapped her hand away. She felt like she shouldn't be touching the tsar's horses, or even be around them. Suddenly, she was struck with the need to escape, but as she turned to leave, a familiar voice said, "Well, Shabbat shalom to you."

Misha stopped by the horse's front leg, the apple bucket dangling from his fingers. He smiled brightly at her, like it wasn't predawn.

"I, um . . ." Anya said, then admitted sheepishly, "I just wanted to pet the goats and horses."

Misha held an apple out in a flattened hand, and the horse munched it up. It reminded Anya of Alsvindr stealing apples, and she felt a pang. The goats around Anya noticed Misha was the one with the food, and they wandered away from her to the apple bucket.

"Well," Misha said, "pet away. What are you doing out here so early?"

She didn't want to tell him she was on her way to befriend the Nightingale. He wouldn't approve. He might want to stop her or, even worse, come with her. "I think the question is, what are *you* doing up here on Shabbat?"

"Oh, you know," Misha said. One of the goats stuck its face into the apple bucket and snatched up an apple. Misha pushed the goat away idly and lifted up the bucket out of their reach. "I have some things to get in order. I'll be in shul all day once I'm done up here; don't you worry about that."

Anya smiled. "I'm not worried." The horse nudged her with his apple-juicy nose, and she laughed and patted him. "He reminds me of my horse back home."

Misha perked. "The Varangian horse, right? With the strange name."

"Alsvindr," Anya said.

"Right," Misha said. "What's a Varangian horse like?"

One of the goats stretched up toward the bucket, then yelled, *"Myah!"*

"Oh, go away!" Misha pushed the goat's nose, then swatted one on the rump. The three of them yelled their displeasure at him and did not go away.

Anya shrugged. "I don't know. He's really big. Bigger than this horse. He gets really shaggy in the winter. He's the color of a thundercloud."

"So you use him for . . . what? For pulling a plow or something?" Misha asked pleasantly as he pushed away a goat nibbling on his coat hem.

Anya's smile melted off her face. "Um . . ." She cleared her throat, trying to mask her upset. That feeling of helplessness welled again. She was just some farmer to Misha. Even though she had showed up with a bow and some arrows, and owned a Varangian warhorse. "Yeah. For a plow."

"Hey!" Misha said. "Do you want to come to shul? My mother is going to make Nava apologize to you for being such a brat last night."

Anya wanted to go but also didn't. After last night, she wasn't sure if she was ready for her very first time in a synagogue. Before she could say anything, Misha lost his patience with the goats swarming him.

"That's it!" he yelled. "Go! Get!" He grabbed three apples out of the bucket and heaved them out into the yard. The goats took off, their little hooves thumping on the cold, packed earth, bleating as they ran after the apples.

Misha looked back at Anya, smoothing his coat down with sharp jerks. "Goats. What a pain."

"That's goats," Anya said, trying to sound pleasant.

Misha brushed off his trousers impatiently, and then said, "So, shul? It starts at nine o'clock. I'll come get you from your room at eight thirty?"

Anya heard herself say, "That sounds wonderful." She winced on the inside. There was no way she'd be back from the Nightingale's tree by then. But she couldn't tell Misha that. "I'll see you then!"

She ran out of the barn, away from the castle, through the frosty predawn streets of Kiev. As she descended the city's hill, something Håkon had pointed out bounced around in her head: the tsar had wanted the dragons alive, just like how he wanted the Nightingale alive. What difference would it make if the Nightingale was brought alive or killed? It would still be the same result: he wouldn't be terrorizing travelers anymore.

Unless the point of his capture wasn't to stop his attacks.

But what would the point be, then?

She didn't have an answer to that.

Anya reached the gates Vasilisa had brought her, Ivan, and Håkon through. Two guards flanked the gate, and they stepped forward as she approached.

"A little early to be going out, isn't it?" one asked.

Anya pulled her coat tighter. "It's almost morning. I need to get an early start."

The other one said, "An early start getting killed? This is the Nightingale's road now. It's not safe out there, little girl."

"I won't get killed," Anya said. "He doesn't kill people."

The guards both laughed.

"Not yet, but he will," the first guard said. "Now, be a good girl and go back home."

He reached out to turn her back toward the city, but she ducked away from him. She sprinted toward the gate, and the guards yelled for her to stop. She didn't. Anya ran across the bridge, past the pile of dead trees, and into the Nightingale's wood.

CHAPTER TWENTY

ANYA HID until she was sure the guards weren't chasing her, and then she hurried toward the Nightingale's tree. It was easily visible, towering over the rest of the forest. She didn't try to find him; she was certain he'd know that she was there, and he would find *her*.

The huge tree loomed above her. She shuffled up to its base, again marveling at its construction. Smaller trees grew overlapping against one another, creating an impenetrable wall that stretched around so far that her house and barn could have fit inside. It was tall, double the height of the forest around it, its branches swaying in a breeze that hit only the very tallest parts. The breeze swept off its golden and orange leaves, sprinkling them down on Anya like confetti.

Anya put her flat palm against the bark, hoping maybe something magical would happen. But nothing did. It was just a tree.

Movement off to her right side caught her eye. She jerked her hand away and turned. The Nightingale stood in the shadow of the leaves, barely visible. She wondered if he had been there the whole time.

Anya held her hands up, showing the Nightingale she had no weapons. Her heart pounded. Fear sat heavy in her chest. If he wanted to hurt her, he could, and she wouldn't be able to fight back.

He stepped forward, out of the shadows, so she could see him in full. Did he really look more like an elf now, or was it because now she knew he was one? He was wearing a long coat, rather than just the meager shirt and pants he had worn when he'd attacked them yesterday. Gold skin, but so pale. Like pine wood. Hair like dirty rocks, or was it like pine bark? If he got closer, would he have pine-green eyes?

"I just want to talk," Anya said.

His painted black eyes never moved from her face. He said nothing.

"Please," Anya said.

He blinked out of sight.

"Oh, come on!" Anya yelled. She hesitated, then ran to the spot he had been a second ago, hoping it would be apparent where he went. But there was nothing.

The wind rustled the branches above Anya's head. They knocked together, and a bird sang nearby. She wished desperately for Håkon or Ivan, or both, to be there with her.

"You haven't killed anyone," Anya said once she found her voice. "You could, but you don't. Why?"

The last word—*Why?*—hung in the air, echoing. She stepped back as the echo of her own voice spun around her, coming from all sides. She shut her eyes, and the echo stopped.

When she opened her eyes, she startled. The Nightingale was standing in front of her, an arm's length away. His eyes were a deep, dark green. Behind the black paint and the dirt, he was so young. Did the tsar know he was hunting someone barely old enough to grow hair on his face?

He brought his hands up, and Anya tensed. When he moved his fingers, though, he wasn't pulling threads. He was doing something else. He pointed to himself. He clawed his hands, palms up, in front of his chest. He drew his thumb under his chin.

Then he did those three movements again, and again, and a realization peppered Anya like falling tree leaves. He was *speaking* to her.

He saw her realize it and he nodded. Faster, he did the same things with his hands, then added more onto the end. Anya got lost in the whirl of intricate gesturing. Is this how elves communicated? By using their hands? Could he not speak?

"I don't know what you're saying," Anya said. "I want to help you, though. Why are you here? How can I help you?"

He let his hands drop as she spoke, his eyes watching her mouth. The next time he moved, he was certainly pulling a thread. Her own word—*help*—came back at her. He was speaking to her, with her own voice. Then he tensed, looking past her with wide eyes. He pointed two fingers at his eyes, and then flipped them around so they pointed to the road.

Anya spun to see what he saw, but no one was there. When she turned back around, he was gone.

"Wait!" she whispered. "Nightingale! Don't leave me!"

Nothing.

She heard the sound then: horse hooves on the road, coming to a stop. Footsteps in the forest, coming toward her. She hurried back, intending to hide behind the tree. Was it Vasilisa and Misha? Or maybe Ilya? Alyosha? Some other guard? If they found her, how much trouble would she be in?

Anya leaned against the tree, and it shifted against her back. Before she could jump away from it, a hole opened up, and a hand reached through.

The Nightingale leaned out of the hole and grabbed her wrist. He put a finger over his lips, shushing her, as he pulled her inside the tree's dark interior.

CHAPTER TWENTY-ONE

THE HOLE that had opened up for Anya snapped shut with a whisper, and she was cast into darkness. She stood still inside the tree for a few heartbeats, the Nightingale holding on to her wrist. Without realizing it, she clutched his arm and clung to him, an anchor in the dark.

The Nightingale tried stepping away from her, but she stepped with him. He slipped a finger between her hand and his arm and tried to pry her off. When she just squeezed harder, he sighed. A moment later, the darkness around her began to lift, and she could see his outline next to her. He was drawing his fingers along threads in the air, rolling them between his fingertips. The light came from stones along the floor, which glowed more brightly the more he rolled his fingers. The glowing stones were bright enough for her to see the entire inside of the tree. It was cluttered with a random assortment of boxes and barrels and bags: things he had taken from travelers, probably. Around the perimeter, the branches of all the trees grew into a narrow, uneven staircase. Anya followed the staircase up with her eyes and noticed a wooden flap covering an opening above her.

"Anya!"

The Nightingale tensed, half fading out of sight. Someone was calling her name from outside the tree.

In the next breath, the Nightingale ran up the staircase. She followed, afraid the lights would go out once he was gone. Anya ran as fast as she felt safe, but he was way ahead of her. At the top was a wide space sheltered by the canopy leaves of all the trees that grew together for the big tree. It was bitterly cold.

The Nightingale hurried to the edge of the tree; he less walked than seemed blown by the wind. Anya followed as he stepped out onto the tree's long, bare branches, fading from view before her eyes.

Voices from down below wound up to her ears. She recognized them.

"Ivan?" she whispered, darting to the edge of the platform. The ground was a long, long way down, and at the bottom, Ivan stood with Håkon and two other, bigger figures.

Ilya Muromets and Alyosha Popovich. Both wore armor now instead of the finery at last night's banquet.

Ivan paced around the tree, rubbing his chin. Håkon stood by Alyosha, his shoulder turned away slightly, guarding himself from the *bogatyr*. Ilya stood still, arms crossed, watching Ivan.

"Anya!" Ivan yelled again.

"What makes you think she's even out here?" Alyosha asked, picking at the sleeve of his undershirt.

Ivan crouched and poked the ground with a finger. "Little, tiny Anya-size footprints."

Anya looked down at her boots. She didn't have tiny feet! She squinted at them. Okay . . . maybe she did.

"Those could be anyone's," Alyosha said, bored. "I'm going back to the castle. The princess can't avoid me forever."

"Alyosha," Ilya said in a warning voice, "give it a day or two."

"I agree," Ivan said from where he followed Anya's footprints. "It's very apparent that she hates your guts."

Alyosha shouted, "Oh, I didn't know fools were experts on love!"

"We are, absolutely," Ivan said. "I thought *bogatyri* were supposed to be experts on bird monsters, and that's why you came."

Alyosha said, "The Nightingale isn't a bird."

"Nightingales are birds," Ivan said.

"Yes, but our Nightingale isn't," Ilya said. "He's called that because of his whistles."

Ivan stopped in front of the tree, right where the Nightingale had pulled Anya in. He straightened and looked up, then put his hand on the tree's side. He dropped his hand, turning back to the *bogatyri*, and pulled something out from the inside of his coat.

Anya squinted. Was that—? Yes. The notebook Lena had given him. He scribbled in it as he walked slowly to the *bogatyri*.

"You know," Ivan said, "I think Alyosha is right. I don't think she's out here. Those footprints aren't even people-prints. They're obviously from a *vila*."

Ilya said, "A *vila*?"

"A beautiful forest spirit who will suck the life out of you!" Ivan said cheerfully.

"I know what a *vila* is," Ilya said. "I didn't realize they left footprints."

"Of course they do!" Ivan said. He showed Ilya what he had been writing.

Ilya leaned closer and read it, then nodded. He spoke slowly. "Yes. You're right. A *vila*."

"Yep." Ivan showed the note to Alyosha, who likewise nodded. "I think you two are safe to go back to the castle."

"What about you?" Ilya asked. "Are you sure it's wise to stay here on your own?"

"Of course it isn't wise!" Ivan said. "But it is my method. I need to do some reconnaissance!" He pointed to Håkon, who had still said nothing, hunched like he expected the *bogatyri* to attack him at any moment. "My assistant and I will be perfectly safe. Don't you worry one single bit."

Ilya and Alyosha exchanged skeptical glances.

The Nightingale appeared in front of Anya then, instantly. One second he wasn't there, and the next he was. She startled back.

He looked angry. Well, she supposed, he always looked a little bit angry, like he hadn't smiled in so long that he had forgotten how to do it. He pointed to where Ivan and Håkon stood, eyebrows furrowed quizzically.

"Those are my friends," Anya said, answering what she assumed his question was: *Who are they?*

The *bogatyri* walked away, heads together, speaking to each other softly. As soon as they left, Ivan ran to the tree and looked up. Anya wanted to wave at him, but the Nightingale pulled her away from the edge.

"Hey!" she protested. "I told you, they're my friends. They're nice."

Solemnly, he shook his head.

"Yes," Anya argued. "Nice. Good."

He didn't shake his head again, but clearly he didn't believe her that they were nice. She couldn't blame him, really. The last time he had seen Ivan, the fool had attacked him.

She looked down. "They're good. I prom—"

The Nightingale grabbed her chin in two fingers and pointed her face to him.

"Hey!" Anya protested.

With two fingers, he pointed to his eyes. Then he turned his fingers to her mouth. Back and forth a few times, from his eyes to her mouth, until it clicked.

He wanted to watch her speak.

"They're good," she repeated. "I promise."

The Nightingale's hand zipped up, and he caught the thread of her last word.

Promise promise promise. His face was a question. *Promise?*

She nodded. "Yes."

He still looked unsure, but he nodded once before winking out of sight.

"Hey!" Ivan yelled. "A hole opened in the tree! Håkon! Look!"

Håkon's voice then: "I'm not going in there."

"Yes, you are!" Ivan said. "Let's go!"

"No!" Håkon hissed. "I don't have any magic. What if something happens? I can't help you."

"We'll be fine," Ivan said. "I think I'm starting to feel it. The fool magic! I have water magic *and* fool magic, Håkon."

"Is it fool magic," Håkon asked, "or are you just being stupid?"

"Both! It's what fools do!"

"I'm not a fool, Ivan."

"And you never will be with that attitude!" Ivan said. "You can't think too much about things, Håkon. You've got to grab life by the horns, and—"

"I told you never to grab things by their horns," Håkon said. "It's rude."

"You know what I meant, you wet blanket." Ivan's next declaration echoed from inside the tree. "It's hollow. There's lights. There's . . . Håkon, there are stairs!"

Ivan's footsteps thumped on the steps, and then Håkon's followed, slower and more cautiously. As Anya watched, Ivan's head appeared at the top of the stairs, and his face broke into a huge grin when he saw her.

"Anya!" He hurried out of the opening. "What are . . ." Ivan trailed off as he looked around the tree and let out a low whistle of appreciation. "This is the best treehouse I've ever seen."

Håkon was still on the stairs, peering up like a surfacing *vodyanoi*. "This is a trap."

Anya jammed her hands on her hips. "It's not a trap! Come up here already."

Håkon narrowed his eyes and stayed on the stairs.

Ivan walked around the platform, inspecting things. "How did you get up here?"

"The Nightingale," Anya said. "He brought me up."

"Is he here?" Ivan peered around, suddenly tense.

"He was," Anya said. "He disappeared. I think he's afraid of you two."

Ivan laughed. *"He's* afraid of *us?"*

Anya crossed her arms. "He's different when people aren't shooting water balls at him."

"Hey!" Ivan said. "He attacked us first!"

Anya shushed him. "He could have killed us easily if he wanted to. But he didn't. He tried to tell me something earlier—"

"What do you mean, tried?" Ivan said. "Does he not speak Russian?"

"He doesn't speak at all," Anya said, then corrected, "Not with his mouth. He uses his hands."

The look of confusion on Ivan's face was absolute but didn't last long. His eyes sparked the way they did when he had a brilliant idea.

"Can you call him back?" Ivan asked, eyes still glowing. He pulled the notebook out of his coat. "We can use this to write to him!"

"Will he be able to read it?" Anya asked.

Ivan shrugged. "Maybe not. We won't know until we try, though."

"Well, anyway, I don't think I can call him back," Anya said. "He just shows up when he wants to." She glared at Håkon, still standing on the stairs. "You're probably not making him reappear any faster!"

Håkon muttered and trudged up the last few steps. He stood by Anya, arms crossed and hands dug up under his armpits. "We're all going to die."

"We are not," Anya said, and then the Nightingale appeared just out of reach of any of them. Ivan and Håkon startled, but Anya was getting used to the Nightingale's popping in and out. She turned to face him, hands up. "They're nice! Just jumpy."

The Nightingale was silent, but he stood like every muscle in his body was ready to snap. He watched Ivan or Håkon; whoever it was, Anya couldn't be sure, because they were both behind her while she faced the Nightingale. She hoped they weren't misbehaving.

She turned. Ivan and Håkon were both staring at the Nightingale, equally tense. The air was tight around them. Anya whacked Ivan's arm with the back of her hand, and he flinched.

"Anya!" he said. "What?"

"Give me your notebook," she said.

He pulled the notebook against his chest, hesitating.

"Wait. What if we charm him?"

"We'll tell him it's a charm book," Anya said. "Maybe that will stop the magic."

Ivan squirmed. "I don't—"

"We don't have all day!" Anya snapped, and he handed over the notebook and the charcoal pencil he had been using.

Anya flipped the book open past the first page, where Ivan had scrawled his "insurance" the day before. The next page was the one Ivan had showed the *bogatyri*, presumably, because it said in Ivan's tall, thin lettering: It's a víla. Go away.

She flipped to the next blank page and wrote, THIS IS A CHARMED NOTEBOOK. SORRY. CAN YOU READ THIS? She held it up to the Nightingale, whose eyes scanned across the page in the proper direction. So at least he knew how to read. But did he read Russian?

He met her eyes and nodded slowly.

Relief. She scribbled more: MY NAME IS ANYA. Then she wrote IVAN and HÅKON, and took turns pointing to each name and then the boy to which it belonged.

The Nightingale watched Anya introduce her friends, and then he took the charcoal pencil from her. With careful, looping letters, he wrote Alfhercht.

"Alfhercht," Anya said, trying the name out: *AWL-furkt*. She wasn't sure she was saying it right, but that was as close an approximation as she could come up with. "Your name is Alfhercht."

"Amazing," Ivan whispered from her side. Even Håkon had come closer and seemed more relaxed. The Nightingale had a name—Alfhercht—and a voice. And, if Anya wasn't imagining things, even the beginnings of a tiny smile trying to unfurl on his lips.

CHAPTER TWENTY-TWO

THE FOUR OF THEM stood in a circle, passing the notebook back and forth as they each took a turn conversing. Anya began, with the question that had been eating her up since the night before: WHY ARE YOU HERE?

Alfhercht wrote: My brother.

She inhaled sharply. There were two of them. Two elves. Was Alfhercht's brother as powerful as he was?

Alfhercht continued writing: The tsar holds him prisoner. For two years. I can't leave him. The tsar won't give him back. The tsar wants me prisoner too. I can't get my brother out. His hand trembled as he finished writing.

Anya glanced between her two friends. Håkon frowned,

his forehead creased. Ivan's eyes were still bright. The tsar held Alfhercht's brother prisoner and wanted Alfhercht as a prisoner too. Why? What had the elves done?

Ivan held out his hand for the pencil. Then he wrote: If we get your brother out, will you leave?

Anya put her hand on Ivan's, covering his question to Alfhercht. "What about Vasilisa? She said she'd get my papa, but only if we brought the Nightingale alive."

Ivan glanced at Alfhercht. "So we should . . . take him to prison?"

"No," Håkon snapped. "Do you remember what Lena told me? She said, 'They need your help.' It's the elves. It's got to be."

"Maybe." Anya frowned. "We should talk to Vasilisa. Tell her the Nightingale just wants to take his brother and go home."

Håkon said, "Do you think she'd care?"

"If she wants the road to be safe, she should care," Anya said. "Whether he's imprisoned or goes back home, it's the same result. The road is safe."

"I don't think she'd care," Håkon mumbled. "She wants to punish him, not solve a problem. She wouldn't let him go."

Ivan held the notebook up so Alfhercht could see his question.

Alfhercht didn't need to write his response. He nodded emphatically and then began to whip his hands through the air, talking, almost frantic.

Anya put her own hands up, palms out and still, signaling for him to stop. She shook her head. "We don't know what you're saying."

Alfhercht huffed, performed a few more gestures, and then snatched the pencil from Ivan. I want to go home.

Håkon wrote next: So do we. Then: Do you know where your brother is?

Alfhercht nodded. Dungeon. A special one underneath the city.

Ivan frowned. If you know where he is, why haven't you gotten him out?

Alfhercht's eyes hardened, and he bit his lip. He wrote with short, stabby strokes: Monster. He underlined the word and tapped hard on it with one finger.

Anya gulped. THERE'S A MONSTER?

He nodded and underlined the word again.

"How does he know there's a monster?" Ivan asked. "Has he been there?"

Alfhercht watched Ivan with a deepening frown. He reached a hand up and grabbed a thread, flicking his wrist up and throwing *monster* back in Ivan's face. Then he snatched the pen and scribbled: I was a prisoner before. I escaped. My brother was hurt. Not fast enough.

Anya looked between Ivan and Håkon. All Alfhercht wanted was to take his brother out of the prison and go home. They could help him do that, and free the city from his attacks.

Papa would have told her that was a good plan. *You should always do what you can to help those weaker than you.*

But Alfhercht wasn't weaker than she was. He could do magic she couldn't even dream of. He was bigger than she was, too. Even without magic, he was stronger.

She could see Papa in her mind, wagging a finger at her. *That's not what strength and weakness are.*

If Anya set two elves loose—two elves that the tsar wanted kept alive in his dungeons—would Vasilisa leave Papa in Rûm? Would she put Anya in prison instead? What would happen to Ivan and Håkon? Did Vasilisa want the Nightingale's threat to be gone, or did she just want to deliver what her father had asked for? Would the tsar be happy that his subjects could use the road safely?

Alive. Like the dragons.

Had the dragons been in a special dungeon too?

Had they been guarded by a monster?

Papa's voice in her head warmed her. *Do what you know is right, Annushka.*

She knew what was right.

WE'LL HELP YOU, she wrote. WE'LL GET YOUR BROTHER OUT. YOU CAN GO HOME.

Alfhercht didn't smile with his face, but something about his countenance changed. He traced one finger over the last word, HOME, and he nodded.

✦ ✷ ✦

Ivan, Anya, and Håkon waited at the bottom of the tree. Alfhercht had let them out after they had agreed that he couldn't go into the castle looking like a feral, forest-dwelling highwayman. He was inside the tree, loudly rummaging through boxes and bags of things he'd collected over the months of robbing people. Anya, Ivan, and Håkon had already rummaged. They'd found the bags Anya had dropped when Alfhercht had attacked them, but those didn't have much in them that would help against a monster. They took away some small weapons—a dagger for each of them—and some long *votola* cloaks that Alfhercht wordlessly insisted they take.

They had all been standing in tense silence, thinking. Anya didn't know what Ivan and Håkon were thinking about, but she definitely couldn't stop wondering what exactly awaited them in the secret prison. She shifted from foot to foot. "What kind of monster do you think it is?"

"Under the tsar's castle?" Ivan asked. "I don't entirely believe there is one. I mean . . . the tsar's spent years and years hunting down all the magical creatures in Kievan Rus' and either killing them or driving them out. A monster sounds like it would be a magical creature. Why would he have one in his own castle?"

"Maybe it's a dragon," Håkon said. "And Alfhercht calls it a monster because he doesn't know any better. If it is, we're going to set it free." His voice was tinged with the barest trace of hope.

"Regardless," Anya said, "we're going to help him get his brother out of there, and send them home."

Ivan and Håkon nodded, then Ivan said, "The princess said she wanted the Nightingale brought to her alive, and then she'd bring your papa back."

"I know," Anya said softly.

"Do you think she'll still do that if you just let him disappear?" Ivan asked.

"I don't know," Anya mumbled, trying her best not to look at Håkon. "But it doesn't matter. And yes, Håkon, if there's a dragon, we're definitely setting it free."

Håkon smiled to himself as the tree opened up and Alfhercht stepped out.

Anya almost didn't recognize him.

He had replaced his torn, dirty clothes with some that, although worn, were clean and without gaping holes. The *rubakha* was simple linen, dyed blue, with a black belt around his waist. His trousers were dark brown, jammed into brown boots. A fur-trimmed cap obscured the crazy haircut he sported, and he had washed the dirt and paint off his face.

"You look . . ." Anya struggled to find a word that aptly described him now.

Håkon said it before she could. "Human."

Alfhercht looked down at himself, appraising the outfit he'd put on, and shrugged.

At that moment, Anya realized Ivan was no longer standing next to her. She turned and looked around for him. He was nowhere. She was about to ask Håkon if he knew where Ivan had gone, and then she saw movement in the trees a distance off. Ivan peered out from behind one, his brown skin blazing red, even from Anya's distance. He had pulled his cap down almost entirely over his eyes.

Anya looked back at Alfhercht. Then at Ivan. To Alfhercht again. And she groaned loudly. "Not now, Ivan!"

Ivan ducked back behind the tree, then popped out with a fake-confident swagger.

"Not what?" he asked, voice shaky. "Oh, Anya." He laughed. "You're so. You're just a. Person. You know. Hey! Alfhercht! Your boots are. Boots." He clapped his hands and rubbed them together. "The dungeon? Off we go!" He marched north.

Alfhercht and Håkon both looked floored, as is appropriate when your friend hides behind a tree and starts spouting gibberish. Alfhercht pointed south of Kiev, eyebrow raised, and Håkon followed him through the forest.

Anya called, "Ivan, this way!"

"I knew that!" Ivan yelled, running past her, following Alfhercht far enough away that, Anya suspected, he was sure Alfhercht couldn't smell him.

CHAPTER TWENTY-THREE

THEY FOLLOWED ALFHERCHT through the woods without speaking, Ivan trailing behind the group by at least twenty feet. At one point, Alfhercht stopped and turned back to look at the group following him, and he stared at Ivan with a puzzled expression on his face. When he moved his hand to speak—one hand palm-up, with a perplexed shrug to his shoulders—it was obvious what the meaning was: *What are you doing?*

Anya answered for Ivan. "He's a fool."

Alfhercht let his hand drop and sighed, then pointed in the direction he had been heading. Then he pinched his fingers almost together.

Almost there. Anya was pretty sure that's what he meant. She swallowed hard.

The elf continued walking, and Håkon came abreast of Anya. "I wish I were a dragon again," he muttered.

"Me too," Anya said. "I mean, you're fine like this. I'm just glad you're here at all."

He nodded toward Alfhercht. "Do you think he's telling the truth?"

"Yes." Anya looked down at her hands. "Why else would he want us to go into the dungeon with him?"

"I don't know," Håkon said. "I just have a bad feeling about all this. Something's going on that we don't know about."

"Like what?"

"I don't know." Håkon nodded at Alfhercht. "The tsar kept Alfhercht and his brother in there for two years. Alive. Do you think . . . maybe the other dragons are still alive too?"

Anya said softly, "I don't know."

"Maybe," Håkon said softly. "Lena said I'm the last, but maybe she just meant the last *free* dragon. I could find them. Let them out."

He looked hopeful. Anya touched the key through her dress. Maybe that was what the key was for. Freeing the other dragons. Or whatever other magical creatures the tsar had stashed in his secret dungeon. She thought of her *domovoi*. How far did the tsar's crusade against magic go? Would he wipe out the creatures of the fields and forests, and then come for the creatures of their home? What would happen to Kievan Rus' as a nation if only the tsar and his henchmen could use magic?

Alfhercht looked back and put a finger over his lips, shushing them. Anya scowled. They hadn't been talking loudly. But he must have been able to see sound threads coming from them anyway. He pointed up to their left, where the towers of Kiev's walls were just visible past the trees. Anya pressed her lips together, realizing his shushing was a warning. A guard on the wall would hear them if they were too loud, so she heeded Alfhercht and didn't say anything.

They stayed off the roads and followed the city wall south and then east. Alfhercht stopped every now and then to look around for a second, and then started walking again. He never cocked his head like he was listening; he always looked instead.

Anya thought of Babulya. She couldn't see anything, threads included. Could she hear the threads instead? Or feel them better than other people? Anya hadn't ever thought about it before. When she got home, she'd have to ask.

They went far enough east to leave the city walls behind, and then Alfhercht went north. He moved through the forest without making a sound. His skin shifted colors and shades, dappled in the autumn light filtering through the trees, and sometimes he matched the trees around him so well that it looked like he was made of bark. If he hadn't been wearing human clothing, Anya suspected he would be nearly impossible to see. As he was, sometimes he looked like a bunch of clothing floating through the forest. Then he'd stop and turn back to them, and his skin would change so she could see him easily.

The forest ended abruptly at the bottom of a cliff. At the top stood the city's wall. Alfhercht led them around, still hidden in the shelter of the trees, until the Dnieper thrashed ahead of them. In the side of the cliff was a cavern, mouth gaping open like a snoring beast.

Alfhercht pointed at the cavern, eyebrows up.

"In there?" Anya said softly.

Alfhercht nodded.

Anya heard Ivan approach carefully behind her. He said, "Does he want us to go in there?"

"Yep," Anya said.

Ivan let out a slow breath. "To fight a cave monster."

"I like caves," Håkon said.

"We're not all drag—" Ivan glanced at Alfhercht, even though the elf wasn't looking at him. Still, what would he think if he knew Håkon was a dragon in disguise? Ivan amended his comment. "We're not all what you are." He took a deep breath. "Well, unto our fates we go, right?"

Before Ivan could march out of the trees, something moved at the cavern's mouth. The four of them scrambled for cover, each taking shelter behind a different tree or bush, as two men walked into the forest.

Ilya and Alyosha spoke as they emerged from the cave.

"Those are some nice caves, Ilya," Alyosha said.

Ilya beamed. "Aren't they? Tsar Kazimir is working with me to turn them into a monastery. That way, we can provide a place for study and prayer, away from the business of the city."

Alyosha said, "But it's under the city."

Ilya ignored the younger *bogatyr*'s jab. "Someday."

Alyosha laughed. "Someday, when you're done battling evil?"

"I think I'll be done soon," Ilya said. "You're young.

You've got so much time ahead of you for more adventures. But I'm old. I'm tired. I want to settle down."

"Like Dobrynya?"

"No," Ilya said. "Though Dobrynya is no young man either, he's been at the tsar's side since he was a boy. He'll be there until there's no side to be at, I think. But I want no adventure. No obligation to the castle or to Kiev. I just want to read until I'm too old to see." He laughed. "I'll get better at reading, hopefully."

Alyosha nodded, plucking at his sleeve. "I'll settle down soon."

"And you sound so happy about it."

Anya wrinkled her nose. Alyosha didn't sound happy at all. He sounded more like he was talking about a prison sentence.

He sighed. "She hates me. I don't even know why."

Ilya laughed. It boomed through the forest, echoing away. "You don't? I do!"

"Well," Alyosha snapped, "aren't *you* so wise?"

"No!" Ilya continued laughing. "I don't need to be wise to know the princess doesn't want to be married at all. It's not *you*. It's *anyone*." He paused. "Well, it is you, some. You broke her things!"

"It was just a stupid sword!" Alyosha said. "She has a hundred others!"

"And you didn't apologize, either," Ilya said.

"Apologize for breaking a flimsy—"

"Yes, Alyosha."

"She's got to get married sometime," Alyosha said. "What else is she going to do?"

Ilya clapped Alyosha on the back with a force that would have broken another man in half. Alyosha jerked forward but was unharmed. "She's going to be tsarina some day, and she's going to be great at it. That girl's got the heart of a bear inside her."

"Are you saying a bear should be tsar?" Alyosha said sourly.

Ilya patted Alyosha on the back again, softer, several times. A *There-there* pat if Anya had ever seen one. "When that bear sits on the throne of Kiev, I will gladly serve her. And you will too."

"I'll be her husband."

"Will you?" Ilya stroked his chin.

"Yes!" Alyosha walked away from Ilya.

The older *bogatyr* put his hands on his hips. "I think, my dear Alyosha, that if you want to win that bear's heart, you should stop expecting it to be happy in a cage."

Alyosha paused in his storming off, glancing back momentarily, and then he continued away. Ilya let out a soft laugh that ended in a sigh and lingered at the cavern mouth. He put a hand on the rocky lip. "He's still young. He'll figure it out."

Anya waited for Ilya to leave, but he didn't. In fact, it didn't look like he was about to go anywhere at all. He stayed at the cavern mouth, deep in contemplation. Anya looked up. The day was getting on. It would be dark before they knew it. She didn't want to be in a spooky, monster-guarded dungeon at all, but especially not at night.

Anya waved to Ivan to get his attention, then Håkon, and Alfhercht last. She pointed to herself and Ivan, then to Ilya. She moved her hand like it was a mouth, talking. Then she pointed to Håkon and Alfhercht. With her fingers like legs, she pantomimed sneaking.

She and Ivan would distract Ilya so Håkon and Alfhercht could sneak into the cavern. Then Anya and Ivan could go in after Ilya had gone.

Alfhercht looked unsure, and Håkon frowned. Ivan may or may not have been paying attention to her between his furtive glances at Alfhercht.

Anya scowled and stood. She grabbed Ivan's sleeve

and marched to where Ilya brushed soil off the stones around the cave mouth. She called, "Gospodin Ilya!"

He whirled, eyes wide, then confused. When he noticed them, he said, "You must be Anya!" He looked at Ivan. "Where did you find her?"

"Uh," Ivan said. "In the woods. She was just, uh—"

"I was collecting leaves," Anya said. "What's this place?"

Ilya said, "Well, this is one entrance to a whole lot of caves under the city."

"Oh wow," Anya said. She scooted around Ilya with Ivan, positioning herself so Ilya would have to turn his back to where Håkon and Alfhercht were hiding. "All the way under the city?"

Ilya nodded, his hand resting on the stone cliffside. "They go all over." He pointed an admonishing finger at them. "But they're not safe for children to be running around in! I'm not sure if all the branches are safe. Some of them might fall down. The tsar has closed them off to keep people safe."

Anya watched Håkon and Alfhercht sneak toward the cave out of the corner of her eye. She was noticing that the tsar took away a lot of things in the interest of safety.

Ilya continued. "And part of the caves go out to the

river. There are whole sections that are underwater. You could get trapped and drown." He laughed and indicated Ivan. "Well, not you."

Ivan's cheeks flared red. "Why not me?"

Ilya laughed again. "You're a funny one!" He continued to laugh, but when Ivan didn't join in and instead looked confused and embarrassed, Ilya's own laughter trailed off. "Wait. You . . . Are you not . . ." He scratched his beard.

"Not what?" Ivan asked.

Behind Ilya, Håkon and Alfhercht were nearly out of the bushes and into the cavern's mouth.

Ilya shook his head. "I'm sorry. It was my mistake. You look like one of the eastern peoples, that's all. The Dvukh people."

Quietly, Ivan said, "My mama is from the East."

"Oh?" Ilya asked. "Is she Dvukh?"

"I don't know," Ivan said. "She doesn't talk about her home."

Ilya said, "Well, ah, does she . . . Are there any sealskins in your home at all?"

"What?" Ivan wrinkled his nose. "Just lying around, or part of clothing?"

"An entire seal skin," Ilya said. "Or it could be

something else. A leopard, or a wolf, or something like that." He tilted his head and studied Ivan. "But you look like a seal to me. The ones I've seen."

Ivan gawped. "I look like a *seal?*"

"Well," Ilya said, "those are the oldest. Do you really not know about the Dvukh?" When they both shook their heads, he sighed. "Who's in charge of your education, anyway?"

Ivan and Anya glanced at each other and shrugged.

Ilya said, "I have a minute to explain. Do you at least know where Lukomorye is?"

They exchanged another glance.

"Lukomorye isn't anywhere," Anya said. "It's not a real place."

"It's pretend," Ivan agreed. "For little kids."

It was where the fairy tales happened. It was the land beyond their own. It wasn't real . . . was it?

Ilya shook his head, a faint smile on his face. "No. No, it's real. That's where they came from. The Dvukh. Lukomorye is an island in the northern ocean, shrouded in mists and ice, and finding it is nigh impossible." His eyes glazed over, as if he were seeing something far away.

As Ilya spoke, Håkon and Alfhercht crept behind him,

past him, into the cave, sticking close to the opposite wall. Anya tried not to watch them, tried to pretend they weren't even there. But it was impossible to keep her eyes off them. Håkon's toe caught on a rock and he kicked it. It clattered on the floor of the cavern.

Anya gasped. Ilya paused his story, and Anya yelled, "*A-choo!*"

"God bless you," Ilya said, and then continued on like nothing had happened. "The Dvukh swam from the island to the Thrice-Nine Kingdoms, back when the land was brand-new, and they settled in the East. They mostly stayed there, in a place we call Ashina. In Ashina, the Dvukh are mostly wolf-people now, I think." He waved a finger at Ivan. "Unlike you. The Dvukh are doubled: human and wolf, or seal, or some other animal. They can change between the two forms. Seals with eyes that are too smart. Huge, gray wolves who can't be caught in any trap. I've seen them out there." Ilya blinked, and his eyes cleared. He directed his gaze to Ivan. "And the people look just like you. Similar to the Polenitsi, too." He paused. "Is your mother a Polenitsa, perchance?"

"I don't think so," Ivan said. Anya noticed him trembling. "How would I know?"

He laughed. "She'd be horrified to have a son, for one."

"My mama has seven sons," Ivan said.

"Oh God." Ilya crossed himself. "Your poor mother."

"Our poor village," Anya said. As Håkon and Alfhercht vanished into the cave's darkness, she said loudly, "Gospodin Ilya, this has been a fascinating discussion. But Ivan and I are . . . going to go throw rocks into the river." She hesitated. "Would you like to throw rocks with us?" She figured they could lose him in the forest somehow. Hopefully.

Ilya laughed. "Oh, I'm too old to throw rocks. But I should be getting back to the castle anyway." He pointed a thick finger between her and Ivan. "Don't rile up any *vodyaniye*."

"Of course not," Anya said.

"I'm surprised there are still some in the river," Ivan piped.

"They're tough to get rid of," Ilya said. "If you get them upset, I'll have to fish you out of the river!" He pointed at Ivan again. "Maybe even you. I'm a good swimmer, though!" He laughed and walked past them, south toward where they had just come from. "God protect you, children."

They waved goodbye to him, waiting for him to vanish before they darted into the dark cave. Inside, Anya couldn't make out the shapes of her friends, so she whispered, "Håkon! Alfhercht!"

"Here!" Håkon's voice came from a few feet back. As he whispered, a glow rose. Alfhercht held a stone in his hand, glowing like the ones in his tree. Its warm orange light threw shadows over their faces, turning them ghoulish.

Håkon said, "I thought he'd never leave."

"Did you hear him?" Ivan asked.

"I heard him say you look like a seal," Håkon said.

Anya laughed, then noticed Alfhercht watching them all intently. He squinted and frowned. She looked at Ivan and Håkon. The shadows on their faces warped their mouths, making their top lips vanish and their lower lips move strangely. He was trying to watch them speak, and couldn't.

Anya fished the notebook out of Ivan's jacket and wrote on it: IVAN LOOKS LIKE A SEAL.

Alfhercht held his glowing stone over the notebook, then peered up at her with a scrunched face. Anya laughed, Håkon laughed, and then Alfhercht reached over to Ivan and pressed the pad of his finger to the tip of Ivan's nose. And he laughed, silent but unmistakable.

Ivan startled when Alfhercht touched him, like he

hadn't seen the elf's finger coming. He turned red so fast, his face seemed to be on fire. No quick quip back. No laugh. It wasn't like him. Under his embarrassment, he looked shocked.

Still laughing, Alfhercht shook his head, pointed to Ivan, and with his free hand made a bunch of gestures. Then he wrote on the notebook: His face is too flat to be a seal's. And he drew a quick sketch: the outline of a seal.

Håkon took the pencil from Alfhercht and drew a crooked cap on the seal's head.

"You know what?" Ivan squeaked, then cleared his throat. "None of you are funny!"

Anya hugged him around his arms. "We're hilarious." She leaned her head on his shoulder. "I bet your mama would talk to you about it when we get back to Zmeyreka."

Ivan shrugged, frowning.

Alfhercht handed the notebook back to Ivan, who took it with trembling fingers, and then the elf crooked his thumb back toward the cave. His meaning was obvious: *This way.*

He led the way, holding the glowing stone out to light the path. Anya followed, then Håkon, then Ivan, until the cavern had swallowed them up.

CHAPTER TWENTY-FOUR

THE STONE'S ORANGE GLOW cast a narrow circle of light, but in the deep darkness of the cave, it was more than enough. Anya, Ivan, and Håkon crowded close to Alfhercht, shuffling along with him to make sure they didn't get lost. If they fell behind or took a wrong turn, they'd never find their way back out.

The tunnel split, and Alfhercht stopped. He lifted his light up to the walls, inspecting them for something. Anya watched him, wondering what he could be searching for, and then he reached a hand up. He drew the tips of his fingers over a dark gash. Someone or something had gouged a long, deep line into the cave wall. Alfhercht pulled his fingers back and wiped them on his pant leg, then took the passage to the right.

Almost immediately, the tunnel sloped down and down and down, growing colder and damper with every step. The stone under their feet began to feel slick with slime and mold, and Anya almost lost her footing several times.

"Håkon," Ivan said in the dimness, "I don't care how comfy you think caves are. This one is a dump."

"It could use some sprucing up," Håkon agreed. "At least a good mopping."

Anya twisted her apron in her hands idly. "Ilya said the caverns went under the river. That some of them were full of water."

"Well, those won't be the right way," Ivan said. "He's taking us to a dungeon, right? That human beings use? The passages would have to be clear. Regular people can't use magic to get through underwater tunnels." He paused. "Maybe there's just some puddles to wade through."

"Maybe," Anya said softly, and then Alfhercht stopped.

He held out his glowing stone, and it reflected on the water. The tunnel in front of them continued to slope down, and a few feet in front of them, it was full of water.

Full, from side to side, all the way back until it touched the ceiling. Impassable.

"Oh no," Ivan murmured.

"They must have flooded since he came through here," Anya said.

Alfhercht turned to them and pointed at the water.

"Go in there?" Anya asked, pointing.

Alfhercht nodded.

Anya shook her head. "Swim?"

Håkon inched closer to the water. "We can swim that, no problem."

"You can't swim!" Anya said.

"Says who?" Håkon said, crossing his arms.

Anya huffed. "Says me! No. We don't even know how far the water goes." She and Ivan could swim, but could Håkon? As a dragon, he swam better than any of them. But as a boy? With his unfamiliar body? He had learned to walk only the day before. Maybe he wouldn't be able to swim. Maybe he'd drown.

"I'm a *river dragon*," Håkon snapped. "I can swim this better than any of you!"

He was being so stubborn, but Anya wasn't about to let him risk his life. Her skin crawled at the thought of

Håkon drowning, and she shook her head harder. "We'll just have to find another way."

"*This* is the way." Håkon stepped to the water's edge and moved to walk straight into it.

Alfhercht shot a hand out and grabbed Håkon around the arm. He pulled Håkon back and sighed, exasperated. He thrust the glowing stone at Anya. She took it, surprised at its warmth. With two free hands, Alfhercht turned back to the water and wove his fingers in the air. The water flowed apart, leaving a ditch of air down the middle. He parted the water in the tunnel the way Moshe had parted the sea. Except there wasn't freedom on the other side. There were even deeper, even darker tunnels.

Ivan stepped closer to Alfhercht, seeming to forget his fear of smelling bad. He was gaping at the elf's manipulation even more than Anya was. After all, he could see the threads Alfhercht pulled. There was a level to Alfhercht's magic that Anya would never be able to appreciate.

Ivan traced one finger in the air, following a thread. "The perfect prison door. Only water magic can get past it."

Peering at Ivan, Alfhercht nodded. His eyes lingered on Ivan's enthralled face for a breath, and then he turned back to the water. He stepped into the ditch, and Ivan followed him.

"Come on," Ivan said to Anya and Håkon. "Whatever water Alfhercht can't keep away, I will. We'll be fine."

Anya and Håkon stepped down. Anya held the glowing stone up so they could see. They walked, staying even closer to Alfhercht now, with Ivan behind them. They passed under where the water touched the ceiling, and then Ivan pulled threads to close the ditch of air behind them, forming an oblong bubble around them instead. Anya remembered the last time she was in an underwater bubble. She had been trapped inside a bag that smelled like earth and rotten cabbage. Ivan had tried to save them, but he wasn't as good at magic back then as he was now. It had been Håkon who had pulled them out, saving them both.

But who would save them if they got stuck this time?

Anya's chest felt tight. She held her breath like she was underwater and not inside a magical bubble, shuffling through a cavern as dark as a midnight storm. Her hands trembled, and the stone in her hands reflected on the water wall. Past it, slipping through the inky water, Sigurd's ghost leered at her, leaving bloody trails behind him. *None of your heroes are here to save you this time.*

Anya shut her eyes and gasped in a breath.

A warm hand on her arm made her open her eyes. Håkon looked at her, blue eyes sparkling with concern. He didn't know about how Sigurd still haunted her—his actual ghost or his memory or whatever it was—or about her nightmares, her panic in her own cellar, her fear that one day she'd wake up and Håkon would be gone. Murdered by the tsar, or by another hero. He didn't know. Ivan didn't know. Only Zvezda knew.

She was afraid Håkon would want to know what was wrong and would press her for an answer. She didn't want to tell him. But he didn't ask. He just squeezed her arm and whispered, "I'm here. I won't let anything happen."

A smile tugged up the corners of her mouth. She knew he wouldn't. He was a good dragon. A good friend. And he was shaping up to be a good human, too. She slipped her free hand over his and squeezed it back.

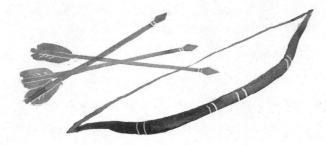

CHAPTER TWENTY-FIVE

AN ETERNITY LATER—or maybe it had been only ten minutes—the air bubble around them was beginning to feel stale and stifling. Just as Anya began to itch with the need to get out from under the water, the top of it breached the surface of the tunnel, and fresh, cold air cascaded over them. Anya sucked in breaths as she hurried away from the water. She relaxed only once she was on dry ground.

Suspiciously dry ground.

They were no longer in a rough cavern. The floor and walls were smooth, sanded down to resemble an actual hallway inside a building. In the stone's glow, Anya could make out unlit sconces every few feet, where there could be torches if needed. Some of those sconces sat beside doors.

Heavy wooden doors.

With keyholes.

The key seemed to get heavier around her neck and warmer against her skin. Behind her, the boys all followed into the tunnel. Alfhercht let his threads go, and the water of the ditch slapped together as it engulfed where the group had just walked up. He touched Ivan on the shoulder. Ivan whirled, eyes wide, face red.

Alfhercht smiled and said something to Ivan with his hands. When it became clear that Ivan didn't understand what he was trying to say, Alfhercht just shook his head and clapped Ivan on the shoulder. He turned, taking the glowing stone from Anya, and led the way toward the eerily smooth hall.

Ivan stood still. One hand wandered up to the spot where Alfhercht had touched him.

Håkon razzed Ivan's hair. "I think he was saying you did a good job."

Ivan didn't try to duck away from Håkon. He just stood there and let his hair go wild.

"Yeah," he murmured. He might have been smiling, or it might have just been the way the shadows crossed over his face.

Håkon followed Alfhercht, and Ivan trailed after. Anya brought up the rear, stopping at every door she came across and slipping her key into the keyholes.

Just like up in the castle, nothing happened.

They wound around corners and past cold torches mounted on the walls, until they reached a thick wooden door. Alfhercht stopped in front of it, holding his stone up, examining it.

"Wait!" Anya whispered, darting forward. Maybe this was her key's chance to shine! She reached for the keyhole with her key, and Alfhercht grabbed it. When he did, his hand trembled.

She understood. "The monster."

Ivan blinked slowly. "Cave monster."

"You're kind of our only hope if it shows up," Håkon said. "Anya and I don't have any magic. We have these knives, but . . ." He gulped.

Anya jammed her hands onto her hips. "We're not *useless*. Your da taught us how to fight."

"Yeah, against people, " Håkon argued. "Not against a monster."

Anya snorted. "Ivan, give me the journal."

He did, and she wrote a message for Alfhercht on it: HOW DOES THE MONSTER ATTACK?

Alfhercht wrote, Magic.

SO WE USE MAGIC AGAINST IT? Anya wrote.

Alfhercht shook his head. Steals magic.

Ivan squeaked, "Steals magic?" He pulled his hands close to his chest, like that would prevent his magic from being taken.

"Steals?" Anya read what Alfhercht wrote out loud. Alfhercht could steal magic. Did the monster do the same thing he did? LIKE HOW YOU DO?

Alfhercht frowned. I don't steal. I pick up.

Anya wasn't sure of the difference, and it must have shown on her face, because Alfhercht continued.

I can take threads from someone, but they can pick them up again. The monster steals forever. You can never use your magic again. Don't try to fight it. Run away.

Next to her, Ivan sucked in a short breath. *You can never use your magic again.* How could the monster do that? What kind of creature could tear someone's magic ability away from them?

But Anya realized something. If Alfhercht and Ivan got their magic taken away, it wouldn't matter how fast she ran. She'd get stopped at that water tunnel. She'd never be able to swim to the other side.

All of them would be trapped forever.

It was too late to turn back. Anya had promised Alfhercht she'd help him save his brother. She had the ability to help. So . . . she would.

She nodded. GET YOUR BROTHER. RUN AWAY. BE SAFE.

Alfhercht read her words, nodded, and pushed on the door. It opened on shrieking, rusted hinges, swinging inward.

CHAPTER TWENTY-SIX

T HE ENORMOUS ROOM beyond was lit dimly through narrow windows in its stone ceiling. It was hugely long and tall, mostly circular in shape. The door Anya stepped through was on an upper level, near the ceiling. She could look down over a short stone wall onto an oval dirt field. They all peered down.

Ivan whispered, "What is this place?"

Håkon stared, eyes wide. "I don't know."

Alfhercht stared at the room with hard eyes. His jaw tightened. He reached for Ivan, hand out, palm up. When Ivan didn't do anything, Alfhercht pantomimed writing something on his palm.

"Oh!" Ivan pulled his journal out of his pocket and handed it to Alfhercht.

We had to fight here, Alfhercht wrote. He underlined "fight" with a shaky hand.

Anya traded looks with Alfhercht and Ivan. FIGHT WHO?

Alfhercht shook his head and shoved the journal back at Ivan. He snatched up his glowing rock and headed around the level toward a distant door.

Down on the lowest level, the low stone wall around the arena field itself was partially destroyed. It looked like something had blown a chunk of the wall apart. Similar blast craters had crumbled a middle tier, where there were a handful of seats for spectating.

"What kind of fighting did that?" Håkon asked.

"Magic did that," Anya said softly. "Alfhercht's sound magic."

He squirmed. "Do you think all elves can use sound magic?"

"Maybe," Anya said.

Ivan said, "Do you think all of them can't hear?"

"Maybe," Håkon said. "Maybe they use sound magic because they can't hear. Or maybe they can't hear because of sound magic."

"I guess we'll find out when we find his brother," Anya said.

Ivan cleared his throat. "Have we considered what's going to happen if Alfhercht's brother is, uh . . ."

He trailed off, but his suggestion was clear.

Anya shook her head. Håkon did too.

Ivan drew a little invisible chart in the air. "If his brother's been in here for so long, it's very possible that he's not alive anymore." He drew a line a few inches away. "So Alfhercht will probably be really sad." He drew a horizontal line. "Or really angry." He drew a line down. "And he might start blowing stuff up."

Anya swept Ivan's hand out of the air, away from his chart. "We'll just have to be here for him."

Håkon said, "I'll be here for him as long as he doesn't start freaking out."

"Håkon!" Anya glared at him.

"What?"

"We said we'd help him," Ivan said.

"Look." Håkon put one hand on Ivan's shoulder. "I know you like him and all, but—"

"You know *what?*" Ivan yelled. "I like *who?* That's. You know? I don't appreciate your assumption!"

Håkon just stared at him.

Ivan plucked the ex-dragon's hand off his shoulder. "Why would I like an elf?"

Håkon shifted his eyes to Anya, eyebrows up. She matched his stare. Neither of them had to say anything.

Ivan scoffed. "This was your idea, Anya! Not mine!"

She laughed and raised her hands up. "Yep. My idea."

Ivan scowled. "You're both the worst."

"It's okay if you like him," Anya said. "Without all that dirt on him, he's sort of handsome."

Movement from the floor below them drew their attention. Alfhercht stood at the edge of the arena, looking out onto the dirt floor. His fists were clenched at his sides, his shoulders bunched.

Ivan watched Alfhercht with sad eyes. "He'd be just like Sasha or Verusha. I can't tell either of them that I like them. I don't know why I let myself like them." He sighed, long and slow and trembly, like he was holding in a thunderstorm.

Anya hugged him tight, squeezing him to her. Then she kissed him on the cheek and said, "You're wonderful. And if any of them think you're less than wonderful, they don't deserve you."

He just nodded and hugged her tighter.

Håkon crept up beside them and wrapped his arms around both as far as he could. "If anyone hurts you, I'll fight them."

Ivan snorted a laugh and pulled away from them both. He rubbed his face hastily with his sleeve and then pointed down at where Alfhercht stood. "We should go down there, I think."

Anya and Håkon agreed, and the three of them descended a dark flight of stone steps and emerged onto the floor under where they'd stood a moment before. On the arena level, it looked so much more massive, like it never ended. Like it was inescapable.

Alfhercht didn't turn when they arrived behind him. Anya wasn't sure if he knew they were there, and she didn't know how to get his attention without startling him. She cleared her throat a couple of times, thinking maybe the sound magic would float by him and he'd see it. If it did float by him, he didn't notice it. He seemed lost in the arena.

Ivan stepped beside him, an arm's length away on Alfhercht's left side but still in his peripheral vision. After Ivan stood there for a few breathless seconds, he stretched his hand out and set it on Alfhercht's shoulder.

The elf didn't flinch. He didn't turn to look at Ivan

either. He remained trapped in his contemplation. He brought his right hand up and across his body, and set it on Ivan's hand.

Ivan's face flushed and his eyebrows rose up so far that Anya thought they might just melt into his hair and be gone forever.

Anya and Håkon exchanged a glance paired with matching smiles. Holding someone's hand wasn't something you did if you didn't like them. If only they were somewhere without an alleged monster prowling around, she and Håkon could have just left Ivan and Alfhercht on their own. But there was a monster, supposedly, and these dungeons were spooky, and she just wanted to figure out which door her key opened up, and she wanted to get out of there.

"Ivan," Anya whispered. He looked at her slowly, like if he moved too fast, he'd spook Alfhercht. "We should go. The monster."

Ivan mouthed, "Oh right," and pulled his hand away from Alfhercht.

Anya stepped forward, poking Ivan's coat where he had the journal tucked. He handed it to her, and she wrote, WE SHOULD GO BEFORE THE MONSTER COMES.

Alfhercht nodded, cast one last sour glare at the arena,

and brushed past them. Anya gave the journal back to Ivan.

They followed Alfhercht through a heavy door, and they found themselves in another oblong room, but much smaller. The meager light from the arena spilled around them, barely lighting the room enough to make out shapes. Alfhercht held out his glowing stone so they could see. A rack of rickety weapons stood in the center of the room. Four columns jutted from the floor, going only halfway to the ceiling. On each side of the columns, a pair of shackles hung from heavy iron chains at varying heights. The columns themselves were the same stone as the walls and mottled with dark splotches. Anya didn't want to venture closer to see what the splotches were. Around the periphery of the room, a dozen heavy doors were built into the walls. A couple of them stood open, but most were shut.

Anya stepped past Alfhercht and went to the rack of weapons. She inspected them without touching them. They were all in such a state of ill repair that Anya probably could have snapped them all with just her hands. Like the columns, they were stained with dark splotches.

Ivan and Alfhercht took in what they could in the dimness. Alfhercht stayed by the door, tense, trembling.

Anya watched him. He said he'd been a prisoner there too. Had he been locked in one of those rooms behind the heavy doors? Had he ever been shackled to these columns? Had one of these weapons been used against him?

Anya pulled the key out from her dress and marched to the door closest to where they'd come in. She jammed the key in the lock.

Click!

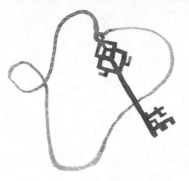

CHAPTER TWENTY-SEVEN

T HE SOLID SNAP of the lock disengaging rippled through Anya's hand. She just stood there in shock, staring at the key grasped in her fingers and at the keyhole beyond. The door started to swing out, and she smashed it shut again with an open palm. She wasn't ready to see what was in there. Not yet. And especially not alone.

"Ivan! Håkon!" she hissed. She turned back to them, her entire body thrumming. "I found it! It opened!"

They looked up from where they stood. Ivan said, "Found what?"

"The door!" she said. "The door my key opens! It's this one! I unlocked it!"

They both hurried over to her. Ivan inspected the key in the lock. Håkon set another hand on the door to help Anya keep it shut.

"What's inside?" Ivan asked.

"I don't know," Anya said. "Lena didn't say. She just said to open it." She swallowed hard. "That means it's probably safe, right?"

Ivan shrugged and said, "Could be," at the same time that Håkon said, "There's no way of knowing for sure."

Anya twisted to look back at Alfhercht while she kept her hand on the key, as if letting go of it meant it would vanish into the keyhole. He watched them from the door but still hadn't moved inside. She jerked her head toward the door. "It's open!"

He stared at her, glanced around with trepidation, and then slunk into the room. He squeezed next to Håkon on his side opposite from Ivan, positioning Håkon between them.

The four of them stood there, unmoving, until Ivan said, "Are we going to open it?"

"We should," Anya said.

"Should we, though?" Håkon asked.

"Yes," Anya said. "Lena gave me this key for a reason. She told me to open this door. I have to."

Håkon shifted on his feet. "We haven't seen a monster yet. What if it's in there?"

"Why would Lena tell us to open a door with a monster behind it?" Ivan asked.

"I don't know!" Håkon snapped. "Why would she turn me into a human?"

Anya sighed. He would have been killed immediately in Kiev if he were a dragon. "You know why." She pulled her hand away from where it kept the door shut, and she slipped it around the handle. "Move your hand. I'm going to open it."

Håkon left his hand there. "Anya—"

"Maybe his brother is in there," Anya said, nodding to Alfhercht. "Didn't you say you think Lena sent you for them?"

Håkon hesitated and then let his hand drop from the door. He stepped back, arms crossed, while Anya readied herself for what was inside. Would it be a monster? Or Alfhercht's brother? Or maybe just a skeleton. She gulped. *Not a skeleton. Please, not a skeleton.*

She glanced at the boys around her, who all looked

ready for whatever they found inside. Anya sucked in a deep breath, let it out, took another one, let it out, and then inhaled sharply one more time. She yanked the door wide open.

CHAPTER TWENTY-EIGHT

ANYA WAS PREPARED for anything. A monster? They would run. Alfhercht's brother, alive? They would help him. Alfhercht's brother, dead? They would help Alfhercht. Another *ibbur* like Lena? They would help it, too, if they could. Lena didn't seem to need help with anything, but she also wasn't being imprisoned by a monster.

But Anya wasn't prepared for what actually met her when the door swung open, eerily silent on its hinges, blowing a gust of stale cavern air over them as they stood in the doorway.

Nothing.

The cell was empty.

It was large enough for Anya to stand in the center and almost stretch her arms straight out. The stone floor was bare but for some straw gathered along the edges of the room. A bucket was on its side in one corner. It smelled of abandonment.

Anya hesitated. She waited for something to drop from the ceiling or climb up from under the straw scattered in the corners. But no. Nothing emerged.

Ivan let out a rush of held breath. "Where is he?"

"I don't know," Anya said. "Is he . . . invisible?"

Ivan scooted toward the room, pausing at the door. "Don't let the door shut."

"I won't."

He went the rest of the way inside, shoulders hunched, while Anya held the door open. He turned a slow circle, arms out. When he completed his circle, he let his arms drop. He shrugged. "Nothing."

Anya looked at Alfhercht, who remained squarely outside the room.

Where was his brother if not in here? Why would Lena give her a key to an empty room?

Ivan started inspecting the straw, as if something was actually hidden beneath it. Anya leaned in and looked up at the ceiling. Nothing there. Ivan declared nothing was under the straw. Otherwise, the room was bare.

Anya pulled the key out of the keyhole and stared at it. Heavy iron, dark and solid. Worn smooth on the end, where it had been held by a thousand hands. No carving, etching, adornment. Just a plain old key that could have gone to any door in the—

She looked around at the other doors.

The key could have gone to any door in the dungeon. Maybe it *did*.

She dashed away from the room toward the next door.

"Hey!" Ivan yelled, scrambling out of the room before the door shut him inside. "Rude!"

"It opens all of them!" Anya yelled, hoping she was right. She stuck the key in the next door and—

Click!

She yanked the door open without waiting for the others. This one was bare too, the same size as the first one. She left it and went to the next door, and the next, and the next. Five nearly identical prison cells, all empty. There were seven more. One of them had to hold *something*.

The boys trailed behind her as she went. Ivan helped

her inspect each room. Håkon had at some point grabbed a sword off the rack in the middle and held it, ready to stab anything that needed stabbing. Alfhercht followed reluctantly, his glowing stone held up to light the way.

Anya plunged the key into the sixth door and turned it. It opened, but without any satisfying heavy click. It was smooth. It rolled open like the mechanism inside the lock had been oiled.

She hesitated. When Ivan tried to yank the door open, she stopped him.

"It was different," she said.

"What?"

She felt fluttery inside, excited. "It was smoother. Like it's used a lot."

Ivan breathed hard, then grabbed the handle. "Let's see why."

They pulled the door open together. The room beyond was the same size as the others, and the same layout. Cramped. Tiny. Straw dribbled on the floor.

But it wasn't empty.

A man sat in the corner, leaning against the wall. His skinny legs were tucked up against him, and his arms were crossed protectively over his chest. His clothing was ragged and stained. His long brown hair looked like it hadn't been washed or brushed at all, ever. The skin of his arms was pale and dull, as if it would crumble if Anya touched it.

For a moment, Anya thought he was dead, but when the glow from Alfhercht's stone fell over him, he shifted and squeezed his eyes further shut.

Alfhercht inhaled sharply and shoved past Anya. He dropped his stone as he ran; it clattered to the floor. Alfhercht fell to his knees next to the man huddled in the corner. He grabbed him and hugged him tight, sobbing as he clutched him.

"His brother," Håkon whispered.

Alfhercht's brother recoiled away for a second, then looked up. His eyes widened when he saw Alfhercht, and his face crumpled as tears winked at the corners of his eyes.

"No." His voice was raspy and hoarse, like a dried leaf. That answered one question: Some elves could speak with their mouths. Alfhercht was unique.

He grasped Alfhercht's face, holding his pale, pale hands against Alfhercht's golden cheeks. Then he pulled a hand away and made very deliberate, trembling gestures as he said aloud, "He got you."

Alfhercht shook his head and spoke with his hands as

well, fingers flying. He pointed back to Anya, Ivan, and Håkon. They all lifted their hands in greeting.

When Alfhercht's brother spoke, he used both his mouth and his hands. "You're helping him? Helping *us?*"

Anya nodded. "Yes." She didn't know what else to say, really, but Ivan did.

"He's been trying to get you out for a long time," Ivan said. As Ivan spoke, Alfhercht's brother used his hands to speak, but not his mouth. It took Anya a moment to realize he was translating for Alfhercht. Alfhercht couldn't hear what Ivan said, so his brother was making sure he could see it. "But he couldn't on his own. So we're helping take you out of here . . ." He blinked a few times. "What's your name?"

Amazingly, impossibly, bizarrely, Alfhercht's brother coughed out a raspy laugh. "He didn't tell you? Of course he didn't." He looked at Alfhercht and said, "You have no manners."

Alfhercht lifted his hands, palms up, in a clear message: "What?"

"You didn't tell them my name," Alfhercht's brother said, then looked back at Ivan. "I'm Wielaf."

"I'm Ivan," Ivan said.

Wielaf nodded. "Everyone in this country is named Ivan."

"I'm not," Anya said. "I'm Anya."

Håkon said, "I'm Håkon. We should go."

Anya shot him an annoyed look, even though he was right. They hadn't run into a monster yet, but that didn't mean there wasn't one. "We should," she said. "Wielaf, can you walk?"

"I'm mostly dragged places," he said. "But I'll try. Help me up."

Alfhercht hauled Wielaf up onto startlingly thin legs, which buckled under Wielaf's weight. Alfhercht let him slide back down to the floor. Wielaf panted with exertion.

"Give me . . . a moment . . ." he said. "Just . . . a moment."

Anya stepped away from the room to give Wielaf a chance to stand without being stared at. Across the oval space, six more doors stood uninspected. Two of them were open, but the other four were locked up tight. She looked down at the key in her hand. What was in the other rooms? Were there more prisoners? She couldn't leave without at least checking to make sure no one else was being held down here.

While the others waited for Wielaf, Anya hurried across the room. In the gloom, she could barely make out anything in the two open rooms, but they were very plainly empty. So were the first three doors she opened.

The fourth room wasn't empty. But, unlike Wielaf's room, there wasn't a person inside to save. Not alive.

A skeleton lay on the floor against the wall, like the person who it belonged to had died scrunched up there. A dirty dress covered most of the bones. Anya sighed, sad. This person had died a long time ago. Anya couldn't have saved her. But she still felt guilty, like if she had somehow gotten here sooner . . .

A dull glint caught Anya's eye as she stood in the doorway. On the skeleton's finger was a ring, dirty and tarnished but unmistakably gold. Anya remained at the door. She wasn't about to go grave-robbing a poor skeleton who had been left in a dungeon.

She studied the skeleton's dress again. It had been white at one point. It was a nondescript shade of dirty cloth now. The apron half hung off the top, and Anya could make out embroidery along it. She shuffled closer to get a better look.

When she did, her mouth dried up.

Blue thread, in curling waves, marching across the top of the apron.

The key in her hand felt hot. Now she understood.

Her lip trembled as she pulled the gold ring off the skeleton's finger. She slipped it into her pocket, tucking it at the bottom so it wouldn't fall out.

Anya knew she needed to get going. They had to get Wielaf somewhere safe. And they had to get away if they were going to escape the monster—although she was starting to doubt that there was a monster at all. But she couldn't go. She couldn't leave the skeleton in the dress down there. She had to take it with them. She had to give it a proper burial.

At first, she thought of taking the skeleton's dress and making a bag out of it, but one tug on the fabric was enough to tear it. She didn't want to risk losing the bones if the dress tore apart. So she pulled her own apron off, though it wouldn't be big enough to just toss the bones in willy-nilly. She grumbled with irritation.

Then it hit her.

She took the skeleton's dress off—apologizing in quiet whispers the entire time—and laid it out flat on the floor. Then she took each long bone and stacked it on top of the dress. The oddly shaped ones sat on top, and the tiny bones, like fingers and toes, went into her pocket with the gold ring. Then she tied the skeleton's dress over the bones, gently, just tight enough to hold them in place.

"Anya?" someone called. It sounded like Håkon.

She called, "In here!" and kept working. She laid her own apron on the floor, set the bundle of bones on top of it, and tied the apron the other way, so there was cloth all around. The skeleton's dress should be able to hold the bones enough to keep them from sliding out of Anya's sturdier apron on the outside.

She felt strange without her apron on, but this whole situation was sort of strange.

Håkon peered in just as Anya stood, hefting the bundled bones. They were much lighter than she assumed they'd be. His eyebrows furrowed. "What are you doing?" He nodded to her bundle. "What's in there?"

"Another prisoner," she said. She didn't want to tell him who, not yet, so she squeezed past him and into the larger room outside.

Ivan and Alfhercht supported Wielaf, who had finally gotten his legs to hold him up. Sort of. He was flushed and panting.

"I'm sorry," Wielaf said. "He doesn't . . . feed me."

"You can eat once we're out of here," Ivan said. "Let's get you safe."

Wielaf nodded and let them help him out of the smaller room and into the arena. They hurried to the door that would take them into the stairwell to the top level, where they could go through the water lock, out the caverns, and into freedom in the forest. Håkon and Anya followed behind. Outside the arena perimeter, Wielaf sighed and said nothing. His stare at the place was the same as Alfhercht's had been. What had they been forced to do in there?

Fight, Alfhercht had said. Fight what? Fight who?

The stairwell to the upper level was just ahead of them, standing open.

And then the door slammed shut.

A cold wind rustled the hair on the back on Anya's head.

Maybe they were about find out who the elves had fought after all.

CHAPTER TWENTY-NINE

IVAN DASHED to the door and yanked on it. Håkon, still wielding his rusty sword, spun to look behind them. Wielaf gasped in a breath and groaned, "He's here."

The monster. Anya clutched the bones to her chest and turned to where the cold wind came from. In the center of the previously empty arena, a swirling tornado of stone gray and loamy black whipped up gusts of frigid air and threw stinging clouds of arena dirt into Anya's face. As she took steps back, a figure stepped through the tornado, in the same way that someone might walk through a waterfall. Once it emerged entirely, the tornado vanished, dissolving into tendrils of ominous smoke that curled upward.

The wind died, but the cold grew deeper. The thing was roughly man-shaped, but that was where its humanity ended and its monstrosity began. It wasn't just thin; it was desiccated. Anya had seen frostbitten fingers and toes before, back in Zmeyreka when fishermen weren't careful enough during winter ice fishing, shriveling into black sticks before they fell off entirely. This thing's entire body looked frostbitten. It was wearing a shredded *rubakha*, dingy and rusty and matted to the thing's body with some kind of metallic bands like frail armor. The bands wrapped around its hands, too. Its fingers were stacked with dirty rings.

No wonder Alfhercht had been afraid.

It said nothing. It just stared at them with eyes glittering in the dim light like fresh copper coins. Its eyes made Anya feel sick, like they could see straight inside her.

She had backed up to the point of being next to Ivan as he struggled with the door. It wouldn't open, no matter how much he banged on it. He snatched at the key around her neck.

"Use your key!" he said.

She let him take it, and he wiggled it around in the lock for a few seconds. It wouldn't open. "We have to get out of here!"

"Of course we do, Ivan!" Anya snapped.

Ivan glanced back at the creature, and his panicked breathing stopped as he held his breath.

"Do you see his eyes?" Ivan whispered. "Like coins?"

Anya nodded.

"They used to do that in Greece." He took a few rapid breaths. "When people died, they'd put coins on their eyes. For the ferryman. But what if . . . what if *that thing* is the ferryman?"

"You don't believe in a ferryman," Anya said, as though not believing in something would make it any less real.

When she spoke, her breath clouded in the air before her. Whatever the thing in the arena was, it was stealing all the heat away.

Håkon stumbled backwards, sword pointed at the creature, and said, "What is that thing?"

Anya and Ivan both shrugged. From behind Anya, Wielaf said, "It's a sorcerer."

Håkon turned only his head to look at Wielaf. "Just a sorcerer?"

Wielaf nodded.

"So it's a man, then?" Ivan asked, mouth hanging open.

"It used to be," Wielaf said. "But it's not like any sorcerer I've seen before." He directed his next warning at Ivan: "Don't use magic against it."

Ivan looked down at his hands. "Alfhercht told us. It steals magic."

Wielaf nodded. "That's why it would make us fight it. If you use magic against it, it will pull the threads away from you. And you'll . . . you'll never be able to . . ." He pressed his lips together and let his head drop forward.

A cold wrapped around Anya, no longer just from the creature. He had taken away Wielaf's magic. She was sure of it.

She took inventory of the people around her. Håkon had no magic as a human, so he was safe. Ivan had his water magic, but there was no water in here, so he was probably okay. Wielaf had already been stripped of his. Anya had never had any at all.

That left Alfhercht. The only one with magic. And with powerful magic, at that.

So they couldn't use magic to get away from this thing. But they couldn't just stand there, either. They had to use regular weapons, like Håkon's rusty sword and their insignificant knives. And that was it.

The creature moved forward.

Ivan shrieked.

Anya smacked his shoulder. "Stop it!" She could feel her own shriek beating against her chest, trying to force itself up her throat like vomit. Håkon held out his sword; the thing jangled as his arm shook.

"Alfhercht got out of here before!" Ivan said. "How did he get out?"

The creature continued to approach. Håkon backed up and over so he was half blocking Anya from its path.

Wielaf's free arm was moving, translating Ivan's question for Alfhercht. The elf responded to his brother with short, irritated gestures.

"It was different then," Wielaf said. "There were more of us. The thing was distracted. And if you'll recall, he had to leave me behind. So it's not the best plan."

The creature walked slowly. Not in a hurry. It knew they had nowhere to go.

"It's the only plan we've got," Ivan said. "What was it?"

Alfhercht nodded toward the other side of the arena, where the wall was crumbled, and spoke with one hand. Wielaf said, "He made the debris to the upper level by blasting out some columns and stuff. He climbed it. Then left the way you all came in."

Ivan grunted. "And you can't climb that."

"I cannot." Wielaf sighed. "I'll just . . . I'll stay."

Alfhercht looked furious. He snapped his fingers in the air, slamming his pointer and middle fingers against his thumb.

Wielaf said, "I was prepared to die down here. I still am."

The creature was at the edge of the arena. This close, Anya could see its knobby fingers with ragged fingernails jutting from the ends. One of the rings on its fingers was strangely shiny. A diamond on it flashed in the dim light. The creature grinned, ghoulish, teeth like tombstones. Anya braced herself for some kind of foul smell, but there was none. Just cold. Biting, gouging cold.

Its glowing copper eyes were focused on . . .

"Håkon," Anya whispered.

"I see it," he said. He moved away from the group. The creature followed him. "I'll distract it. You all go. Get Wielaf up top."

Anya said, "No, Håkon! That's insane!"

"You have a better idea?" he snapped.

"Anything *but that*."

Ivan grabbed Håkon's sleeve and yanked the sword away from him. "You don't know how to use a sword.

And you're the last . . . you know what you are. There are a million of me. Go help Wielaf."

Ivan shoved Håkon back toward the group and faced the monster. "Hey!" he yelled, waving the sword in the air. "I've got the sword now, you nasty-looking shrivel-beast!"

The creature glared at him with ice-cold irritation.

Then turned away.

And walked toward Håkon again.

CHAPTER THIRTY

HÅKON SCURRIED BACK to where Ivan waved his arms in the air. The creature followed. Then Håkon ran past Ivan. The creature followed again.

"Hey!" Ivan yelled.

The creature ignored him. It wouldn't stop following Håkon.

It knows. Anya shuddered. How could it know what Håkon was? And even if it did, why would it want him? He was a human and not magical, and—

Unless the creature could turn him back into a dragon.

"Håkon, don't let it touch you!" Anya yelled.

"Wasn't planning on it!" Håkon ran toward the other

end of the arena, canting this way and that, not entirely able to run as well as Ivan or Anya could.

The creature followed.

To Wielaf and Alfhercht, Anya said, "Let's go." They had to get Wielaf out of there. She'd have to trust that Ivan and Håkon could manage the monster on their own for a while. "Wielaf, we'll distract the monster while Alfhercht gets you through the water lock. Once you're out, Ivan can get me and Håkon through."

Wielaf watched the creature follow Håkon around on the other side of the arena. "Your friend . . . he's got a special magic."

"No," Anya said. "He doesn't have any at all."

"He's got to." Wielaf nodded toward Alfhercht. "Like this one does. The sorcerer collects magic. Alfhercht has one the sorcerer doesn't: sound magic. Your friend does as well."

Anya shook her head. "He doesn't." *Just dragon magic. Nothing special at all.*

They reached the rubble pile as Ivan let loose a battle cry and ran at the creature, sword raised. Anya didn't even have time to yell at him for being stupid. The creature lifted an idle hand and flicked a finger at Ivan. Ivan flew backwards, while his sword dropped from his hand and tumbled several feet away.

Håkon continued to zigzag around the arena while Ivan picked himself up.

Anya had to turn away from them to help Wielaf up the rubble. First she tossed her bundle of bones to the upper level, wincing at the dull clatter of bone against bone inside the cloth. She hoped nothing broke.

Alfhercht climbed up first, and Anya stayed behind Wielaf for support. Between the two of them, they maneuvered Wielaf to the upper level; the very end involved a lot of Alfhercht pulling and Anya pushing and Wielaf biting his lip so hard that he made it bleed a little.

All the while, from the arena behind them, Ivan shouted and screamed and yelled at the creature. And then he yelled as he flew through the air, lifted and thrown by the monster as it continued its slow advance toward Håkon.

Håkon, who was very clearly getting tired.

Once Wielaf was panting and wincing on the floor of the upper level, Anya gathered up her bones and lifted him to standing. She and Alfhercht helped Wielaf hobble toward the exit door.

"Hey!" Ivan yelled, out of breath. His sword was gone, but that wasn't stopping him. He grabbed a loose stone from the floor and hurled it at the creature. It hit the thing in the back of the head, making it stumble forward.

Up until that point, the creature hadn't made a single sound. But when Ivan's stone hit it, it bellowed out a sound like an avalanche of rocks and snow flattening a mountain forest. It whirled away from Håkon, who limped along a distant wall, toward Ivan.

Its eyes were no longer copper. They blazed white.

"Ivan!" Anya breathed.

Alfhercht looked down at Ivan. He was scrambling away from the creature, but it was moving faster now. Its strides lengthened, and it reached Ivan in seconds. It snatched his collar and dragged him up into the air, his feet swinging uselessly under him.

Alfhercht left Wielaf with Anya. He ran back the way they'd come, sprinting along the low wall.

Ivan kicked his feet outward, but they hit nothing. The creature continued to boom and scream.

Alfhercht whistled while he was running. Anya saw him twist his fingers in the air in front of him, and the familiar sound of his whistle turning into magic reached her ears.

"Alfhercht!" Wielaf gasped. "No!"

Håkon had gathered some stones and was throwing them at the monster, trying to distract it away from Ivan while staying away from it himself. He stopped as he watched Alfhercht run to the balcony closest to where the monster was. It hadn't noticed him yet, focused as it was on wringing the life out of Ivan.

Alfhercht stopped on the balcony and flung the whistle at the creature. The sound parted the air in front of him, a low rumble Anya felt in her marrow.

It hit the creature, slamming into its body like an invisible boulder.

The edge of it caught Ivan, too, smashing the side of his face. Blood squirted out of his nose.

The creature collapsed to the ground in a heap, dropping Ivan. Håkon limped as fast as he could toward his friend. He grabbed Ivan from where he lay on the floor, gasping and bleeding. Håkon half dragged Ivan to his feet, and the two hobble-ran toward the rubble pile.

The creature was up, rising like a *strigoi* from a crypt.

It blew toward them, arms up, pulling threads.

The rubble pile shifted.

"Look out!" Anya screamed.

Håkon grabbed Ivan and pulled him away from the

shifting stones, clearing the rubble just before the top of the pile crashed down.

Ivan and Håkon stood together as the dust settled, watching as their only means of escape rolled in various directions.

Alfhercht whistled, hands up, and the monster turned toward him.

"Don't!" Anya and Wielaf screamed at the same time. Anya dashed to Alfhercht and grabbed his arm. Irritated, he shrugged her hand away.

"It will take your magic!" Anya said.

Alfhercht turned to Wielaf and gestured rapidly. Wielaf said, "He says it has to see him work the magic. If he waits for it to turn . . ." He sighed and shook his head, then said to Alfhercht, "You surprised it! You won't a second time. It's not worth the risk!"

Alfhercht gritted his teeth, but he didn't try his magic again.

"How do we get them up here?" Anya asked. Panic was settling into her.

Wielaf shook his head and whispered, "I . . . I don't think we do."

CHAPTER THIRTY-ONE

IVAN AND HÅKON stood tall and grabbed rocks, wielding them as weapons. Ivan's nose still bled, and he wiped at it as he swayed in place. Even from her distance, Anya could see his eyes swimming in their sockets. Alfhercht's magic had hit him hard. But he was trying to stay on his feet and be of help. Ivan stared down the creature, which hadn't advanced at all. It just lingered outside the stone pile, grinning.

It pointed a gnarled finger at Håkon.

"No way!" Ivan yelled, slurring. He ducked, grabbed a rock, and hurled it at the creature.

The rock went wide. The creature lifted a hand, and the rock froze in midair. Then the creature clenched its fist shut, and the rock ground itself into dust as it hung there. The creature unclenched its fist, and the dust blew to the ground.

A rhythmic pounding vibrated the floor under Anya's feet.

"What's that?" she whispered to Wielaf. "Is the monster doing it?"

He shook his head. "I don't know. I've never—"

The door behind them flew open so hard, it ripped off its hinges. Anya grabbed Wielaf and Alfhercht and shoved them away, all of them diving to the floor as the door blasted past them and a huge, armored person charged into the room.

Water spattered all over the floor as Ilya crashed through the low wall of the balcony, a club stretched out in front of him as he soared through the air.

Anya gaped at him as he sped past. How had he known where they were? How had he gotten through the water lock? He was soaking wet, leaving water in a splattering trail behind him. He had realized they were missing, he had followed them, and he had swum the flooded cavern.

He'd said he was a good swimmer, hadn't he?

Anya scrambled up in time to see Ilya drop toward

the creature, the club up over his head, poised for what would surely be a fatal blow.

Fatal for a non-skeleton-monster, maybe.

Ilya brought the club down, cutting through the air, and the creature swung an arm back.

Ilya stopped in midair. His club jerked out of his fingers and flew across the room.

The creature turned its head to look at Ilya, copper eyes burning. It threw Ilya like a half-full sack of flour. He crashed into the edge of the balcony, slamming his head against the stone and dropping to the floor. He didn't get up.

As Ilya fell, the creature grabbed Ivan's hair and flung him away. Håkon scrambled backwards, but the creature reached him anyway. It held him in place and advanced until they were face-to-face.

Anya didn't realize she was running until she was around the edge of the balcony. The creature loomed over Håkon, one ragged fingernail stretched out toward him. It slashed at his arm, splitting his skin.

Håkon cried out and tried to grab for the gash in his arm, but the creature twisted his hand away. Past his skin, red blood welled and glittered. Impossibly, it didn't run down his arm. It just stayed inside the gash, sparkling like—

Like rubies.

His human skin had been torn away. His dragon scales were under. Shining through.

Håkon struggled against the creature, but it held him in place, so close that it was on the verge of enveloping Håkon in the cloud swirling around it.

Anya looked up. Ilya was climbing unsteadily to his feet, but he looked too groggy to be of help. Ivan was shakily raising himself up. Neither of them looked like they could do much.

So it was up to her.

In the back of her mind, Sigurd roared with cruel laughter.

No magical dagger to save you this time. You can watch the dragon die now.

He was right about the first part. She didn't have a magical dagger. Or her bow and arrows. She didn't have any magic. She just had herself. What could she do against a monster like the one below her?

Then Babulya's voice cut in.

Pray with your feet, Annushka.

Anya's lips parted a little. *Yes.* That was it.

She backed up to the wall, then ran as fast as she could. At the broken balcony edge, she leaped as far and as forcefully as she could, feet first. She pointed her toes up and jutted her heels down, praying this didn't break her ankles.

The creature held Håkon by the throat with one hand, and with the other he continued peeling Håkon's skin off his arm, revealing even more scales. Håkon screamed in pain, struggling, clawing at the creature holding him down.

Anya hit the creature with her heels. Its head snapped to the side, neck broken. Anya felt more than heard the wet crunch of his bones under her feet, and she would have gagged if she hadn't hit the ground just then, tangling up in the creature's ragged *rubakha*, then flying clear, her momentum shooting her across the floor. She scraped every exposed inch of her skin, and her dress tore as she rolled.

She looked up, head spinning. Håkon clutched at his arm near the creature, which lay motionless. Ivan was farther away, where the creature had thrown him. Ilya was—

Oh no.

Ilya stood, staggering toward the creature. If he got too

close, he'd see Håkon's scales. He'd see that Håkon wasn't a normal human boy. He'd kill him. Anya clawed her way to her feet, limping and hobbling to where Håkon knelt on the floor, holding his arm and moaning with pain.

She dropped to her knees in front of Håkon, frantic to hide his scales from the approaching *bogatyr*.

"M-m-my arm." Håkon's voice was shrill and hoarse. He lifted his hand up for a second. The scales under his human skin were wet with blood. He moaned again. "It burns!"

Anya tore a strip off the bottom of her dress and wrapped it around Håkon's wound. She wasn't sure if it would help his pain, but it would make it harder for Ilya to see what was under Håkon's skin.

Håkon watched her wrap his arm between nervous glances at the creature. "Did you kill it?"

"I don't think it can die," Anya said. "Especially not by someone like me."

The creature shuddered, as if agreeing with her. It moved one arm, and then the other.

Ilya stopped a few feet away from it, then held his hands up, plucking at threads. They glowed golden, shining, and he wrapped them into a ball as radiant as a fiery angel.

Anya stared. *Light magic.* That's what it had to be, right? It looked like Ilya held a tiny sun in his hand.

From the other side of the arena, Ivan yelled, "Gospodin, wait!"

They all looked up. Ivan limped toward them. He was scraped up and bleeding. Ivan's nose and chin were caked with blood, as was the front of his shirt. He still walked like he was half-asleep.

"It can steal magic!" Anya finished for Ivan. "If you use magic against it, it will take it away from you."

Ilya stared down at the creature, which was still trying to get up. Its head hung, floppy, on its broken neck. Dark liquid rolled off its head and spread into a puddle on the floor. Anya felt a deep sickness in her gut. No one could touch that puddle and live.

Ilya looked like he was going to use his magic anyway, lifting his glowing hands into the air.

Then the light vanished, and he ran to Anya and Håkon. He grabbed Anya and lifted her up, practically flinging her onto the balcony.

"Get that other boy out of here," Ilya said. "I've got your friends. We'll be right behind you."

Anya nodded. She hurried to where Wielaf and Alfhercht watched by the broken balcony wall. Wielaf held Anya's bundle of bones. She took it from him as Alfhercht got him to his feet, and the three of them limped out of the arena, scrambling into the long, dark hallway.

CHAPTER THIRTY-TWO

T HE DARKNESS MEANT they went slowly, carefully feeling along the walls, until brightness began to rise up behind them. They paused and turned. The golden glow grew brighter and brighter, and then Ilya appeared with his light magic held out in front of him again. Ivan and Håkon were behind him.

"Go!" he snapped, and they did.

The light skipped ahead in the air in front of Ilya. It trembled, and then an avalanche of rage made the cavern walls shudder and dust drop from the ceiling.

"The creature," Anya mumbled.

"It's up!" Ilya shouted. He came to a halt and waved

everyone else in front of him. "Go ahead of me! I'll stop it if it catches up!"

They obeyed and ran until they reached the water, where they stopped long enough for Ivan to tear a canyon in it. Ilya stared at it, then sighed.

"Well," he said, "I swam this when I came through this way. If only I had water magic, I could have walked it."

Ivan gawped. "You *swam this?*"

Ilya nodded. "I told you I'm a good swimmer."

"I'll say," Ivan mumbled, still shocked.

"Let's go!" Ilya said, herding them into the dry spot between the walls of water. Ivan went in front, and Alfhercht followed at the rear. Anya caught him pulling threads behind Ilya's back, expanding Ivan's bubble to fit them all.

They weren't far into the water at all—the top of the bubble was still open to the air—when the walls began to shake. More dust fell, and smaller stones. A crack splintered the wall, and a huge slice of rock slid out, crashing to the floor.

"It's pulling down the caves," Wielaf said, his voice barely above a whisper. "It knows it's losing us."

The cavern shook again. More stones fell; more cracks spread up the walls. Alfhercht pulled the bubble top shut, blocking out the falling dust and rocks, and the group went as fast as they could with their various injuries.

The cavern shook under them. The water around them sloshed, pressing against the water magic holding it back. Ivan strained, clenching his teeth and groaning with effort as a particularly strong wave hit his magic. A bucket-size spear of water shot through the bubble and hit Ilya's shirt, splashing over all of them.

"Ivan," Anya whispered, not wanting to distract him from keeping them safe.

Out of the corner of her eye, she saw Alfhercht reach out a hand and hook his finger in the air, drawing down and out. The bubble near Ivan bowed out, reinforced, and Ivan shot Alfhercht a grateful glance.

The floor under them shifted.

"Faster!" Ilya said.

Ivan went faster. He splayed out his hands, pushing the water apart as the wet floor under them cracked. Water squirted up through the cracks, tiny geysers until Alfhercht could press them back down. But doing that took his attention away from Ivan at the front. He left the geysers then, and they waded through water up to their ankles, then calves, then knees.

Over them, the ceiling of rock shook loose and fell.

One huge rock bounced against the water magic, then smashed through. Water poured in around it, and they all screamed until Ivan patched the hole.

His chest was heaving. The blood that had dried around his nose was wet again; with water or with new blood, Anya couldn't tell.

A strand of Anya's hair floated in front of her face, singularly annoying. She swept her finger, trying to clear it away.

It caught on her finger, and Ivan groaned. He collapsed to his knees, his head and shoulders just clearing the water.

Everyone stopped. Ilya grabbed Ivan's shoulders. "Ivan! What's wrong?"

Ivan shuddered. "We're going to die in here!"

Another strand of hair floated in front of Anya as she realized what it actually was.

Not hair.

Magic.

It wound out of Ivan's chest, reaching its other end toward her.

"We're not!" Ilya said. "Get up! We can make it."

Ilya had the threads too. From his chest. His face. All reaching toward Anya.

Ivan shook his head, hugging himself. "No. No, this is the end. I . . . I don't want to die down here." The threads multiplied, jutting out from him.

"Then don't!" Ilya bellowed. Water rushed in. Alfhercht was doing his best, but it wasn't enough.

There were threads everywhere, clogging up the bubble. Everywhere. Coming out of everyone. Even her.

She put her finger on one of the threads coming out of her own chest, and that barest touch brought a flood of terror into her mind. They would drown. The creature would catch them. Håkon would die. Ilya would kill Håkon. Alfhercht would kill them all.

They would drown.

They would drown.

Sigurd laughed from the water sloshing around them.

Anya grabbed the thread and drew her fingers along it. Rolled it gently, willing it to go away. It softened under her fingertips, and the fear softened too. The thread faded, fraying away, until it was gone. She didn't know how she knew how to do it. She just did.

The water was up to Anya's waist.

Anya reached out, grabbed the threads coming out of Ivan's chest, and frayed them. His shoulders un-bunched. His tears stopped. He blinked, surprised, and then he looked up at her. His eyes widened as he watched her roll his fear away, and he stood.

"Did you just—"

Her chest felt tight with excitement, even with everyone staring at her. "Maybe."

"Anya!" he yelled, and another jet of water blasted through the bubble.

"No time!" Anya said, pushing him back toward the front of the rapidly diminishing bubble.

Ivan trudged forward, moving his arms through the magic like he was treading the water that slowly filled the bubble. Alfhercht was at the rear, trying to push water out so they could move faster. But it was like bailing water out of a boat with a hole in the bottom. Sooner or later, the water would win, and the boat would sink.

Anya did what she could, still stunned at the threads all around. She frayed them away, one by one, and everyone moved faster and more purposefully.

Wielaf struggled to wade through, so Håkon hoisted him up and nearly carried him through the water, with Wielaf barely supporting himself on weak legs. Ilya's light shone out through the turbulent water around them, and Anya searched for the end of the tunnel. Dark rock stretched as far as she could see.

More rumbling, more cracks beneath them, more rocks from above. The cavern was coming down.

Håkon grabbed Anya's hand and pulled her to him. "Take him."

He meant Wielaf. She shook her head. "But what are you—"

"If that monster can peel my skin off and . . ." He glanced at Ilya and lowered his voice. "If he can make me a dragon, then I can do the same to myself. If I peel my human skin off, I can use magic. I can save you all."

"That's insane!" Anya hissed. "Ilya would kill you!"

"We're going to die anyway," Håkon said.

Wielaf stared at him, eyes wide. "A dragon?"

"Mind your own business," Håkon snapped.

"I'm not letting you do that," Anya said. "No way."

Håkon pulled the bandage down his arm, exposing his scales. "It's not your decision to make." He grabbed a piece of skin at the edge of the wound and pulled it up in a strip, sucking in a pained breath as he did.

"Stop!" Anya knocked his hand away and pulled the bandage up again. "No. I won't let you!"

"It's not up to you!" Håkon argued.

"It is so!" she snapped, tears burning her eyes. "I brought us here! This is my fault! I came here to get back someone I love, not to lose someone else. And I'm probably not going to get Papa, so if you disappear, I'll—" She bit her lip to keep it steady, but it didn't work, so she said nothing else.

Wielaf looked back and forth between them both, then grabbed Håkon's unbandaged arm. "Hold me up. I'm going to fall. So hold me up."

Håkon didn't right away, but Wielaf didn't wait for him. He pulled threads, pushing the water out and down. He almost immediately crumpled downward, the effort of the magic draining him of any strength he had left. Håkon caught him and hoisted him up. Wielaf's eyes closed, but he kept plucking strings.

Anya breathed out in relief. "I thought that monster had taken your magic, Wielaf."

He grimaced. In a voice like rustling leaves, he said, "Just the one that matters."

Wielaf pushed the water away around their feet, and Ivan could wade more easily. He tunneled through the watery darkness, and then the rock above them vanished. Ivan slammed the tunnel upward, and fresh air rushed over them.

They had made it.

They scrambled out of the water as the roof of the

tunnel finally gave out and collapsed. It sent a wave crashing up on Anya's legs where she stood on the shore. She watched the water rise and listened to the cracking and booming of caverns collapsing.

The bundle of bones in her arms seemed lighter. Like they knew they were free and were celebrating.

"We're out," Ivan whispered. He dropped to his knees, exhausted, and made the sign of the cross. "We're alive." He kissed his knuckles as he clasped his hands to his lips and prayed.

Håkon tried to set Wielaf down, but the elf's legs buckled beneath him and he hit the floor. Alfhercht dashed to him and held him up, cradling him in his arms.

In Alfhercht's trembling embrace, Wielaf's arms dropped and his eyes shut. He went limp.

Alfhercht gasped harsh breaths as he shook Wielaf gently, trying to rouse him. He looked up at Anya in panic.

Then he slipped his hands under Wielaf's shoulders and dragged him toward the mouth of the cave.

CHAPTER THIRTY-THREE

IVAN WAS THE FIRST to follow Alfhercht. He helped him carry Wielaf out of the cavern and into the purple twilight. Anya, Håkon, and Ilya followed. Ivan tried to stop outside the cavern, but Alfhercht kept going, into the woods.

"Wait!" Ilya called. "We can take him to the castle infirmary!"

Anya winced. Even if Alfhercht could hear what Ilya said, she knew the elf would never allow his brother to be taken into the city, let alone the castle.

He didn't go far into the woods. He set Wielaf down against a tree, turning Wielaf's head so the skin of his cheek touched the tree's bark. He set Wielaf's palm against the tree as well and held it there, watching Wielaf's face.

Anya stood next to Ivan and Håkon at a distance as threads laced around Alfhercht, a cocoon of fear. Ilya stepped up beside the three of them and murmured, "What's he doing?"

Anya had no idea, so she said nothing. The four of them watched the elves in silence, not quite knowing what to expect.

Nothing happened.

Just the one that matters.

Anya stepped forward and knelt by Wielaf, still crumpled against the tree. Alfhercht was frantic, pushing his brother's hand harder against the tree's bark, like something was supposed to happen.

Anya put her hand on Wielaf's shoulder. It rose and fell with shallow breaths. She looked at Alfhercht's panicking face and said, "It took his magic."

Alfhercht watched her speak, then shook his head. He pressed Wielaf's hand harder. Nothing. He was smashing his brother's hand against the tree's bark, so Anya put her fingers on top of his and pulled them back. She set Wielaf's hand in his lap and said to Alfhercht, "I'm sorry."

Alfhercht hitched a breath and knelt by Wielaf, brushing his dirty hair off his forehead. Wielaf's eyelid twitched at the touch but didn't open.

Håkon was at Anya's side then, blue eyes wide. He stared at Wielaf's chest, reaching a trembling hand up to point.

Then he darted his hand forward and pinched the air. He breathed fast.

He had grabbed a thread. What else could it have been?

"Anya," Håkon whispered, "can you see it?"

"No," she said. "A thread?"

He nodded. "It's . . ." He shuddered. "I don't like it."

"What is it?"

"I don't know," he said. "But it's breaking."

Anya put her hand against Wielaf's neck. He was pale and cool. Under her fingertips, his heartbeat was slow and stuttering. He was limp everywhere. He had been through so much, and now . . .

She held her breath. He was dying.

What thread was Håkon holding?

"Don't let go," Anya whispered.

Håkon squirmed. "It feels different from my other

magic. It's so heavy." He pinched the thread with his other hand and then said, "Anya! It broke!"

Under Anya's fingertips, Wielaf's heartbeat stilled.

Alfhercht grabbed Wielaf's shoulders and shook him. Håkon cried out and pinched his fingers tighter. "He's going to make me drop it!"

"Alfhercht, stop!" Anya yelled.

He didn't. He grabbed Wielaf's face and tried to lift it up. Wielaf was limp. Floppy.

Ivan was there then, grabbing Alfhercht around the arms and hauling him backwards. Alfhercht kicked and struggled, but Ivan succeeded in pulling him away. He wasn't shaking his brother anymore. Meanwhile, Håkon panted with exertion.

"Can you un-break it?" Anya asked. Her throat felt so tight, she almost didn't get the words out.

"I don't know." Håkon strained, trying to bring his fingers together. They wouldn't budge.

Threads of fear came off him, sharp. Panic. He was sweating. His breath came fast and shallow.

"It won't move," he said through clenched teeth.

Anya touched his threads of fear, rolling them between her fingertips. Fraying them away, like she'd done to Ivan. "Keep trying."

He nodded. His breaths came slower. He pulled again, and his fingers inched closer.

Behind them, Alfhercht had gone still. No more sounds of struggling reached Anya's ears.

Håkon gritted his teeth so hard, they squeaked. His hands were white from pinching, and he shook as he strained against the thread. Fear kept coming back, sprouting up anew as soon as Anya frayed those threads away. She kept at it.

Then his fingers touched.

Wielaf inhaled hard.

Ivan let go of Alfhercht. The elf collapsed next to Wielaf and pulled him into a tight embrace. Wielaf's arms rose up and pushed at his brother. When Wielaf spoke, his words were slurred. "What are you doing?"

Alfhercht refused to let him go.

Anya looped her arm around Håkon's shoulders. He shook, damp with sweat, and looked down at his hands.

"I have magic," he said. "I don't like it."

From behind Anya, Ilya spoke. "I never thought I'd see that kind of magic used for good."

Anya and Håkon turned. Ilya's arms hung at his sides, and he stared at Håkon.

"What magic?" Håkon asked.

"Death."

Anya opened her mouth to speak, but beneath their feet, the ground rumbled. Anya tensed, certain the creature from the arena had followed them somehow, but the sound of whinnying replaced that fear with a new one. Horses—a ton of them—were riding closer.

Soldiers. Horsemen. The tsar.

Alfhercht glanced toward the noise, and Ilya took a step toward them. Wielaf didn't notice, but Alfhercht did. He put himself between the *bogatyr* and Håkon, fingers curled into claws, glaring darkly.

Alfhercht inhaled and pursed his lips.

"No!" Anya put herself between Ilya and Alfhercht. She held her hands up, hoping neither of them would be willing to go through her to get to the other. "Ilya, just let them go. Please."

Ilya stood his ground, his face pulled into a scowl. "That boy is the Nightingale."

"We know," Anya said. "He wanted his brother. That's all."

Ilya nodded toward Håkon. "And this one's a death magician."

"He's not going to hurt anyone," Anya said. "Right, Håkon?"

"R-right," Håkon said.

Ilya looked down at her and then pointed to Ivan. "And you two are helping them?"

Anya nodded, knowing that the confession was going to get her in trouble.

Ilya and Alfhercht stared at each other as the rumbling of the horses came nearer. Then Alfhercht ducked beside Wielaf and pulled him to his shaking feet. He carried his brother back toward the trees, and both of them vanished into the dark woods.

Anya stayed where she was, arms still up. Ilya didn't move to chase the elves. He just looked down at Anya and said, "That was brave, little girl. Foolish. But brave."

"I guess Ivan's rubbing off on me, then," Anya mumbled. Suddenly, horse after horse emerged from the trees around them. They were warhorses like Alsvindr, bedecked in plating and royal standards. The first person to approach looked very familiar, and only after Ilya dropped to a knee and bowed did Anya realize who he was.

The tsar.

Everyone around him was dressed for war, but he wore a deep green silk *kaftan* and a long fur-trimmed robe rather than armor. His leather boots were shined and reflected the torchlight from the riders near him. His eyes had glowed like fire at the banquet, but now they looked less fiery and more like . . . copper. Anya's tongue stuck to the roof of her mouth as she gazed at his eyes, then at his finger. His diamond ring flashed.

Riding beside him was Vasilisa, and behind her were Misha and her retinue of archers. Packed into the forest behind them were dozens of soldiers with torches. The density of threads rising from the assembled army was almost overwhelming, and Anya gaped at them.

Before she or anyone else could bow, the tsar reached out a hand. "Rise, Ilya, my friend. Be cautious! The Nightingale is in these woods."

Anya's heart seized. It tried to beat but seized again. Would Ilya tell the tsar where Alfhercht and Wielaf had gone? Would he tell the tsar about Håkon? She scooted closer to her friend, ready to shove him toward escape if Ilya gave them away.

Ilya licked his lips, then shook his head. "I haven't seen any sign of the Nightingale, Your Majesty. But there's something even more troubling."

Anya glared at Ilya. He was going to tell the tsar about Håkon! She grabbed Håkon's arm, fingers digging into his skin. She tried to tell him to run, but she couldn't get out a sound.

"Oh?" the tsar said. He turned a hard stare toward Anya. "These troublemakers?" Without waiting for Ilya to answer, the tsar shouted, "Guards! Take them!"

From the trees behind the tsar, armored guards advanced toward Anya.

Her tongue unstuck. "No!" Anya yelped.

"Wait!" Ilya protested.

"Father!" Vasilisa spoke louder and sharper than anyone else. They all fell silent. The guards stopped in their tracks. Vasilisa pointed to Ivan. "This is one of your fools, Your Majesty. He came here to find and capture the Nightingale."

The tsar lifted his chin. "Did he? Well, fool, have you done what you came here to do? Have you freed my people from the violence of the Nightingale?"

Anya felt herself simmering, wanting to speak up in Alfhercht's defense, but knowing it would only get her in trouble. She wanted to grab those threads of fear over the army, fray them away. But she was too far away, and the tsar was right there. It was one thing to do magic in Zmeyreka or in a flooded cave. It was quite another to do it mere feet from the tsar himself.

Ivan said, "Well, er, Your Majesty, we—"

"Yes, we did," Anya said.

The tsar frowned at her, and her blood froze in her veins. "Who. Are. You?"

"Ivan's companion," Anya said, surprised her voice was still holding. She stepped in front of Håkon. "We, um, found the Nightingale. And we drove him away. He'll never bother any traveler to Kiev ever again."

"I decreed the Nightingale be brought alive," the tsar spat. "How dare you defy your tsar?"

Ilya put his hand on Anya's shoulder. "There was no other way. They did what was necessary."

Anya was grateful to Ilya, but she still shook so hard, she was afraid she was going to collapse. She wished the tsar would speak to someone else, but he kept talking to her.

"Letting him escape is even worse than killing him," the tsar hissed. "How is he to be punished, then?"

Anya didn't think he deserved punishment, but she couldn't say that. So she just stood and trembled.

The tsar looked disgusted. He turned to Vasilisa. "Was this your idea?"

"No," she said angrily. "I told them to—"

"To let a criminal escape justice." The tsar's nostrils flared. "That's a move of weakness. Is that what you're going to be? A weak ruler?"

Vasilisa pressed her lips together into a bloodless line.

He held her eyes for a long few seconds and then said softly, "I know you won't be a weak ruler. Because you won't *be* a ruler at all. Return to the castle." Vasilisa opened her mouth, but the tsar silenced any protest with a single word. "Now."

She snapped her mouth shut and jerked her horse's head around. The horse leaped into a gallop right away. Misha and the rest of her guard followed.

When they'd gone, the tsar pointed a finger back and forth between Anya, Ivan, and Håkon. In a tired, exasperated voice, he said, "Take them into custody. Put them in interrogation. We'll find out where they've hidden the Nightingale."

Guards stepped toward Anya, and she backed up into Ilya. He set his hands on her shoulders, and she expected him to shove her forward into waiting manacles.

But he pulled her back, putting himself between her and the guards. He corralled Ivan and Håkon behind him as well.

"Ilya," the tsar growled, "move."

"No." Ilya squared his shoulders. "These children are not a danger. The Nightingale isn't even a danger. There's something beneath Kiev, Your Majesty. Something malevolent. Something . . ." He took a deep breath. "Something evil."

"Ridiculous," the tsar said. "They're lying to you."

"I saw it!" Ilya roared. "I fought it! I stood close to it, my king, and I could feel the rot of its evil intent. There is a sickness spreading in the foundations of Kiev. These children are not important. Let them go. You have more dire problems to address."

The tsar snarled at Ilya. "You presume to tell me how to run my kingdom?"

"I do!" Ilya dug his heels into the earth. "You asked us, the *bogatyri*, to make Kievan Rus' a holy place. And I'm telling you, it has an unholy boil festering within it. You must do something!"

The tsar's eyes slid away from Ilya and settled on the trio behind him.

Or did they?

No. They looked past Anya. Past Ivan. And dug into Håkon. The tsar glared at him, his eyes searing copper rings in the torchlight. His hands tightened on his charger's reins. Was he staring because he had noticed how much Håkon looked like the princess? Or had he noticed . . . something else?

"Very well," he said, looking away from Håkon. "You're

right, my friend. As always. Yes. Come back to the city. Tell me about this thing under Kiev." He waved an idle hand at the trio. "Bring them. Not as prisoners," he clarified. "Let them stay as guests and leave in the morning."

Ilya thanked the tsar. A moment later, the entire regiment had turned around and was heading back to Kiev.

Anya, Ivan, and Håkon lingered with Ilya as the horses moved ahead of them. Ilya loomed over them and said, "There's more going on here. I can feel it."

"You saw what we saw," Anya said.

Ilya nodded and then looked around. "Those boys can't go home, you know. The elves."

"Why not?" Anya asked. She had thought Ilya was on their side. Was he not going to let Alfhercht escape the tsar's cruel injustice?

Ilya's answer was possibly even worse than demanding they be turned in. "They have no home anymore," he said softly. "They used to have cities everywhere in the western forests. But after Grand Princess Olga toppled the Drevlian capital, the rest of their cities started collapsing too. The Alvolk, the Álfish . . . I think you'd be hard-pressed to find even one village anywhere south of Ál-fheim, and that's even shrinking now." He shook his head.

"I hope I'm wrong. I hope they can reach their home and live in peace."

Anya watched the dark forest. No home? She knew the feeling of being faced with homelessness. Alfhercht and Wielaf were free from Kiev, but where would they go?

Ilya interrupted Anya's thoughts with a huge hand on her kerchief, mussing her hair. "You did very good down there. You're all very brave to stand in the face of such evil."

Ivan's voice, small and forlorn, came from behind them. "What was that thing, anyway?"

Anya remembered what Wielaf had said: a sorcerer. But sorcerers were just people who had gotten very good at their gifted magic. She had always considered Babulya a sorceress, but now she wasn't so sure. Could Babulya do what that creature in the arena had done? What kind of magic had that sorcerer gotten good at?

Ilya cracked his knuckles. "I don't know. Something that shouldn't be there, whatever it is."

Anya agreed with him. "Gospodin Ilya, thank you for not telling the tsar about the Nightingale."

Ilya nodded, then looked out into the forest. "I wish them luck, wherever they end up. If they come back here, though, I won't be able to let them go again." He looked at Håkon. "And you. The boy with death in his fingers."

Håkon shook his head. "I don't—"

"You do," Ilya said. "That's a rare magic. You can do evil things with a magic like that."

"I won't," Håkon said. "I would never."

Ilya nodded. "See that you don't, or I'll have to come have words with you. Now, should we get back to the castle, where it's warm?"

Anya said, "I don't think we should go into Kiev again."

Ilya looked down at her, surprised. "Is that right?"

Anya had a terrible feeling in her gut in the form of copper and diamond, but she couldn't figure out what it meant. She knew what made it worse, though: the thought of returning to the castle.

"We want to go home too," she said.

"Well, I won't stop you," Ilya said. He squatted in front of her so they were eye to eye, and he said, "I'm blessed to have met you. Your parents would be proud."

Anya's lip trembled. Her heart felt too big for her chest. She nodded, unable to thank him or tell him he was her hero or ask which way the road north was. He smiled at her and stood, then nodded to Ivan and Håkon before sparking golden threads of light magic in one hand. He walked away, his self-made light the last thing to fade in the dark forest.

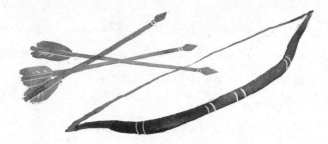

CHAPTER THIRTY-FOUR

ANYA, IVAN, AND HÅKON stood in the dark forest for a few minutes, trying to put their thoughts together. Håkon looked particularly troubled, staring off into the distance.

Finally, Ivan said, "I wish we were home."

Anya did too. Desperately.

Håkon just sighed.

Footsteps made all of them tense up. For a moment, Anya thought it might be the elves, but she banished that thought the moment she remembered Alfhercht's complete silence in the trees. They wouldn't have made noise.

The person coming out of the trees was dressed in

armor, her golden hair braided around the crown of her head. Vasilisa, with Misha behind her. Why were they there? Had they come to take the three of them to the castle?

Anya squared her shoulders. "We're leaving."

"I know." Vasilisa seemed less prickly than usual. She was bordering on casual. "I wanted to thank you, since my father won't."

"For what?" Anya said.

"You got rid of the Nightingale," Vasilisa said. "You didn't do it the way I wanted you to, but he's still gone. He won't attack people anymore. That's what matters. So thank you."

Anya watched Vasilisa, scanning around her for threads that would betray any fear in her. None. Misha, on the other hand, had a few wafting up from him.

"You're welcome," Anya said.

"Here." Vasilisa reached behind her to where something was secured to her back. She pulled it off and tossed it at Anya, who realized what it was even before she caught it.

"My bow!" Anya gripped it close. She'd forgotten all about it in the madness of the day. Vasilisa also had her arrows, and Misha had Ivan's staff.

Vasilisa said, "I know I'd want my weapons back if I left them somewhere, so we brought them to you."

"Thank you," Anya said. She hesitated, then pressed forward. "I know our deal was that you were going to send for my papa if I brought the Nightingale back alive, and we didn't hold up our end, but—"

Vasilisa shushed Anya with a hand in the air. "I already sent for him."

A warm feeling spread out from Anya's heart. "You did?"

"I did." Vasilisa's mouth cracked upward, a smile that seemed uncomfortable on her face, and then she punched Misha in the arm. He came forward, holding two small pouches in his hands.

"Rewards," he said as he handed one to Anya. "Some rubles."

He hesitated handing her the other one. It was a little bigger than the pouch with rubles. Finally, he said, "And this one is from my family. When I couldn't find you this morning . . ." He frowned. "We were all worried. My father said blessings for you. And when I came back to the castle to look for you, I brought a gift from us."

Anya took the second pouch as she said, "You didn't have to bring me a gift."

"My mother likes you," Misha said. After a slight hesitation, he added, "We all do."

Anya suppressed a blush and opened the pouch. Inside was a small cloth square wrapped around a handful of rubles. The cloth was embroidered with a colorful hand. In the center of the hand's palm, a blue eye stared out at Anya.

Misha pointed. "That's a *hamsa*, the hand of Miriam. It's for good luck. Ilana was making it for me, I guess, but she told me today that you need it more than I do. She said sorry it's not finished."

Anya ran her finger over the embroidery. It didn't look unfinished. "It's beautiful. Tell her thank you."

Misha nodded. "I will. And those rubles are for *tzedakah* when you get back home. Because *tzedakah* is a mitzvah, and someone doing a mitzvah can't be harmed. So you'll be safe as you travel." He shrugged and smiled.

Anya laughed. "I should do *mitzvot* more often."

"I think you're doing plenty." He surprised her by pulling her into a hug. *"Leich l'shalom."*

Anya nodded against his shoulder. *Go toward peace.* *"Leich l'shalom* to you, too."

They broke apart, and Anya stepped back to where

Ivan and Håkon waited. Håkon had one hand on his bandaged arm, and he was staring openly at Vasilisa.

She was staring back.

Anya glanced back and forth between Ivan and Håkon. Ivan shrugged.

"You should go," Vasilisa said finally. "Before my father figures out you've gone."

Anya nodded. "Thank you."

Vasilisa returned the nod. Her eyes found Håkon one last time, and she said, "You're welcome."

✦ ✹ ✦

It took Anya, Ivan, and Håkon a while to find Alfhercht's tree again. The darkness didn't make anything easy, and neither did the fact that they were afraid to travel too long on any road near the castle. When they finally came upon the tree, Anya knocked her knuckles on the side of it and whispered loudly, "Alfhercht? Wielaf? Are you here?"

No response. Just the dry rustling of autumn leaves.

Ivan stood with slumped shoulders, and Håkon kept inspecting his torn skin beneath the bandage around his arm.

"They must have left already," Ivan said. "Gone back to wherever their home is."

"Ilya said their home is gone," Anya said.

Håkon moved the bandage back so it covered his entire swath of exposed scales. "How would Ilya know all that?"

"He's a *bogatyr*," Ivan said. "That's his job."

"We should go back home too," Anya said. "It's going to take a while."

She wasn't looking forward to the long walk north. They had some money now, thanks to Misha and Vasilisa, but they didn't know exactly how to get back to Zmeyreka. It would be a long, long journey.

Anya sat down next to the tree, her back pressing against its smooth bark, and set her bundle of bones to her side. She pulled her knees up to her chest and wrapped her arms around her legs. She ejected a shaky sigh. This trip hadn't been a complete disaster, but it was close. Anya had made a fool of herself in front of the first rabbi she'd ever met. She had gotten her friends stuck in the woods with no food and no way to get home. And now the tsar knew who she was, but not in a good way.

Håkon sat down next to her, on the other side of the package, and put his arm over her shoulders. He said nothing while Ivan sat on her other side and likewise put his arm around her. They sat like that for a while, and then

Håkon said, "It could be worse. We could have drowned in that cave."

"We could have gotten arrested and dragged back to Kiev," Ivan added.

"Or the tsar could have shown up a minute earlier and caught Alfhercht and Wielaf," Håkon said.

Ivan nodded. "Ilya could have seen Håkon's scales."

"I'd be a dead dragon, Anya." He said it with such matter-of-factness that Anya snorted out a laugh.

"I think the worst thing that could have happened," Ivan said, "is that I could have lost either of you. But I didn't. We have a long journey home, but we'll manage. We'll make it."

Anya sniffed, smiling but still sad. "You lost Alfhercht, though. You liked him."

Ivan flipped a hand in the air. "Oh sure, he was handsome. And magical. And he saved my life. His hands were so warm." He sighed. "But he did make my nose bleed. I'll find someone just as amazing as him. Or I'll pine for him for the rest of my life."

Håkon nodded. "That's probably more likely."

"You're not allowed to make fun of me," Ivan said. "Only people who have been in love can make fun of my pining."

"Ah well," Håkon said quickly. "I can't say anything, then. Because I've never been in love."

"Me neither," Anya said.

"I have," a voice said from around the other side of the tree. Wielaf materialized into being, leaning against the side of the tree. "So can I make fun of you?"

He smiled weakly. He didn't look healthy by any means, but he didn't look on the verge of death anymore. His skin was darkening toward a gold similar to his brother's, with even darker swirls patterning his arms. His hair was still ragged, but his eyes were a brownish orange.

Anya scrambled to her feet. Håkon followed. Ivan stayed on the ground, blushing furiously.

"You're still here!" Anya said. "And you look so much better! Your magic *does* work!"

Wielaf ran his hand over the tree's bark. "No. It's gone. But I'm still Alvolk. There's something in my bones that not even that creature can take away." He craned his neck, looking upward. "The trees won't talk to me. But they'll heal me. I'll take it."

He didn't sound like he was ready to take that. Anya said, "I'm sorry."

Wielaf shrugged. "Alfhercht wanted to stay in case you came back. I wanted to stay and see what the deal is with . . ." He paused. "Are all of you dragons, or just him?" He pointed to Håkon.

Håkon clutched at his arm. "It's just me."

"Ah." Wielaf used his hands to speak as he said words aloud. "That's interesting. Alfhercht had no idea."

"Where is he?" Anya asked.

"Oh," Wielaf said. "He's hiding. Because of what—"

Alfhercht appeared then, dashing out of the trees, smacking Wielaf's hands down. He spoke furiously, sharply with his hands. Wielaf didn't translate for the others. He just laughed as he and Alfhercht spoke back and forth. At one point, Wielaf very clearly pointed at Ivan. Alfhercht tried to snatch his hand out of the air, but he wasn't fast enough.

"Anyway," Wielaf said, focusing on Håkon, "we wanted to make sure you three were all right. We thought dragons were extinct. The tsar would turn himself inside out to get his hands on you."

"I know," Håkon said dourly.

Anya watched Ivan and Alfhercht pointedly not looking at each other. She smiled to herself a little, then pulled Ivan to his feet. "We're grateful that you stayed. Could we ask you a favor?"

Wielaf bowed to her. "Anything for you. We will never repay you for what you did for us. But we'll try."

"We need to get home," Anya said. "But we're pretty ill-equipped. Could you help us get there?"

Wielaf beamed. "Absolutely!" He pointed his thumbs at Alfhercht and Ivan. "That will give these two a chance to—"

Alfhercht's hands were up, and Wielaf's voice cut off. His last words—*chance to*—bounced around the clearing before ricocheting off into the trees.

Wielaf tried to speak again, couldn't, and sighed. He crossed his arms and looked exasperated.

"It will give us all a chance to talk," Håkon said.

Wielaf nodded, grinned, and clapped Håkon on the shoulder of his uninjured arm. The tree opened up, and they gathered some supplies from inside: backpacks, blankets, an assortment of random items they'd be able to trade for food or board if they needed it. Anya put her bones inside her own pack, making sure they were cushioned. Alfhercht put one of his glowing stones into his pack, and another into Håkon's.

While everyone else continued to pack, Anya cleaned the blood off Ivan's face so he wouldn't horrify any other travelers they came across. Her scrapes and bruises were all superficial, and she cleaned them off as much as she could. There wasn't much she could do about Håkon's arm past bandaging it. All of them put on clothing from Alfhercht's tree so they weren't traveling in torn or bloody clothes.

Ivan suffered Anya's scrubbing of his face, then went back to shoveling things into his pack until it was bursting and lopsided. He shouldered it crookedly and zipped away from the tree, not waiting for any of the rest of them. Anya and Håkon exchanged a knowing look as he ran off.

They followed him out to the road, Anya and Håkon in front, Wielaf and Alfhercht behind. Anya ducked her head close to Håkon.

"Obviously, we can't travel on the road much," Anya said. "But I think with Wielaf and Alfhercht, we'll be able to—*oof!*"

She bumped into Ivan, who had come to a stop at the edge of the road.

"Ivan!" Anya snapped. "What—"

She stopped when she saw the hut sitting in the middle of the dark road. The door was open. Lena stood in the doorway, grinning. "Want some help?"

CHAPTER THIRTY-FIVE

THEY DIDN'T GET a chance to answer. Anya blinked, and they were inside Lena's hut. The door was shut, and the hut was swaying as it flew, however it did. The two children and the dragon in human skin stood around the crackling fire. Alfhercht and Wielaf lingered by the front door, far away from the flames, blinking with alarm.

Lena patted Håkon on his torn arm. "I see you figured out how to remove your disguise." She tutted. "There's a less painful way, you know."

Håkon scowled. "I thought we were going to die. And I wouldn't have had to take it off if I still had magic as a human."

"Oh, you." Lena smooshed his cheeks with both hands, puckering his mouth. "Of course you had magic."

Håkon frowned. "Death magic."

She kept smooshing his cheeks as she said, "How was it?"

"I didn't like it," he said.

"Well, lucky for you, when you're a dragon, you don't have it."

Håkon pulled his face away from her squeezing hands. "How does that work?"

"Dragons have their magic," Lena said. "And humans have theirs."

"That doesn't make—"

"It does make sense if you think about it," she said, flitting away from him before he could say anything else. She went to where Alfhercht and Wielaf stood. "You picked up friends."

Wielaf said, "Who are you?"

"I'm Lena," she said. "I think you'll like it in Zmeyreka." She winked at Alfhercht and then turned from them.

Anya remained by the fire. Her backpack seemed to weigh a thousand pounds. Inside, the bones sat, safe and wrapped up. The ring in her pocket seemed to whisper to her. But she didn't want to present either to Lena. She was suddenly struck with the fear that Lena hadn't ever meant for her to pick up the ring or the bones, and that she'd just desecrated a corpse for no reason.

But the skeleton's apron. The blue waves. She looked at Lena's white apron with its own curling blue waves across the top.

Håkon and Ivan sat by the fire, chatting and poking at Håkon's arm. Wielaf and Alfhercht stayed by the door, their hands flying. Lena walked closer to Anya and said in a soft voice, "Did you use my key?"

Anya nodded. "That's how we got Wielaf out."

"Oh good." Lena stopped just in front of Anya. "Did you find anything else?"

Anya swallowed hard and pulled the ring out of her pocket. Before she handed it to Lena she said, "You knew my papa wasn't in Kiev."

Lena nodded. "I did."

"Why did you take us there?"

Lena sighed. "It was dishonest of me to do that. I'm sorry." She nodded toward Alfhercht and Wielaf. "They didn't deserve to be trapped there anymore."

"It's okay," Anya said softly. "Neither did you."

Lena smiled, and Anya opened her palm. The ring

glowed in the firelight. Lena's lip trembled when she saw it. Her eyes brightened. She picked up the ring.

"I got something else, too," Anya said. She went to swing the pack off her shoulder, but Lena stopped her with a gentle hand.

"I know," Lena said. "Thank you. You don't . . . I don't need to see those. You know what to do with them."

Anya nodded.

Lena held the ring in her palm, clutching it close to her heart. She sighed, kissed the ring, and handed it back to Anya.

"Tell him I still love him," Lena said. "Please."

Anya knew who. She put the ring back in her pocket. "Lena, how did this happen? Your ring . . . You died—"

"I knew a secret," Lena said. She glanced at Håkon, who picked at his peeling human skin. He wasn't paying attention to Lena and Anya. None of them were.

"Is that why you're helping us?" Anya asked. "For Håkon?"

Lena's sigh was heavy on its way out. "Of course for him. Always for him." She smiled with tears gathering in her eyes. "It doesn't matter that we found him in a wrecked boat in a river. He's my son, and I would die a thousand more times to protect him."

"Are you going to tell him who you are?" Anya asked.

Lena sighed. "I don't know. He was so little when I left. He wouldn't remember me."

"I think he'd want to know," Anya said.

"Hmm." Lena watched Håkon replace the bandage over his arm. "Maybe I will."

Anya smiled, but then the memory of the creature in the dungeon snuffed her smile out. Lena had been there. She had probably met it. Anya trembled. "Do you know what that monster was? The one under Kiev? It cut his skin off. It knew."

Lena sucked in a sharp breath, but before she could say anything, the hut came to a stop.

"We're here!" Lena trilled, her voice steady. She wiped the tears out of her eyes and swept to the door. "All right, all right. Ivan and Anya, I'm going to drop you off on the road. Håkon and Alfhercht and Wielaf, I'll take you into the woods near Håkon's house."

"Can you just drop us off *at* my house?" Håkon asked.

"No." Lena put her hands on her hips. "I know of a nice tree I think the elves will like."

Wielaf translated for Alfhercht, and both of them lifted curious eyebrows. "Do you expect us to stay in their village?" Wielaf asked.

"For a while," Lena said. "I know you feel better, but you've still got some healing to do."

Alfhercht looked like he was going to argue, but Wielaf put one hand on his brother's arm. "You're right."

Lena smiled and scooted up next to Håkon. "So. Håkon. What was it like being a human?"

"Terrible," Håkon said, and Lena laughed.

"Pretty weird, huh?"

He stuck his tongue out and plucked at his *rubakha*. "I hate clothes."

"Clothes are the worst," Lena agreed. "Would you like to go back?"

Håkon's eyes widened. He looked so excited, and Anya knew she should be happy for him. But for some reason, her heart sank. She didn't want him to be a dragon again. She liked his more animated expressions, and the way it was easy to hug him. But it wasn't Anya's decision, was it?

He looked up at her, and she plastered a smile on her face. "You could be a dragon again!" she said, trying her best to sound glad. "And you'd have your old magic back."

"Yeah," Håkon said, but he didn't sound as happy as Anya thought he would. He peered at Lena. "There's no way I could be both, could I?" He flexed his fingers. "I kinda like hands, now that I'm used to them. And I like being able to go places without having to be afraid of being seen."

She shook her head. "It's one or the other. I'm sorry."

"Figures," he mumbled. He glanced at Anya. "I . . . I don't know."

"Well." Lena leaned close to him. "I bet we can figure something out." She kissed his forehead as she'd done before, and where her lips touched, a red light burst out of his skin. It was warm and shone so bright, Anya had to shut her eyes. Just like the first time. The red light filled the hut, encasing all of them in its warmth, and she tucked her face into the crook of her elbow to keep out the searing brightness.

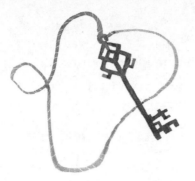

CHAPTER THIRTY-SIX

WHEN THE LIGHT FADED, cold air replaced it. The road was dark, but a distant light rose over the familiar cliffs of the river valley. Dawn. How long had they been gone? Three nights and two days, since Thursday night. Long enough to panic everyone.

The hut was still there, and as they watched, it blew away like it was made out of dust. When it was completely gone, Ivan stuck his hand where it had been.

"Amazing," he whispered.

Anya said, "What are we going to say to your family?"

Ivan shrugged. "We were gone for two days. Where could we have walked to and back from in two days?"

"Nowhere," Anya said. "Mologa, maybe, but—"

A commotion bounced around the trees in the cold night air, and Anya very clearly heard Ivan's father, Yedsha, say, "Okay, we can search for Vosya and Anya in a line. We'll do the west side of the road this morning, and the east side . . ."

Yedsha rounded the corner, and the words died on his tongue. Anya had never seen him looking so haggard and so frantic. As soon as he saw Ivan, he blurted, "Vosya!" and ran to him. He grabbed Ivan in his arms and hugged him, squeezing so tightly that Ivan squeaked out a breath and made no other sounds.

Marina and Ivan's brothers minus Dvoyka and Troyka came around the bend. But they weren't alone. Verusha and Olya Dragutinovna and their mama were with them, and Mila Nikolaevna and her mama, and Father Drozdov, and the entire Lagounov family, and the Melniks, and Demyan Rybakov, and Kin, and even some of the old fishermen, who lagged behind the main group.

When Ivan's brothers saw him, they yelled his name and joined their father, jumping on him and knocking him over. Six Ivans rolled around on the road, hollering at the youngest one that they were all so happy to see him.

Marina followed, but she didn't go to Ivan. She ran to Anya instead, hugging her close. In a whisper heavy with emotion, she said, "You're back. Oh, thank the heavens, you're back."

Anya embraced Marina as others ran to them, barely managing to hold back a flood of tears.

Marina said, "Your mama is going to be so happy to see you. She hasn't rested a second since you and Ivan disappeared. She showed up to come with us this morning, and I made her go home to get some sleep." She laughed. "If only I'd known!"

Anya couldn't keep the tears from pouring down her cheeks. Marina and Anya cried in each other's arms. Verusha and Olya hugged Anya and Marina, then Mila joined. All five of them cried while the rest of the villagers murmured exclamations of relief, and Father Drozdov did the sign of the cross and thanked God over and over. Then Anya, Marina, and the three girls let go long enough to compose themselves. Marina laughed and wiped a tear off Anya's cheek with a finger. "What on earth were you two thinking? Running off like that?"

Anya wiped her wet face with her coat sleeve. "I was being so foolish. I was going to march down to Rûm and get my papa and bring him back. And Ivan came with me because he wanted to make sure I was safe. But then we stayed the night out in the cold, and it was terrible."

On the road, Ivan's brothers were taking turns shoving dirt down the back of his tunic. Ivan just lay there as they did, his face swapping between a grimace and a grin.

With Anya clasped to her side, Marina said, "Help your brother up, boys! We need to go warm these two up before their toes start to fall off!" She swept her arm out and said, "Everyone, thank you so much for helping us search! We'll see you at the church!"

As the crowd dissipated, Anya got hugged or patted by every person who had been searching, except Kin. Then he, too, pulled Anya into a tight hug and said, "I'm glad yer back."

Anya squeezed him, arms barely fitting around his barrel chest. "I've got something for you."

"Oh?"

She nodded. "But not until everyone is gone."

Ivan's brothers got off him, smooshing dirt into his hair as they did. Even Yedsha sprinkled Ivan with dirt. Ivan smiled and, not bothering to brush the dirt off, went to his mother. "Mama," Ivan said, slipping his arm around her waist, "are your people called the Dvukh?"

Marina looked startled. "Y-yes. How did you—"

"Will you tell me about them?" Ivan asked.

Marina's look of shock remained for a second, and then she smiled. "Of course I will, Ivanushka."

All the Ivanovs, plus Kin and Anya—who was as much Ivanov as anyone could get, she thought—walked back up the road to Zmeyreka as Marina told Ivan about the East, about the magic that ran deep through the earth there, and about seals.

CHAPTER THIRTY-SEVEN

ANYA STOPPED OFF long enough to let Marina pour a warm drink down her throat, and then she and Kin left the Ivanov house. In the village, Anya shifted her backpack straps on her shoulders. The bones seemed to get heavier and heavier with every step.

"Ye've got something for me, eh?" Kin asked. "Is it information on the whereabouts of my boy?"

"Sort of," Anya said. "He's safe."

Kin nodded. "I believe ye. What's this other thing, then?"

They reached the bridge going north over the river.

No one was around as far as Anya could tell. She stuck her finger in her pocket and pinched the ring between two fingers. "I think you're going to be upset."

Kin's face darkened. "What—"

Anya held out the ring. It flashed in the sunlight, and Kin's mouth fell open. His eyes were wet in seconds, and he grasped the ring from Anya's fingers.

"Where?" he whispered. He cradled the ring in his big, callused palm. He still didn't sound cross, but the pain in his voice tore at Anya's heart.

"In Kiev," Anya said, voice cracking. "She was in a secret dungeon."

Kin leaned hard against the bridge. "Oh, Lena," he whispered, voice hoarse. "Oh, my girl. What were ye doing?"

Anya shifted on her feet. "I have more, but first I need to know something." She thought she already knew the answer—an *ibbur* was the soul of a Jewish person, after all—but she asked anyway. "Was Lena Jewish?"

He nodded. Tears soaked into the top of his beard. "She belonged to an old Khazar family. They escaped the old tsar's slaughter. Fled north, like yer *babushka*. They had neighbors who . . ." He frowned. "Well, let's say her village wasn't as kind to Jews as Zmeyreka has been. Her parents were killed. Lena was sold to a *jarl* who came through. She was lucky. He wasn't cruel to her." Kin kissed the ring. "And that's where we met."

Anya slipped her small hand into Kin's large one and walked with him to the other side of the bridge. She wanted some shelter before she gave him a pile of bones. On the other side of the bridge, standing in the autumn shade, Anya slid her pack off her shoulders and pulled out the apron-wrapped bundle of bones. She handed them to Kin, who took them with trembling hands.

"She was a healer," he said. "And so kind. She'd tie herself in knots if it meant helping someone in trouble. Ye brought her back to me."

"I couldn't leave her there," Anya said. "Alone. In a dungeon."

"Yer a good person, Anya." Kin stared down at the bundle. "Ye remind me of her."

Anya didn't know what to say to that. She thought he was being awfully generous. She wasn't sure she could do the things Lena did, or be so strong. But she didn't argue. She just stood with Kin by the bridge, saying nothing.

After a few minutes of tearful silence, Kin looked up at Anya. "Kiev, you said?"

Anya nodded.

Kin wiped his wet cheeks with the heel of his hand. "You fool children went to Kiev and back in two days?"

Anya hesitated. "Uh . . . yes. We did."

"How the—" Kin sputtered. "How'd ye manage that?"

Anya smiled. "Lena did it."

"She what?" Kin asked. "How?"

Anya said, "I'll tell you all about it while we walk."

When they got to her turnoff, Anya had just finished telling Kin about how Lena had helped her kill Sigurd. Kin was speechless for a moment, then said, "Ye'll have to tell me the rest later."

She nodded. "I will. Or Håkon could tell you."

Kin nodded to her, lip stiff, and pulled the bones close to his chest. "Thank you, Anya. For bringing her home."

Anya smiled, and Kin continued north. She wondered if she should go with him, but she decided not to. He needed time alone with Lena. So she let Kin go and hurried down the road toward her house.

Zvezda stood in the middle of the road, facing her. As

soon as she was halfway down the road to the house, he started bleating as loudly as she'd ever heard him bleat.

She reached the goat as the house door flew open. Mama was out first, in her nightgown, running so fast that she was across the garden before Anya could blink. She grabbed Anya in her arms, squeezed her close, and sobbed.

Dyedka and Babulya came out next. Dyedka hollered, "I knew it! I knew she was home! That dang goat's been standing there since sunup!"

"Anya," Mama whispered, "I'm so glad you're safe."

Anya buried her face in Mama's shoulder. "I'm sorry I worried you."

"You're in big trouble," Mama said, but she didn't sound angry.

Anya took a deep breath and nodded. "I deserve it."

Mama squeezed her tight. "You have to make another sukkah. Zvezda ate your other one."

"Nooooooo," Anya groaned. Then she laughed.

"I'm just so happy you came back to me," Mama said. "Where did you go?"

Kiev.

To meet the tsar.

To have dinner with a rabbi.

To free two brothers from their captivity there.

"Up the road," Anya said. "We didn't make it far. But I met Ilya Muromets."

Mama pulled back and blinked. "You met who?"

"I'll tell you all about it," Anya said, thinking she would be very careful about exactly how much she said. "Can we go inside? I'm cold."

"Of course." Mama kissed the top of Anya's head and hugged her again. "Inside to warm up, Annushka. And to write a letter to your papa."

Anya's heart thumped at the mention of him. "Papa?"

"Germogen arrived last night," Mama said. "When we were frantic for you. Papa's okay inside Rûm. He says *Chag Sameach:* Have a happy Sukkot. Write your letter and we'll send Germogen back today."

Anya bounded inside, into her warm home with her loving grandparents and mama, to write a letter to her brave papa, and then—fine, yes—to put together a new sukkah before Sukkot began at sundown. Because that was the least she could do.

✦ ✶ ✦

Inside, Anya snatched up her letter from Papa. Mama hadn't opened it, so Anya was the first to read his strange message:

Annushka,

I got your message, you crazy girl! Do NOT come to find me. I'm glad Demyan got home. Even if they find me, I can't come home now. We've gotten into Rûm itself, but there's no war here. The first villages we passed through were full of people who say they haven't heard from Istanbul in years. As we get closer to Istanbul, the people are gone. There are empty homes full of statues. Something's going on here, and we've all decided to figure out what it is. I don't just take care of the horses anymore —I ride them. You wouldn't recognize your papa, Annushka. I know how to fight. I'll teach you when I get home. And I will get home. I promise. I promise.

Love, Papa

P.S. I didn't tell your mama any of this. I don't want her to worry.

Anya read the letter over and over, her eyes drawn back to the same line.

There's no war here.

That should have made her feel good. If there was no war, Papa wouldn't die in a battle. He could come home. But . . . he wasn't coming home. He was staying.

There's no war here. But he stayed anyway. Impossibly, she would have preferred a war. At least she knew what a war was. She didn't know what it meant that Istanbul had been quiet for years, or that villages were abandoned and full of statues.

Vasilisa hadn't spoken like she knew there was no war.

What was going on?

Mama walked up, and Anya snapped the letter back into its roll.

"Good letter, Anya?" Mama asked.

She nodded. "Yes. He's doing well."

Mama kissed Anya on the forehead. "Don't forget your punishment. You've only got a few hours to get that sukkah up."

Anya stuck Papa's letter in her pocket and hugged Mama before she left.

From above Anya, a raven cawed. It landed on the ground in front of her. It looked at her sideways. She crouched and said, "Did Håkon send you?"

The raven cawed, then took off flying. Anya followed.

Before she built the sukkah, she had business to attend to.

CHAPTER THIRTY-EIGHT

THE RAVEN DOVE AWAY from the farm, crossing the empty field toward the forest beyond. It landed on a branch just inside the tree line, cawed, and then flew up and into the sky.

Anya paused inside the tree line as the raven flew up and away. Where was everyone?

"Anya." She spun as Wielaf appeared with Alfhercht lingering behind him.

Anya pointed to her barn. "That's where I live."

Wielaf nodded. "Yeah, that's what Håkon said. That woman in the hut said we'd be safest here."

"Where is Håkon, anyway?" she asked.

Håkon leaped out from behind a tree, arms out wide, and said, "Surprise!"

Anya's words evaporated in her mouth. Håkon was still a human. She suspected his arm was repaired too. Lena had kept him a boy.

"Anya!" Håkon trotted to her and pulled her into a tight hug.

"Håkon." She breathed his name, unable to return the hug. "You're a human."

He looked down, rubbing his palms over his *rubakha*. "Yeah. But not forever. Just until the end of the day. So, midnight, I guess. Then I'll be a dragon again."

"But why?"

He scratched his head. "I wanted to stay a human." He blushed. "It's stupid. I want to walk around the village without people being afraid of me. I want to touch *everything*."

Anya laughed. "Kin's going to be so surprised."

"Yeah, he is." Håkon laughed with her. "So, how much trouble are you in?"

"None yet," Anya said. "I think they're just happy that I'm alive. Where's Ivan?"

"I sent a raven to his house." Håkon grinned.

Past Håkon, Ivan appeared next to Anya's barn. A raven perched on Ivan's head and flew off as soon as he got to the edge of the field. He stood there with his fists on his hips and yelled, "Very funny joke! Ha ha!"

Anya stepped out of the trees and waved her arm. "Ivan! Here!"

He waved back and started to run across the field. Anya felt Wielaf slide up next to her, and he said softly, "Tell me something about Ivan."

"Okay."

"Is he . . ." He stroked his chin thoughtfully. "When he said he'd pine for Alfhercht. Did he mean that?"

"I think he did," Anya said, worried that Wielaf wouldn't like Ivan's feelings toward Alfhercht. "But if Alfhercht doesn't like him, Ivan's not going to follow him around or anything. He's too shy for that."

"Humans are strange," Wielaf said, almost as an aside to himself. "Alfhercht likes boys. Right now, one in particular." He nodded to Ivan trudging across the field. "And I'd be a terrible big brother if I let him walk headfirst into heartbreak."

Anya smiled. "Ivan is going to act really weird and worry that Alfhercht thinks he smells bad." Ivan was nearly to them. "As soon as he finds out Alfhercht's here, watch what he does."

Wielaf lifted an eyebrow, then turned. Alfhercht stood at the tree line, and as Ivan got closer, he stepped out.

Anya watched as Ivan noticed Alfhercht. He screeched to a halt a distance away from the group. "Wow!" he called, trying to look everywhere that Alfhercht wasn't. "Hi, everyone. Isn't this great? It's. We're gonna. It'll be a great time."

Wielaf whispered, "That's hilarious."

Alfhercht continued walking toward Ivan. Ivan took a step back. Alfhercht stopped.

Anya winced. "Ah, he's such a fool."

Then Ivan stepped forward. Just one step. He said, "Hi."

Alfhercht put his open hand to his eyebrow and brought it out toward Ivan. Almost like a salute, but gentler.

"He said hello," Wielaf murmured to Anya. He waved to get Ivan's attention, and called, "He said hi!"

Ivan repeated the gesture to Alfhercht. They lingered by each other, neither moving closer. Anya couldn't see what Alfhercht was doing with his face, but she assumed it wasn't anything terrible. Ivan was smiling.

Ivan laughed awkwardly, wrung his tunic in his fists, and called to Anya, "Um, where's Håkon?"

"Here!" Håkon bounded out of the trees and waved.

"You're a human!" Ivan yelled.

Håkon splayed his arms out and wiggled them around. "Just for today!"

Anya and Wielaf followed Håkon out of the trees. The five of them stood in a loose group, looking out over the empty field.

"So," Anya said, "Lena brought you here?"

Wielaf and Alfhercht nodded. Alfhercht spoke with his hands, and Wielaf translated: "She told us this was where we'd be the happiest." Then he shrugged.

Anya nodded. "Well, we don't use this field for anything, really. The goats graze in it, I guess. But that's all. We could build a house here."

"No," Alfhercht said through Wielaf's translation. "We'll build our own house."

Alfhercht and Wielaf conferred with rapid gestures, and then Alfhercht paced around the perimeter of the field, studying the ground with a thin-lipped mouth. Wielaf watched as Alfhercht paced to the middle of the field.

"This will be a great place," Wielaf said, then added, "I mean, temporarily. That woman in the hut was right. I'm weak, and it's almost time for us to hibernate. Going back home now would be tough. We might get caught in the open when the snows come. That would be terrible."

"You're going to have to tell us more about that," Anya said. "Is hibernation just sleeping for a long time?"

"From the first frost to the first thaw," Wielaf said. "I haven't hibernated in three years. I'm ragged from it. Him too." He pointed to Alfhercht, who looked up. Wielaf crossed the first and middle fingers of both hands, touched the crossed tips in front of his body, and then swung his hands out. Alfhercht did the same back to him.

Alfhercht knelt. He dug his fingers through the loam on top, down deep to the cold earth below, and then pulled his hand back out. A slender sapling followed his fingers, unfurling its tender buds and shoots up.

When the sapling was up to Anya's knee, Alfhercht stopped pulling it up. He hooked his fingers around a magic thread and walked with it a few paces away. He dug into the dirt again, pulling up another sapling, gathering another thread of magic. Around in a circle he went, drawing up sapling after sapling, until he made a circle out of knee-high trees, with an invisible bundle of magic in his fist.

Anya snuck a glance at Wielaf. His eyes were searching the air. She recognized that squinty, rapid back-and-forth. She did it all the time. Looking for threads. Never seeing any, until now. Wielaf's own fears manifested as threads coming out of him. She wanted to comfort him, but what was she supposed to say to someone who'd had his magic ripped away from him?

Alfhercht fiddled with the invisible magic, and even though Anya couldn't see the threads, she knew what he was doing. He wove the threads together, braiding them up and around, painstaking in his art. The saplings shuddered with every tug he made, and they all grew taller and thicker, doming inward, until they touched at the top.

It wasn't as huge as Alfhercht's tree outside Kiev, but it was a comfortable size. They didn't need a fortress. Just a safe place to stay while Wielaf got his strength back.

Alfhercht joined Wielaf among the group, smiling cautiously. The trees were still too thin to overlap and form real walls, but they were thickening up as everyone stood and watched.

"How long will they take to grow?" Anya asked.

Wielaf looked back at the tree, shrugged, then said, "Tonight?"

"Wow," Håkon said.

"What are we going to do until then?" Ivan asked.

Anya snapped her fingers. "I have an idea."

✦ ✹ ✦

Anya knew there were a lot of rules about how to build a sukkah. The walls were fairly simple—there had to be at least two full walls, plus part of a third, even though Babulya always insisted on four full walls. There were size limits—it couldn't be too tall—but Anya was never worried about those, because she was certain she wasn't capable of making one too high. The *sechach*, the roof, was another story. It had to shade the inside but not be complete coverage. The tree branches couldn't still be alive, and it had to use plants that weren't harvested for another purpose. So no straw taken from the goats as a temporary *sechach*.

She relayed this information to Wielaf and Alfhercht as the group walked toward her barn. Wielaf stroked his chin. Alfhercht spoke with his hands, and Wielaf translated with his voice: "I can do that."

Alfhercht paced out a long, wide area, and dug his fingers into the soil at four points. Slender saplings rose up, the corners of the sukkah. Alfhercht pulled branches sideways out of these saplings, then paced between, pulling up six more saplings. When he pulled branches from these saplings, they converged with the branches of the saplings next to them, forming walls. He left a spot for a door, and left holes as windows. He left the top open per Anya's instructions.

The sukkah frame was perfect. It was big enough to hold half the village, too.

"Thank you," she said. "It looks beautiful."

Wielaf and Alfhercht both grinned, and then Babulya's voice called, "I'll say!"

She came shuffling around the side of the barn, followed by a retinue of chickens. Håkon stumbled backwards, slamming into the side of the barn. He looked terrified, but then settled. He put his hands on his chest, as if reminding himself that he was a human now, not a dragon.

"What on earth was that?" Babulya asked.

Everyone looked at Håkon. "I tripped!" he said.

Babulya listened to his voice. "I don't know you, do I?" She swung a hand out toward Alfhercht and Wielaf. "And I don't know them, either."

"They're—" Anya started. She looked around at everyone gathered. No one offered up any explanation about the newcomers' identities.

"We're Kin's nephews!" Håkon blurted. "We're visiting him. Just for today."

"Just for today?" Babulya narrowed her sightless eyes, then grinned. "How lucky! Tonight we're having a special dinner! You'll all have to join us!" She moved to the sukkah. "After all, you helped my Annushka build quite the sukkah."

Alfhercht and Wielaf looked worried. Babulya ran her wrinkled hand over the corner post closest to her, and the sapling's leaves shifted toward her. Wielaf and Alfhercht's expressions changed from worried to surprised.

"Oh," she said in a soft voice to the tree. "Is that right? Well, what are they doing here?" She leaned closer, then *tsk*ed. "No home? Well, we know about that kind of thing, don't we?"

Wielaf's mouth dropped open. Then Babulya turned to him and Alfhercht and shuffled forward. She reached out her hands, and Wielaf let his find hers. "You're welcome to stay with us as long as you need to. Especially this winter. Do you have a safe place to sleep?"

Wielaf and Alfhercht looked back and forth between each other and Babulya. Wielaf managed to say, "We do, Gospozha."

She nodded toward their growing tree home. "That'll be up fast enough?"

Wielaf trembled. "It should."

Babulya patted Wielaf's hands before letting go of them. "We'll make sure it is, won't we?" Babulya stroked the sapling at the edge of the sukkah. "I think you look very nice. You'll grow into a beautiful little structure right here. But hmm, hmm, Annushka, there's no *sechach*."

"We didn't get there yet," Anya said.

Babulya nodded. "Did you know your papa used to make the *sechach* out of the roses? It was so pretty." She patted the tree and turned back toward the other side of the barn. "Too bad he's not here to do that this year."

CHAPTER THIRTY-NINE

BABULYA WAS RIGHT. Papa wasn't there. But Alfhercht and Wielaf were.

Wielaf followed Babulya so she could show him her roses, while Håkon dragged Ivan with him to take Alfhercht into the forest. When they came back, they carried a pile of birch branches large enough to cover the entire top of the sukkah.

Anya directed them to put the branches next to the sukkah, and then they lifted her up so she could put each branch on, laying them alternating back and forth. Before she got down, Wielaf ran up with lengths of rose vines in his hands. White roses bloomed along them, definitely out of season, Babulya's doing, but Anya didn't care. She hung them as garlands inside the sukkah while Alfhercht coaxed the birch's leaves into riotous golds and oranges so the whole top of it looked like the horizon of the setting sun.

The sun itself was going down, and Mama came around the side of the barn. She stopped dead in her tracks and marveled at the beautiful sukkah, then realized there were three boys there she didn't recognize.

"Kin's nephews," Wielaf piped, even though he had no idea who Kin was. "It's very nice to meet you."

"Likewise," Mama said. She peered at Håkon and said, "Are you Kin's nephew too?"

Håkon stood stiff, nervous. He had seen Mama from afar many times. Anya imagined he had never thought they'd speak.

"Yes, Gospozha," he said finally, then blurted, "Anya says you make very good bread."

Mama smiled. "Well, you'll get to try some tonight if you want to stay. You're all invited."

They thanked her, then set about decorating the sukkah further, between helping Mama and Babulya bring bowls and lanterns and pillows to sit on out to the sukkah. Soon it was like a little second home, lit up and beautiful in the deepening twilight. Håkon left to get Kin—to show Kin his temporary boy form while it lasted—and Anya watched Wielaf and Alfhercht teach Ivan some words with his fingers as she shoved all the goats into the barn and locked the door.

Kin and Håkon came down the road. Kin looked freshly scrubbed, and his eyes were red. Lena's gold ring was around his smallest finger. He couldn't stop hugging Håkon.

Dyedka came out of the house using his walking stick with one hand and carrying a pitcher of water with the other. When he saw Wielaf and Alfhercht, he frowned.

Anya gasped. *The tree people*. Would Dyedka recognize them? If he did, would he be angry? She hurried toward him and said, "Dyedka! These are Kin's nephews."

He frowned. "So Kin's got Alvolk as nephews?"

Everyone quieted. Dyedka eyeballed the elves with his good eye, then handed Anya the pitcher of water.

"Dyedka," she said, "they're nice."

He didn't respond to her. He approached Wielaf and stood close, eye to eye. They stared at each other for a while, and then Dyedka said, "See this?" He tapped his eye patch. "Your lot's quiet in the trees. Didn't even know someone was next to me until he slashed my eye right out."

Wielaf blanched. He didn't translate Dyedka's words for Alfhercht, but Alfhercht seemed to get the idea of the conversation anyway. He charged forward, but Wielaf stopped him with a stiff arm. He was quiet for a while, and then he said, "I'm sorry that happened to you."

Dyedka clapped him on the shoulder. "What are you sorry for? You weren't even born yet! We shouldn't have been there, you know. Burning those forests hurt my heart. Awful. Whole cities gone while they slept. It was a coward's war." He jerked his head toward Babul-ya. "Channah says you don't have anywhere to go. Well, you can stay with us as long as you need. No one's going to hurt you this winter. I'll make sure of that myself."

Wielaf smiled, bit his lip, and nodded. He spoke to Alfhercht in silence, and then they both looked at Dyedka.

"Thank you," Wielaf said with his mouth.

"Thank you," Alfhercht said with his hands.

Dyedka nodded and continued into the sukkah. And just like that, everyone followed him. Even Zvezda had escaped the barn as usual. He meandered up to the suk-kah and sniffed at the living leaves. Then he grabbed a mouthful. As everyone sat down inside, Anya lingered at the door, pushing Zvezda so he couldn't get in. She looked skyward, watching for stars to mark the end of the day. Then Sukkot could officially start, and . . .

She tensed as a thought crossed her mind.

The end of the day.

She looked over at Håkon, sitting beside Kin. He would stay a human until the end of the day. He thought that meant midnight. But Lena was Jewish. To Lena, the end of the day was . . .

"Håkon!" Anya yelled.

Håkon looked up at her, eyebrows up, questioning her outburst.

His eyes were still blue. But his pupils were the vertical slit of a dragon's.

"Get out of there!" Anya screamed.

Everyone turned to her, startled. Mama said, "Anya, what are you yelling about?"

But it was too late.

The skin of his cheek flaked open, revealing red underneath. The split spread out and down, his human skin peeling away. Mama stood and stumbled backwards, hitting the wall of the sukkah. Babulya and Dyedka stayed seated. Dyedka grabbed Babulya and pulled her close.

Håkon's trouser legs shredded away as his long ruby tail with golden spines tumbled out. His human hands blew away into dust, revealing his dragon claws. The human face that he'd been so upset about dissolved, and his red, scaly, dragony face popped out, complete with twisting horns.

He sat there, coiled on the floor of the sukkah, too stunned to move. Mama stared at him. Dyedka stared at him. Alfhercht and Wielaf stared at him. Ivan and Kin stared at each other.

Zvezda poked his head in and said, *"Myah."* Then he walked nonchalantly into the sukkah, crossing to where Håkon curled, terrified, and sniffed the dragon's snout. Then he said, *"Myah,"* again and butted Håkon gently with the top of his head.

Dyedka was the first to move. He slumped back against the side of the sukkah and said, "If that's not the strangest thing I've seen in a long time."

Babulya smacked Dyedka's arm. "What just happened?"

"The boy's a dragon," Dyedka said.

Babulya's milky eyes widened, and she hooted, "I knew it! I knew there was a dragon about!" She waved her hand in Håkon's direction. "The chickens have been laying like crazy for months!" Then she crooked a finger at him. "There'll be good rainfall, won't there? Ha! You better make sure of that, young man."

Håkon just stared at her with huge blue eyes, and then he nodded. "Y-yes, Gospozha."

Mama slid to the floor, hand on her heart. "He talks."

"Aye, he does," Kin admitted. "And he reads, too, when he sits still long enough."

The tent was silent, and then Mama burst into laughter, covering her face with her hands. Then Ivan laughed, and Anya, and soon they all did. Even Håkon. Zvezda bleated loudly, which Anya supposed was the goat's version of laughter.

They let Zvezda stay inside for dinner. He stood next to Håkon, munching on whatever got close enough. Håkon coiled beside Anya, eating as carefully with his little claws as he could. Ivan sat beside Alfhercht, speaking unsteady words with his fingers and grinning stupidly when Alfhercht nodded with encouragement. Wielaf sat beside Babulya, who wondered loudly if a dragon kindling a flame was breaking Shabbat. They all decided that it wasn't.

The lanterns lit up the inside of the sukkah, and when Anya looked up, she could see the stars shining in the sky above them.

THE END

GLOSSARY

Anya Miroslavovna Kozlova: AHN-yeh mee-roh-SLA-vov-neh KAZ-lo-veh

Ivan Ivanovich Ivanov: ee-VAHN ee-VAHN-ov-itch ee-VAHN-ov

Håkon Jernhåndssen: HAW-kohn yarn-HUND-sen

Dobrynya Nikitich: dah-BRIN-yeh nee-KEE-teech

DIMINUTIVES (USED ONLY BY VERY CLOSE FRIENDS OR FAMILY)

Annushka (AH-noosh-kah): a diminutive form of the name Anya, which is itself a diminutive of the Christian name Anna or Hebrew name Channah.

Ivanushka (ee-VAH-noosh-kah): a diminutive form of
the name Ivan

Masha (MAH-shuh): a diminutive form of the name
Maria or Miriam

RUSSIAN

babulya (BAH-bool-yeh): grandma

babushka (BAH-boosh-kah): grandmother

bogatyr (buh-GAH-tihr): an epic hero; a knight-errant.
The three most famous *bogatyri* are Dobrynya
Nikitich, Ilya Muromets, and Alyosha Popovich.

domoviye (DAH-mo-vey-ah): plural of *domovoi*

domovoi (DAH-mo-vey): a house spirit, similar to an
English brownie. They help around the house if kept
happy but can turn into poltergeists if angered or
disrespected.

dyedka (da-YED-kah): grandpa

dyedushka (da-YED-oosh-kah): grandfather

Gospodin (gas-PAHD-yihn): Mr., sir

Gospozha (gas-PASZH-ah): Mrs., ma'am

gusli (GOOS-lee): an ancient East Slavic multi-string
plucked instrument, played while resting on the
musician's lap

Kiev (KEEV): the name of the capital of Kievan Rus'

Kievan Rus' (kee-yeh-VAHN roos): a medieval Slavic nation that existed between 862 and 1242 CE, located in modern-day Western Russia, Belarus, and Ukraine. Named for the Rus, a Scandinavian people.

leshy **(LEH-shey):** a forest spirit that can hurt or harm depending on a person's treatment of the forest

Perun (PEE-roohn): an Old Slavic god. The highest god of the pantheon.

ruble (ROO-bl): the currency of Kievan Rus'

Rûm (ROUM): a general term for the Byzantine Empire to the south, located in modern-day Turkey

rusalka **(roo-SAAL-kah):** a river spirit who is fond of drowning men. Depending on the lore, *rusalki* may be mermaids, fertility spirits, or the souls of women who drowned.

rusalki **(roo-SAAL-kee):** plural of *rusalka*

Semik (SEE-meek): "Green Week" or "Rusalka Week." A Slavic agricultural festival celebrated in early June.

Sogozha (SAH-gozh-eh): a tributary of the Volga River

tsar (ZAHR): king

Varangian (va-RAHN-gyan): a term for a Scandinavian mercenary

vodyaniye (VOHD-yeh-nee): plural of *vodyanoi*

vodyanoi (VOHD-yeh-noy): a river-grass spirit that looks like a frog and will drown people by tangling them in the grass. Unlike the *rusalki*, when a *vodyanoi* drowns someone, that person's soul must stay and serve him.

zmey (ZMEE): dragon or snake

zmeyok (ZMEE-ahk): a horned snake indigenous to Anya's village. The name means "dragonling" because people once thought these were baby dragons.

Zmeyreka (ZMEE-ree-kah): "Dragon River," the name of Anya's village

Zvezda (ZVYEZ-dah): "Star," the name of Anya's goat

HEBREW

bat mitzvah: "daughter of the commandment," Jewish coming-of-age, signifying that the child is now responsible for her own following of Jewish law, whereas prior to this event the parents were responsible for the child's following of Jewish law

challah: the name for enriched, sweet bread that is served on holidays (except Passover). Traditionally, a piece of the challah dough is torn off the loaf before baking and burned separately to represent the offering given to priests in the temple.

Hadassah: Esther, the Jewish queen of Persia who revealed herself to be Jewish after one of the king's advisers convinced the king to kill all the Jews in Persia. By revealing that she was Jewish, Esther put herself in danger of being killed with all the rest, but instead, her bravery led to the Jews not being killed, and that particular adviser being punished.

Havdalah: "Separation," the ceremony marking the end of Shabbat, or the sabbath. It divides the holy time of the sabbath from the regular week, and takes place at sunset on Saturday when three stars are visible in the sky.

***ibbur* (ee-BOOR):** "incubation," a possessing spirit that is always positive (whereas a *ru'ach tezazit* is always negative). If a righteous soul needs to complete a task or perform a mitzvah, the soul can enter into a living person in order to perform this task or mitzvah. The *ibbur* needs permission from the possessed person before it can inhabit his or her body, and the *ibbur* will leave as soon as the task or mitzvah is complete.

Juhuri: the language spoken by the Mountain Jews
of Azerbaijan. A mix of Persian and Hebrew,
similar to Yiddish (Hebrew-German) and Ladino
(Hebrew-Spanish).

kippah: a small, circular, brimless hat worn to fulfill the
customary requirement that the head be covered.
Men wear them more often but women can wear
them as well.

Moshe: another name for Moses the prophet

Purim: a holiday commemorating Hadassah/Esther pre-
venting the massacre of the Jews in Persia. It involves
dressing in costumes, reading the Book of Esther,
and eating triangular cookies called *hamentaschen*.

ru'ach tezazit **(WOO-akh tza-ZEET):** an evil possessing
spirit that invades a living body and makes it do bad
things. The opposite of an *ibbur*.

Shabbat: the weekly holiday for Jewish people to take
time away from work and regular life

Shabbat shalom: the greeting used on Friday or Saturday
wishing the other person a peaceful Shabbat. In Yiddish someone may say *"Gut Shabbos."*

Shavua tov: "Have a good week." Said at the end of
Havdalah to wish everyone a good and productive
week until the next Shabbat.

Shavuot: "Weeks," a harvest festival at the end of spring that commemorates the receiving of the Torah from God by Moses. Traditionally, dairy products are eaten on this holiday, especially blintzes (cheese-filled thin pancakes), called bliny in Russia.

Sivan: the name for the month on the Hebrew calendar that usually falls in May to June

synagogue: a Jewish house of worship. Sometimes called a shul or a temple.

Talmud: Jewish civil and ceremonial law discussed and debated by historic rabbis and recorded as a discussion of what the Torah means

Torah: also called the Pentateuch; the first five books of the Hebrew Bible

ACKNOWLEDGMENTS

Writing a first book is fun but tough.

Writing a second book is . . . impossible.

But somehow, they get written. Mine got written with the support of some very amazing people:

Erika Turner, my editor at Versify, who weathered my anxious emails and gave me insight and advice. I'm awed by how you "get" this book and how you're able to really touch the very deepest heart of it.

Rena Rossner, superstar agent extraordinaire, who speed-read an early draft at my request and who, incredibly, endures my silliness and GIF-posting with the bearing of a queen.

Jeff Langevin nailed my cover yet again. He has thus

far taken all my half-baked and unformed suggestions and turned them into visual perfection.

My family: my husband, for literally everything. My daughter, for being proud of me. My son, for keeping me humble. My mother-in-law, my mom, my sister, my nieces and nephews—all their positivity and support and excitement got me through times when I was tired and weary and feeling like giving up.

The SLC Writers Group gang didn't get to read this book the same way they got to read the first one, but that didn't stop them from being jazzed about it. Everyone needs cheerleaders, and I've got the very best group of them.

To the Utah Novel19s: our debut year was WILD and I would have had a much harder time without you. You're all amazing people, talented writers, and incredible friends!

And finally, thank you, thank you, dear reader. I hope you've found what you were looking for.

Sofiya Pasternack